THE HIGHLANDER'S DEMAND

Highland Rogues, Book 1

Mary Wine

Dragonblade Publishing, Inc. is an imprint of Kathryn Le Veque Novels, Inc.
P.O. Box 7968
La Verne CA 91750
ceo@dragonbladepublishing.com

Produced in the United States of America

First Edition November 2019
Print Edition

ARE YOU SIGNED UP FOR DRAGONBLADE'S BLOG?

You'll get the latest news and information on exclusive giveaways, exclusive excerpts, coming releases, sales, free books, cover reveals and more.

Check out our complete list of authors, too!

No spam, no junk. That's a promise!

Sign Up Here

www.dragonbladepublishing.com

>>>><<<<

Dearest Reader;

Thank you for your support of a small press. At Dragonblade Publishing, we strive to bring you the highest quality Historical Romance from the some of the best authors in the business. Without your support, there is no 'us', so we sincerely hope you adore these stories and find some new favorite authors along the way.

Happy Reading!

CEO, Dragonblade Publishing

Additional Dragonblade books by Author Mary Wine

Highland Rogues Series
The Highlander's Demand

*** Please visit Dragonblade's website for a full list of books and authors. Sign up for Dragonblade's blog for sneak peeks, interviews, and more: ***
www.dragonbladepublishing.com

CHAPTER ONE

Lindsey land…

WINTER HAD LOST its grip on the land.

Rhedyn paused to take a deep breath. She held it in as she smiled. Her nose wasn't freezing for the first time in months. The sun had set hours before but the fringed days of winter were gone. It was still chilly enough to see her sister Bree hugging her airside close as she stood on the back steps which led from the kitchens down to the yard.

"Father isn't back yet," Bree said before Rhedyn spoke.

Her sister was still young, just fourteen winters now. Womanhood had yet to settle on her.

"He said he'd return tonight," Bree insisted.

"Father is likely at the Sow's Troth," Rhedyn remarked as she moved up beside her sister. "And ye know it. So ye should no' be out here looking up the road as though his fate is uncertain." Rhedyn hugged her sister. "Let him enjoy some ale with his men."

"Connor is here, and Kain," Bree protested. "I am not being foolish."

The two Lindsey Retainers offered Rhedyn a nod before they returned their attention to watching the back gate. There were also men posted along the walls which formed the outer walls of the Lindsey stronghold. Bree was the laird's daughter. So as long as she was on the back steps, more of the Lindsey Retainers would make certain she was watched.

"Father has plenty of drink here," Bree continued. "Why does he stop at the Sow's Troth whenever he ventures out?"

Connor and Kain both shifted. One rocked back on his heels as the other rolled his shoulders. Rhedyn felt a touch of heat on her own cheeks as her sister unwittingly touched on a very inappropriate topic.

"Father enjoys hearing the news from other travelers," Rhedyn remarked. She cupped her sister's shoulders. "Enough watching the road. Father will be here by sunrise, have no doubt. And he will not be happy to see dark circles beneath yer eyes."

Rhedyn turned her sister around and gently pushed her toward the entrance to the kitchens. Another Retainer was there, surveying what the Head-of-House had left out for the men on night watch. He reached up and tugged on the corner of his cap when he saw the two women crossing through.

Rhedyn kept herself from sighing as she made her way to her room. She knew what the Sow's Troth was. Located on the crossroads where Lindsey, Mackenzie, and Munro lands met, the tavern was a place where clans mingled. She wouldn't go so far as to say it was friendly interaction, but the Retainers from the different clans minded their manners because they didn't want to be barred from the services the tavern had for hire.

Bree was correct. There was ale and drink aplenty in the Lindsey stronghold. But there were not women the Lindsey laird might bed without the rest of the clan knowing about it.

Her sister was too young to know of such things. Rhedyn wasn't sure just what age she'd been when she'd deduced the truth of the Sow's Troth herself, but it mattered little. Her mother was long dead, and her father wasn't interested in wedding again—so why shouldn't he seek comfort in the arms of a woman when he needed to?

It was just the way things were, and Rhedyn couldn't really find it in her heart to think badly about her father. She discovered herself thinking more and more of just how difficult it might be to live in loneliness.

Stop thinking the worst…

It was wise advice. Rhedyn rolled onto her side on her bed and tried to get her thoughts to settle. Rolfe Munro had come to court her. And she didn't doubt he'd come again.

She opened her eyes and stared across her chamber. The window shutters were closed against the chill of the night, but she knew where everything was even in the darkness. The room was where she had lived her entire life. There was a comfort inside it that she felt being shaken by the approach of her twenty-second birthday.

It was time to wed.

Her father had no sons. As his eldest daughter, her future marriage was one of great importance to the Lindsey clan. For heaven's sake, she'd been reared with the knowledge that her wedding would be about the alliance it brought the clan.

So why was she so torn over the issue now?

Rolfe was fine enough to look upon. She could find no fault with the man. He'd come and spent two days under her father's roof when he might have simply gone to her father's study and sealed the arrangement with her waiting somewhere for the announcement to be made.

So why did she feel so discontented?

Why did she suddenly have a deeper understanding of her father's need to visit the Sow's Troth?

Sinful…

Without a doubt, Rhedyn knew many would admonish her for admitting she knew the Sow's Troth had women for hire there.

Well, she wasn't a lackwit. At least in her bedchamber, she didn't have to appear like one. In public, well, she'd kept her mouth shut. Not because it was expected of her. No, Rhedyn would mind her tongue on the subject because she suddenly understood just how little affection there might be in her own marriage. Not because her intended groom was callous, but fate simply hadn't bestowed any affection between them.

Fate was such a fickle beast.

⋙⋘

The Sow's Troth...

THE ALE WAS flowing. The loud booms of laughter confirmed it. Sandra Lindsey contemplated the large common room with a knowledgeable eye. Retainers from three different clans were represented at the long tables. Tonight, they appeared to be men who knew the house rules.

Her rules.

There was no grumbling, and they kept their animosity confined to the games of dice and cards they were engaged in. Sandra nodded approvingly before pointing to ten women waiting for her instruction. The moment she motioned them toward the common room, they picked up pitchers and glided forward. Their bodices were cut a bit lower than the respectable women of the village, and Sandra's patrons smiled with appreciation.

The women made slow progress between the tables. They lingered over each cup they filled, allowing the men in front of them a good look at their cleavage. While they all wore linen caps on their heads, their hair flowed down from beneath those head coverings.

Sandra didn't run a common whore house. Oh yes, she was a madam, but she considered herself a woman who lived her life according to arrangements that she made for herself.

Freedom.

She'd had a husband once. One who had used her as he pleased, when he pleased, and satisfying her had never been something he'd concerned himself with.

Now, when she allowed a man to take her to bed, he knew he'd better see to her needs or it would be the last time he was welcomed into her establishment.

"Evening, lass," Colum Lindsey spoke from the top of the stairs. He'd venture no further until she granted him permission.

The two burly men she kept well fed and near at all times would see to it.

"Colum," Sandra purred. "'Tis good to see ye."

Sandra gestured her guards away. Colum tilted his head to one side and offered her a wink. There was still a hint of a spark in his eyes, even if there were winkles from age on the side of his face.

"Ye knew I'd come, woman," Colum admonished her softly. "I'm helpless against yer allure."

"Hush," Sandra said as she patted the place next to her on the end of the bed she sat on.

Abovestairs there were only beds. Her girls only served one client a night. The men below in the common room understood they'd need more than silver to win one of the beauties' favors. Colum settled next to her, and she smiled as she caught the scent of his skin. He was freshly bathed, a hint of rosemary clinging to him.

A courtesy her husband had certainly never afforded her.

Sandra banished the memory. She turned and offered her full attention to Colum.

Her lover.

Oh yes. Label her scandalous, and she would smile proudly for respectability had never rewarded her with happiness.

So, she'd take a different path. One of her own choosing.

⟫⟫⟫⟫✳⟪⟪⟪⟪

IAIN MACKENZIE HAD heard of the Sow's Troth. He rode into the village at the crossroads, desire making his member stiff.

He paused outside the tavern, taking note of the well-kept look of the place.

"Appears to live up to its name, lads," Iain declared as his men clustered around him. "Let's find some entertainment!"

He charged up the steps. Iain pushed the doors open and grinned when he got a glimpse of the women pouring ale. He rubbed his hands together as he looked each one over. A blonde caught his eyes, but she turned away instead of venturing over to serve him.

He stood for a long moment in the open doorway. A man came forward, wearing an apron. "Welcome, welcome. Would ye have a seat?"

Iain grunted. But he walked over to a table and sat on one of the long benches. Several of his men joined him. He didn't give any attention to the men who had elected to stay with the horses. Let them nurse their righteous principles. All the more ale and flesh for him to enjoy.

"Send the blonde over," Iain ordered.

"If one of our mistresses finds ye to her liking, she will venture forward," the man said in a low voice.

Iain reached up and grabbed a handful of his shirtsleeve. "This is a whorehouse. Send the bitch over here now."

The man surprised him by breaking his grip. "Ye have been misinformed. We run a tavern. With well-known hospitality."

Iain frowned. But across the room, he spied one of the women leading a man toward the stairs. "Do nae lie to me, man!"

The man held up a finger. "Allow me to bring ye a fine supper. Perhaps after ye have filled yer bellies, ye will be more inclined to entice one of our mistresses to invite ye abovestairs."

"Entice?" Iain asked. He kicked the bench back and faced off with the stranger. "I do nae intend to woo a whore! Order that bitch over here now."

The man shook his head.

"Take yerself over to the edge of town if ye want that sort of thing."

Iain turned his head, looking for the man who had spoken. When their gazes connected, the man didn't look away. He sat his mug down and stood up, revealing the colors of the Munro.

"A whore is a whore," Iain declared.

"Then why are ye here and no at the edge of town?" the Munro Retainer asked bluntly. "The whores down there cost a tenth of what ye'll end up paying here. The Sow's Troth only has courtesans."

"Courtesans?" Iain spat. This time the girls pouring the ale took exception to his tone. They looked at him. "Ye are whores," he informed them all.

A moment later, the women turned and walked back to the kitchen without a single word. The men at the long tables abandoned their conversations and dice games, turning to glare at him. More Munro Retainers rose up to back the man who Iain had taken issue with.

"Stop ruining the night for us all," the Munro Retainer said. "The Sow's Troth caters to a man who wants more than a quick rutting."

"I've no' even begun to ruin yer night," Iain declared as he curled his fingers into a fist. "But I will be happy to smash yer jaw for ye."

"Enough," Colum Lindsey said from the stairs. A ripple of agreement went through the common room. "Iain Mackenzie. We've heard plenty from ye. Take yerself off to the edge of town."

"Ye may be laird of the Lindsey, but I am the son of a laird as well," Iain declared.

Colum nodded. "I know who ye are. But in this place, we all keep the peace. It's an understanding, lad. One which seems to be escaping ye. So, go to the edge of town where the rules will suit ye better."

Colum turned and disappeared up the stairs. Iain growled, earning a chuckle from the Munro Retainer who was still standing. Iain turned his ire on the man, but the Retainer only turned his back and sat down again.

"Ye are all a bunch of cockless bastards!" Iain said. "Sitting here, begging for a taste of a whore's sex. Real men use the night for raising."

Iain stormed out of the tavern and a moment later, the sound of horses riding away filled the place.

>>><<<

COLUM LINDSEY HAD almost made it back to the top of the stairs. He stopped though, Iain's words echoing in his head. He caught the scent of Sandra's perfume, which made him mutter a coarse word as he turned and descended to the common room floor.

"Seems we need to leave, lads," Colum spoke firmly. "In case that bastard makes good on his words."

There was a mutter of discontentment, but tankards landed on the table tops as the men all began to stand. Sandra was at the railing of the loft, looking on as her customers paid for their ale. Colum looked up at her and reached up to tug on his cap before he turned and ventured into the night. Iain Mackenzie was going to get the fight he was looking for if the bastard made the mistake of stepping foot onto Lindsey land.

And that was a bloody promise.

>>><<<

THERE WAS JUST a sliver of moon tonight.

Rolfe Munro slowly smoothed a hand along the neck of his stallion. He watched the animal's ears, looking for any sign of trouble.

A low whistle came through the darkness, but Rolfe knew it for one of his men. There was a slight crunch from their steps as more of his Retainers joined him.

"Thought ye'd gone to the Sow's Troth," Rolfe said.

"We did," Donnach Munro replied. "Iain Mackenzie ruined the night by declaring he was going raiding."

Rolfe's shoulders tightened. "Did young Mackenzie say just where he was going raiding?"

"No," Donnach answered. "But we cut the evening short in case he finds his way onto Munro land."

The stallion's ears moved. Rolfe looked up in the direction the horse had turned its ears toward. In the distance, there was a flash of light. It danced and flickered as it grew into a large fire.

"Damn his soul," Donnach declared. "The prick really did go raiding."

Rolfe mounted his horse and wheeled the animal around in the direction of the growing fire. "He's made the last mistake of his life."

"It's Iain Mackenzie," Donnach cautioned Rolfe. "As it stands, ye are both sons of lairds. Neither of ye outranking the other."

"He's raiding me land," Rolfe responded heatedly. "Being brother to the Makenzie laird will no' stop me from protecting what is Munro."

Rolfe spurred his horse forward. Maybe he should have spared a thought for the fact that Iain was the half-brother of the current Mackenzie laird, but as he got closer and heard the cries of Munros suffering through a raid, he closed his heart to any thoughts of mercy.

Two men lay on the ground near the house they'd risen in the dead of night to protect. Dark puddles of blood reflected the fires blazing on the roofs of their stable and house. The flames were greedily consuming the thatch as the light illuminated the brutality being endured by the wife of the dead crofter.

Iain had her bent over a fence as he rutted on her like a beast. He gave a grunt before finishing. Rolfe was certain he'd relive those moments for the rest of his life as he failed to make it across the field before Iain drew a dagger across the woman's throat. Ian turned, his face contorted by his love of violence, and pointed his dagger at a young girl who was being forced to watch. The blade was slick with her mother's blood—the moonlight spared him no details of the brutal attack.

"Ye see?" Iain asked her. "Do ye see what happens to those who do nae understand what I expect of them?" He pointed the tip of the dagger at her as his men held her in place. But he heard the approach of horses at last. The loud roar of the fire had given Rolfe the advantage.

Rolfe and the Munro Retainers came down on the Mackenzie hard. So absorbed in their sport, they'd failed to watch their surroundings. More blood spilled on the ground as the men riding with Iain fought for their lives and the Munros cut them down in defense of the lives they'd taken.

Rolfe didn't give Iain a quick death. He sliced him across the back of one leg first. Iain growled but his temper couldn't help him overcome the crippling injury. He hobbled as Rolfe pursued him mercilessly.

"Spill my blood and the Mackenzie will avenge me!" Iain declared.

"I was no' feuding with the McKenzies," Rolfe said. "Yet, here ye are killing me kin, and ye think to intimidate me with yer name?"

Rolfe thrust his sword through Iain's midsection. It was a brutal motion, one which took all of the strength Rolfe had. The blade sliced through Iain's flesh, emerging through his back. Iain let out a roar. It pleased Rolfe. He tightened his grip and yanked the blade free. Iain sunk to the ground.

This pleased Rolfe even more.

"Yer brother had better have more sense than ye," Rolfe declared as Iain drew in his final breath. "For I will not ever allow the Mackenzies to raid me land."

The fire was burning down, smoke drifting away on the evening breeze. Rolfe felt his body shaking, his strength spent. Yet, what drew his attention the most were the wide eyes of the girl. She was frozen in place, staring at what had been her home and family just an hour before. He'd saved her and yet, Rolfe honestly questioned if he'd shown her any kindness. The emotional wounds she had were as deep as the ones her family members had physically suffered.

"Do ye have other kin, lass?" Donnach asked her softly.

The girl blinked at last, turning to look at him. She extended her arm, pointing at the two men lying on the ground.

Rolfe wiped his sword blade across Iain's lifeless body to clean the blood off. "We'll take ye up to the castle. See ye have a respectable position."

The girl wore on only a shift and her arisaid, but everything else was gone. The stone walls which made up the simple crofter home she'd lived in was naught but a smoking bowl. She clutched the Munro colors close.

Colors he would not allow to be trampled upon by anyone.

Even the Mackenzie.

≫≪

"FATHER."

Rhedyn stopped before the head table and performed a reverence.

"Daughter." Colum motioned her forward. "Ye are up at first light. Good. Come and keep this old man company."

Rhedyn enjoyed the opportunity to sit next to her father at the high table. It was just barely dawn but her mind had still been churning, so there was little reason to stay in bed. Her reward was the chance to sit beside her father because his captains weren't there yet. Two Retainers were standing behind her father though, their duty to see to his protection and evident in the way they didn't take their ease. One pulled a heavy chair out for her.

"Eat, daughter." Colum pushed a platter closer. There was cheese and fruit and a bit of butter left from the day before. Her father used the small dagger he'd been eating with to stab a chunk of cheese and deliver it to the plate which a maid had placed in front of her.

The castle was just stirring. In the kitchens, the first meal of the day would be simple porridge. But work would begin with a rush as the eggs and milk were brought in. Bread would be mixed and left to rise. In a few hours, the scent of roasting meat would mix with baking bread. Rhedyn caught a glimpse of the Head-of-House as the woman came to the opening between the great hall and the kitchens. She propped her hands onto her hips, frustrated by the laird's early arrival.

Colum chuckled and sent the woman a smile. "No hurry." He called out, but the woman had already turned and disappeared back into the kitchens where her authority was absolute.

"I did no' expect ye so early, Father." Rhedyn meant her words as pleasant conversation, but her father stopped chewing. Colum contemplated her for a long moment before he pointed the tip of his dagger at her.

"Ye have grown up daughter," Colum said slowly. "It is good." He resumed chewing. "Aye. As it should be. Ye know enough about adult matters now to understand what a man is about out at the Sow's Troth. I should no' be surprised."

He flattened his hand on the table top and slapped it several times while he swallowed. "Yer cousin is wedding next week. We'll go and enjoy the celebration."

Rhedyn didn't respond immediately. She took a moment to weigh her words, feeling the change between them. Her father was looking at her in a different way now. Seeing the woman she'd grown into instead of the child she had always been.

Well then, she would act like an adult.

"There is no reason to take me to a wedding in the hope I will suddenly be in the mood to wed."

Her father grinned at her. "As it seems ye are no longer a child, I would no' need to resort to such games in order to bring ye around to doing yer duty."

Rhedyn felt responsibility land on her shoulders. But she decided she liked the feeling. Yes, there was a demand which came with being seen as an adult, however, there was also a compliment in seeing her father gaze upon her as someone he might look to for assistance in managing the clan. In all the times she'd thought about her need to marry, she had never realized how much good it would bring to those she loved.

"Do ye have no feelings at all for Rolfe Munro, lass?" her father asked seriously.

Rhedyn swallowed the lump which suddenly formed in her throat. "I see his good points."

"He has much demand on his time with his father being ill and yet he came to court ye."

"I know father." Rhedyn quelled the urge to duck her chin. A woman didn't cower.

"Ye have no affection for him."

"I have no deep affection for any man," she offered.

Her father perked up, his gaze filling with approval. "Ye have a fine mind in that head, daughter. Looking for the logic in a situation and no' being led by yer emotions. We'll go to the wedding, see if any of the other laird's sons attend."

He then gave his full attention to the meal. The Head-of-House returned soon after with steaming bowls of porridge. His captains arrived, but when she made to rise and relinquish the chair beside him, her father clasped her wrist and bid her remain. His captains turned an inquiring look toward their laird, but Colum remained steadfast.

That feeling inside her grew. It seemed to glow, like coals did in the hearth on a cold winter morning when everything else was chilled to the core. Her life appeared to have naught but sharp edges with all its duties and requirements.

But inside, she felt the rewards of performing as she was expected to. Deep down in her heart she realized she was earning respect, instead of being afforded it because of who her father was. Something which was completely hers alone because she'd cultivated it.

She wouldn't disappoint her clan.

Not ever.

>>><<<

COLUM LINDSEY SAT at his desk late in the evening. He'd dismissed his secretary, preferring to pen a letter with his own hand. He dipped the quill into the inkwell, withdrawing it. A sheet of paper was laid out in front of him. He applied the tip to the parchment with care, forming his letters slowly, just the way his tutor had instructed him when he was a lad.

When he dipped the quill again, he looked at his fingers. The skin was no longer youthful. There was more than one scar from countless hours spent training with his sword.

That was a skill lost now. Age, it seemed, had no mercy for any man.

But as time had taken his vigor, it had also seen his daughter raised up into a fine woman. Colum smiled as he continued writing. Rolfe Munro was a good man. Given enough time, Rhedyn would find the affection she didn't yet have for him.

Colum finished his letter and nodded.

Aye. Just a bit more time together and the pair would make a perfect match.

Once the ink was completely dry, he folded it and sealed it with hot wax. He pressed his signet ring into the puddle of wax before it cooled.

"Connor," Colum called out. The Lindsey Retainer came into the study a moment later, his hand reaching up to tug on his cap.

"Take this to Munro land and make sure ye tell Rolfe I wrote it with me own hand."

Connor nodded before he turned and left. The study was silent, but Colum found himself humming a little tune as anticipation warmed his insides.

‐›››‹‹‹‐

"HURRY, RHEDYN!" BREE was excited. Her sister's eyes sparkled and her hair flowed freely for a change because it was a wedding. Maidens might forget their lien caps in favor of head wreaths. "They are coming back from the church doors now!"

Rhedyn smiled as her sister picked up huge handfuls of her skirts and yanked them to her knees as she ran.

"Go on with ye, daughter," Colum encouraged Rhedyn.

The Lindsey laird settled down with his men to watch the celebration. The couple had gone to the church doors for the blessing and were now returning to the green for dancing and merriment. A hogshead of ale had been newly tapped. The bride's father was happily filling mugs with nut-brown ale and handing them out as fast as the brew flowed.

Even the weather appeared to be in a good mood for the sky was blue with only a few clouds floating by. Everyone hurried up to the center of the green to take advantage of the lack of rain. Musicians gathered together to produce a melody that soon had the assembled company mopping their brows.

More people arrived. Different tartans mixing together as the first celebration of spring was at hand. Months of being locked behind walls because of snow had everyone in the mood to join in.

But the air of celebration died as swiftly as a man being dropped through the trap door of the gallows. A new group arrived, riding hard and nearly into the mass of wedding guest. Only at the last moment did they pull their horses to a stop and jump from the saddle.

"Colum Lindsey!"

Hamish Mackenzie stood at the far end of the field. He held his sword out with one arm, proving just how much strength he had. Not that Rhedyn might have missed it. From the way his shoulders blocked out the bright afternoon sun to the firm placement of his feet, there was nothing about him which said anything but strength. At his back were over two dozen Mackenzie Retainers. Each and every one of them intent on spilling blood.

"I demand satisfaction, Lindsey! Satisfaction for Iain Mackenzie who is newly dead due to yer actions!"

The accusation was sharp, cutting through every last conversation and leaving the assembled guests staring as they waited to see how Colum Lindsey would react.

"I never betrayed Clan Mackenzie," Colum declared firmly.

Rhedyn wished she didn't hear the hints of age in her father's voice. Yet, she couldn't force her ears to be deaf to the gravelly sound. Her father was well past his prime, his hair nearly white now. He presented a stark contrast to Hamish whose hair was dark as midnight and his face hard instead of sagging. In a straight fight, the victor was not likely to be her father. Yet, she knew that he would rather face the Mackenzie himself than allow the Lindsey Retainers to battle on his behalf because it would begin a feud.

"Me brother drank with ye before he rode out a week past," Hamish insisted. "He trusted ye to be his companion while his tongue was loosened, and ye betrayed him by telling the bloody Munro where he was going!"

The people gathered were intent on what was being said. Rhedyn watched as the women began to tug their children away. The tension was increasing as the group of Mackenzies moved closer to where Colum Lindsey sat with his men.

Rhedyn stepped in front of her younger sister, urging Bree back a few steps.

The sound of horses being ridden hard came closer. Almost anything would have been a welcome intrusion at that moment if it meant it distracted Hamish Mackenzie from his argument. But the men riding toward them were wearing the same colors as Hamish. Their leader was atop a huge stallion. The beast was more than fourteen-hands high and powerful enough to raise up chunks of earth with its hooves.

"Hold, Hamish!"

The leader of the new group of Mackenzie's issued his order in a tone which made it clear he expected obedience. Hamish Mackenzie's expression turned to one of frustration, but he lowered his sword.

The newcomer had three feathers on the side of his bonnet. They were secured with a gold broach which had the Mackenzie crest on it.

"Laird Buchanan Mackenzie," Colum greeted him. "Ye have fine timing, lad. Yer clansman is no' thinking matters through and ruining a fine celebration."

Buchanan landed in a wide stance before he was tossing his reins to a younger lad, who appeared quickly to see to the chore. The new laird of the Mackenzies was striding toward his clansmen a moment later, the longer pleats of his kilt swaying with the powerful motion of his stride. His face was a grim mask.

"Ye can nae mean to allow yer brother's murder to go unaccounted for?" Hamish Mackenzie demanded of his laird. "A half-brother is still blood."

Buchanan was taller than his clansman. Rhedyn watched the way he flashed a stern look at Hamish before stopping beside him.

"I have never called Iain anything but brother," Buchanan spoke directly to his clansman.

The two Mackenzies stood for what seemed like a very long moment before Hamish was nodding and reaching to place his hand on his laird's shoulder. "I knew I could count on ye to see justice done."

"Aye, I'm seeking justice," Buchanan spoke in a controlled tone. He lifted one hand and pointed at Colum Lindsey.

"Think man," Colum declared from where he was. "The Lindseys have long been allies with the Mackenzies. I would no' betray ye."

Hamish turned on Colum. "Do ye deny that Iain was drinking with ye at the Sow's Troth before he went out to raid the Munro?"

"I do not deny he was at the Sow's Troth at the same time I was," Colum stated. "We did no' drink together, for he was in a foul temper. Plenty of men saw it."

"And then…" Hamish raised his voice so it carried to everyone watching. "Ye shared a drink with Donnach Munro!"

"The Sow's Troth is a tavern, man," Colum answered. "More than one clan can enter the establishment. I do nae have the right to stand between the owner of the place and his customers."

"Ye besotted old goat!" Hamish declared. "After ye passed out, Donnach Munro rode after Iain and cut him down. Everyone knows ye are negotiating with the Munro for an alliance! Did ye seal the deal with Iain's spilt blood?"

There was a rumble of anger from the Mackenzie Retainers. In response, Colum's men puffed out their chests, making it plain they wouldn't back down. Rhedyn felt her fingernails cutting into the palms of her hands as she clenched her fingers into tight fists. Spilled blood would only ever be paid for with more bloodshed.

"The Munro share a border with me land as well as the Mackenzies," Colum replied. "Rolfe Munro has come to meet me daughter."

"Which means ye are guilty!" Hamish roared.

The burly Highlander lunged toward Colum. Rhedyn realized too late that she was on the wrong side of the fight. It hadn't seemed so great a distance while the music had played and she and her sister had joined in the dancing.

Now, her own clansmen were too far away to help her and Bree. Rhedyn turned toward her sister, intent on running, but her motion drew attention to them.

"Perhaps we'll simply deal with the matter by striking down yer own blood." Hamish's gaze settled on her. "An eye for an eye."

Rhedyn turned back around to shield her sister.

A fox will always chase a fleeing rabbit...

Her heart was beating so fast, it felt like it would be bruised from the impact with her ribs. But she stood in place, lifting her chin even as she felt her eyes widening in spite of her determination to face up to the Mackenzies.

She would not flee like frightened prey...

She was a Lindsey. And the laird's daughter. She would stand her ground.

"A fair enough exchange," Hamish snarled. "Our laird only had two children, ye have only the two daughters...each will be left with only one..."

Hamish came closer, allowing Rhedyn to see the hate distorting his features. There was a savage gleam in his eyes, and it chilled her to the bone, for she recognized it as the sight of a man who had no mercy in his soul.

"Mackenzies, do nae cut down women." Buchanan stepped into the path of his clansmen. "Much less a half-grown lass."

Hamish shifted his attention to Buchanan, offering Rhedyn the chance to escape. She turned and shoved her sister away. With a single, wide-eyed look, Bree grabbed fistfuls of her skirt and lifted the fabric high enough to expose her knobby knees. She ran toward the safety of her father's men.

Rhedyn intended to follow her sister, but a hard grip on her upper arm jerked her back.

"Blood for blood," Hamish declared. "The Lindsey have taken an heir to the Mackenzies, we are owed one of their laird's line in return."

Rhedyn felt her heart suddenly stop. She was somehow suspended between heartbeats as she heard the Mackenzie Retainers muttering in agreement.

So, this was what blood lust was...

She drew in a stiff breath to fend off a wave of blurry vision. If she was to die, she'd bloody well face her fate with courage. Her vision sharpened, allowing her to stare straight into the eyes of Buchanan Mackenzie. He gripped her by the upper arm, pulling her in front of him.

By Christ, he was big.

Wide shoulders gave way to arms which were thick with muscle. His eyes were topaz and flickering with temper.

"Killing that old goat will no' be an even exchange for Iain," Hamish pressed his opinion. "The price paid must be equal to what the Lindseys have taken from the Mackenzies."

The Mackenzie Retainers grumbled in agreement.

"Ye bastards," Colum Lindsey said from across the green. "Are ye the bloody English, then? Settling business between men with me daughter?" He grunted and reached for a sword. "Bring yer fight to me, Buchanan Mackenzie."

Rhedyn felt her breath freeze in her chest. "Nae...he is an old man...ye must not. Please do...not fight him." She curled her fingers around his forearm, unconsciously attempting to keep him from meeting her father's challenge. His eyes narrowed, his jaw clenching.

But all around them the rumblings were increasing and growing in volume. Blood lust was contagious it would seem.

⟫⟫⟪⟪

BUCHANAN MACKENZIE SETTLED his attention on Colum as he raised his hand, making it plain he was going to render his decision. The Mackenzie Retainers went silent.

Rhedyn could only wait helplessly.

"Since ye have naught but daughters," Buchanan began, "it seems there is no way to even this score without them."

Colum was turning red with rage, but Buchanan didn't wavier.

"I do nae spill women's blood," Buchanan said. There was a rumble of approval from those watching. "But Hamish is correct in saying that the loss of me brother can only be paid for by taking one of yer direct kin."

The grip on her arm tightened past the point of pain. But it was nothing compared to the look of raw anguish on her father's face. Her sire was struggling to draw in a breath, his lips moving as he attempted to force an argument past his horror.

"Me daughter—"

"Belongs to me now," Buchanan finished for him. "The next man who thinks to betray the Mackenzies better hear of this matter and know we will extract a high price for betrayal."

>>>><<<<

RHEDYN BLINKED MORE than once throughout the rest of the afternoon and into the evening as she attempted to wake up from the living nightmare and leave the Mackenzies behind.

Luck didn't favor her. They rode hard and long before stopping to rest the horses. In spite of how badly she wanted to leave the saddle, Rhedyn didn't because such an action would leave more vulnerable to the Makenzie Retainers.

"Get off the horse."

The Mackenzie Retainer who spoke didn't give Rhedyn time to comply with his demand. He hooked her arm with his large hand and pulled her over the side of the beast she sat on. The only mercy he afforded her was to keep her from crashing to the ground, because both her legs weren't beneath her as she landed.

His mercy was short lived. With a snort of disgust, he flung her away from the horse and turned to take the reins. Rhedyn stumbled, stepping on her skirt. She fought against the motion of her body, succeeding in avoiding falling face first in the dirt. There was an ominous sound from the waistband of her skirt as stiches were ripped. With a little hop, she managed to get her feet off the wool fabric and back onto the ground.

Several of the Mackenzie Retainers offered her disdainful glares.

Rhedyn straightened her back. One of the men didn't care for her lack of fear. He had a scar running across his forehead from a knife blade, and it served to make him appear nightmarish. The way his lips curled into a sneer only completed the moment.

"Ye'll soon learn yer place, Lindsey bitch," he said.

He raised his hand to strike her, but she didn't lower her head. She stared straight at him. Since pride was all she had left, she'd hold tight to it.

A hard tug on her skirt sent her back before the blow landed.

"Relieve yerself," Buchanan ordered without any care for the delicate topic. He jerked his head in the direction of an outcropping of trees. "Quickly, or ye can wet yerself for all I care."

Her cheeks heated, but she turned and went the direction he'd indicated. She had the feeling having her bodily functions mentioned was going to be the least of her concerns while she kept company with the Mackenzies.

But obeying her captor did take her away from the men who had so very recently demanded her blood be spilled.

She'd never hated her father's neighboring clan. However, she'd been raised with a healthy respect for their strength. The younger lads of the Lindseys might be brazen enough to talk about lifting a few head of cattle from the Mackenzies, but none of them actually did it. At least not very often. The Mackenzies were known for making certain they took twice as much as someone stole from them. The current circumstances were proof of that.

Rhedyn looked up after finishing her business and drew in a deep breath. She caught the scent of rain coming on the night breeze. Her heart thumped, and her nose felt chilled as the moon began to rise.

She mustn't allow herself to despair. Better to put her strength to use in thinking of a solution.

The Mackenzies were powerful, but that didn't make the Lindseys weaklings. Taking a man's daughter wouldn't reflect well on the Mackenzies. They might be the stronger clan, but if the Munros and Lindseys united against them, the Mackenzies wouldn't be assured of victory.

Rhedyn felt her fear receding. She couldn't be the only one who realized the facts. Buchanan wouldn't have lasted as laird for a year if he didn't have any sense.

An owl cried out somewhere in the distance. Darkness was deepening around them, the moon a sliver in the sky. Rhedyn realized she was very much alone. Could it be Buchanan was giving her a hint to run and allow him to save face with his men?

In any case, she couldn't afford to waste the chance to escape.

But her first step caused a crunching sound as she set her foot down on a stick, which had dried out in the warm spring weather.

Do nae panic...

She might be a lass, but she was also her father's daughter. She set out again; this time, she lowered her foot slowly. She felt the debris on the forest floor depress beneath her weight, but no sound came. Satisfaction filled her even though she battled the rise of frustration over how slow her progress was. Every tiny sound was cause for alarm. Still, she'd press on.

"I should have let ye wet yerself."

A half cry got past her lips as she was shoved into the thick trunk of a tree by a single hand placed across her throat. Buchanan's grasp was impossibly strong. She withered against it, unable to quell the urge to struggle. He held her without any strain, staring at her silently until she went still.

"I do nae fancy having a stinking woman riding near enough for me to suffer the stench, or I would no' have allowed ye a bit of privacy," he groused.

Buchanan was only a shadow in the moonlight.

But that was enough to send fear through her.

In the darkness, the Mackenzie laird embodied every whispered tale of marauders she'd ever heard by the hearth in the dead of winter when the old women had done their best to frighten the younger girls into obedience by recounting stories of what happened to those who didn't stick close to the kitchens and chaperones. Tales of girls left dead by the side of the road who walked the night as ghosts because their souls were so tormented.

"Ye are no very bright, are ye Rhedyn Lindsey?" Buchanan had leaned toward her, his voice a rough whisper. "Why are ye making me take ye in hand?"

It was strange the way her name sobered her. Somehow, hearing it cut through her rising fear, leaving her once more holding tightly to her identity and the need to maintain her dignity, no matter the circumstances. She'd thought the matter through. Reasoning was the way to gain her freedom.

"Why…keep me?" Her voice was a ghost of a whisper. "Ye can let me go…and no one will be the wiser. Ye have appeased the tempers of yer men by taking me. But keeping me will enrage more than just the Lindsey. Ye must see it's best to allow me to escape."

"Ye'd have me tell men I expect to follow me into battle that I can nae keep control of one small lass?" He let out a snort. "They'll rip these feathers off me bonnet, and me balls as well, to make certain I do nae father any idiotic spawn to insult the Mackenzie name."

His hard retort threatened to undermine her composure.

"Ye needn't be vulgar," Rhedyn admonished. Perhaps chastising him wasn't the wisest choice, but the words were across her lips before she managed to think twice about the matter.

His fingers tightened in response. "Ye will no' be telling me what to do."

She glowered at him and discovered she preferred boldness to meekness.

"Allow me to leave, and ye can be certain I will not give ye any trouble," she said. "Ride away and take yer men. Be wise enough to see taking me along will only end in bloodshed for both our kin."

Bold, impulsive words.

Well, they felt better than being strangled by her own fear…

"By the sound of ye," Buchanan moved in closer, "I may have made a grave error in taking ye. Colum might just consider himself well rid of the shrew ye sound like."

Rhedyn gasped. She was suddenly trying to tear at the fingers clasping her throat. Her captor leaned in so that he could use his body to keep her pinned in place, but she wasn't finished fighting. She lifted her knee, jamming it up toward his groin as she'd been taught by her father's war chief.

"Christ." Buchanan growled as he shifted, so her knee collided with his thigh instead. His grip tightened on her neck, making it impossible to draw even breath into her body. Her eyes burned, and her vision began to waver. Still, she fought on, digging her fingernails into the skin on his forearm.

"Ye label me vulgar for mentioning them," Buchanan spoke so close to her face, she felt his breath against her lips. "But someone sure as hell told ye where a man's balls are."

"I was taught to defend myself against villains!" Rhedyn cried.

She felt him stiffen. A moment later, she was sagging against the trunk of the tree, her throat free from his grip. She sucked in a deep breath as she lifted her gaze, ignoring the weakness threatening to buckle her knees and sweep her away on a wave of blackness. She would not crumple at his feet. But the time it took for her to catch her breath also saw her temper flickering out. Buchanan stood silent, as though she was questioning his actions.

Ye are seeing what ye want to see in him…

Perhaps she just couldn't stop herself from trying to get him to see the logic in allowing her to escape. Huge and hulking as he was, she still didn't see him as a blaggard. But how to awaken his sympathy?

Buchanan had retreated several steps and hooked his hands around the wide, leather belt holding the pleats of his plaid in place.

"Ye do nae care to be called villain?" she asked, more stunned by the way such a simple word had succeeded in making him release her than she ever could have imagined.

"Yer father betrayed me blood," he answered. "What I have done is seek justice."

"There is no proof that my father is guilty," Rhedyn said. "Simply because he was at the Sow's Troth doesn't mean he betrayed yer kin."

"And there is still plenty of proof that he did spill the information on where my brother was bound," Buchanan responded. "If I release ye, me men will insist I fight yer father. Ye asked me no' to do so. Hence, ye are coming with me."

Stalemate…

They locked gazes, neither of them looking away. Duty was something sitting on both their shoulders in that moment. She should have been thinking about how to convince him that he was doing wrong but instead, Rhedyn discovered herself seeing what they had in common.

He grunted a moment later, reaching out to close his fingers around her upper arm. "Ye are coming with us, mistress. Step one foot beyond where I tell ye, and I'll have ye bound to make certain ye are where I place ye. It's up to ye how uncomfortable ye will be on this journey."

There was a look in his eyes which sent a shiver down her spine. But what chilled her blood was the fact that she was very certain Buchanan was a man who would back up his words without hesitation.

She was his captive and the worst part was, she could see the logic in his actions.

"YE MIGHT HAVE waited until we got home to toss her skirts."

It was Hamish who made the vulgar comment.

But what made Buchanan shove Rhedyn toward his captain, Graham, was the fact that several of his men made approving noises in response.

It sickened him.

"Rape is an ugly thing." Buchanan spoke carefully for his men were still spoiling for a fight. "It leaves a stain on a man's soul. Taking Colum's daughter is one thing. Committing an act of violence on her, well, that is another matter altogether."

"The daughter of a traitor deserves no better," Hamish insisted. "How else are ye planning to gain justice for Iain's death?"

Hamish faced off with him, clearly discontented with Buchanan's handling of the matter.

"Fighting an old man would no' have served the Mackenzie name well." Buchanan informed Hamish. "Nor would have turning that wedding into a massacre. Think, man. If we'd acted like savages, every clan represented there would have united against us fearing they would be next. Justice is what ye crave but as yer laird, I have to keep me mind on what will serve the clan best."

His men had been set to stand firm with Hamish, but they considered his thinking, many of them nodding reluctantly in agreement.

"Taking Colum's daughter accomplishes naught if we plan to do nothing with her," Hamish said, clearly unwilling to see reason.

"I left a slice across Colum Lindsey's heart that will no' ever heal so long as he knows his daughter is mine to do with as I please," Buchanan delivered his opinion in an icy tone. "If she's dead, she no longer suffers. He can console himself with the knowledge that she is at rest."

Hamish snorted. He looked past Buchanan to where she stood. Hate burned brightly in his eyes.

The man Buchanan had shoved her toward caught her by the wrist and tugged her over to where the horses were. The disgruntled expression on his face made it plain he had no liking for his task. But he started to lean over and interlace his fingers to help her mount.

>>>><<<<

"I CAN MANAGE quite well," Rhedyn muttered. She wanted to sound more composed, but the truth was Buchanan's words had chilled her to the bone.

'If she's dead, she no longer suffers…'

Rhedyn fought back the need to retch in response. Was she truly so lacking in courage that simple words were enough to make her sick? By Christ, she refused to allow it to be so. She'd managed a conversation with the beast, so there was no reason to be sick now.

She reached up and grasped the bridle. The horse they'd given her was mild tempered as far as stallions went. Which was to say, she'd be wise to make sure she kept a watchful eye on the animal if she didn't care to end up tossed off its back.

Not that she blamed the creature. In fact, she decided the horse and herself were rather well matched. Both of them were expected to endure what the Mackenzies burdened them with.

Graham watched as she led the horse around to where there were several large rocks. Rhedyn spoke softly to the animal. With a final pat, she lifted her skirt and used one of the rocks as a stepping-off spot. The beast shifted when she settled into the saddle. She ran a hand along its neck in a soothing motion.

"Glad to know I don't have to be mothering ye," Graham said before he turned to see to his own horse.

Rhedyn looked down at the reins.

So tempting…

One good dig with her heels into the sides of the stallion and it would take off into the night. She could feel the strength of the beast, felt how wide it was across its back. Of course, she expected no less from any horse the Mackenzies had ridden out of their stronghold.

"Ye are coming with us, mistress. Step one foot beyond where I tell ye, and I'll have ye bound to make certain ye are where I place ye. It's up to ye how uncomfortable ye will be on this journey."

Rhedyn cast a look toward Buchanan as his words rose from her memory. The Mackenzie laird was testing the strap securing his saddle to the back of his horse, but he turned his head so their gazes met.

She wished she didn't feel that connection so keenly.

The urge to flee intensified with knowing he was staring at her.

Don't be foolish…

Rhedyn listened to her instincts and forced herself to take in her surroundings. Over half of Buchanan's Retainers were mounted. They'd run her down with pathetic ease.

Her plight was pitiful enough without ending in the dirt at their feet.

Even knowing that, she discovered her legs frozen to the sides of the horse. Graham gave her a jerk of his head, and still she found it impossible to urge her horse into motion.

But the horse knew which direction home lay in. As the rest of the Mackenzies fell into line, her horse tossed its head and began to follow. She bit her lip to contain the sound of despair which tried to escape from her.

She must be smarter than her captors, for they'd win when it came to a matching of strength. Out thinking them, well, there was where her opportunity lay. Such would be just as much of a challenge as matching blow for blow with them.

All of her life, she had heard tales of courage and bravery. Such traits had been expounded upon as virtues which offered rich rewards to those who displayed them in times of adversity. Right then, she knew without a doubt she was engaged in the battle of her life.

She had only her own resources to draw upon. Lessons learned through her childhood were going to be put to the test, her mettle proven. She drew in a breath and looked at the fortress growing larger with every step of her horse.

Well, if she was alone, then she would simply have to measure up to the challenge her life had become.

She was still her father's daughter, after all.

⇒⇒⇒⇐⇐⇐

FIRST LIGHT CAME early.

Colum Lindsey was already in the yard by the time the birds started singing.

"Laird…"

Colum turned on his captain. "Do nae lecture me! I am no' some woman to be sent back to her bed. Me daughter has been taken, I have me honor to reclaim."

Rory shut his mouth and ran a hand down his beard. The man was clearly contemplating his next argument.

"How can I rest when me daughter is in the hands of Buchanan Mackenzie?" Colum reached for the saddle sitting over the rail between stalls.

But another man lifted it up. "Ye can rest, because I will see to the matter."

Colum stood in silence as he watched the other man place the saddle on the back of a horse. His hands were skilled as they secured it and soothed the stallion. Colum had thought there wasn't a man alive who might have convinced him to forgo riding out after Rhedyn.

God had a twisted sense of humor at times, for standing there in the Lindsey stable was a young man Colum had spent countless nights praying to catch a glimpse of. He'd begged on his knees for the Almighty to grant him the opportunity to speak with the man.

"So," Colum began but stopped because he needed to swallow the lump in his throat. "It seems ye have finally decided to come and listen

30

to me side of the tale at last."

Vychan's hands stilled on the horse. Colum drank in his wide shoulders and height. Vychan turned and offered Colum a look which reminded him of himself thirty years before. But Vychan stared at him with a pair of green eyes, the same eyes Colum had fallen in love with so long ago. Tears prickled his eyes.

"Yer father," Vychan began roughly, "forbid ye to wed me mother. What more is there to say?"

Memories rushed back to Colum; it seemed the years had done little to dull the edges of his emotions. He recognized the same flare of youth in Vychan's eyes which Colum hadn't felt stir in himself in a decade. He swallowed his anger and drew on his experience to temper his mood. He'd been yearning for a chance to tell his only son his side of the story.

He didn't need to bungle it. The righteousness in Vychan's expression betrayed how much the younger man wanted to be done with the matter altogether. One good bout of temper, and Colum would never see his son again.

"Me father," Colum began, "had my respect as the scripters say is me duty, but he was no' long for the world when I met your mother."

"Ye put a babe in her belly." Vychan skipped to the thing most important to him. "Yer actions condemned her to birthing a bastard."

"Yer mother and I…" His son's jaw tightened. "Yer mother and I were both made fools of by love. Me father was a callous man who never valued such tender emotions. Yer mother showed me they were worth risking everything for. And I was set to leave with her, until I suddenly realized I had to find a way to provide for ye both. Suffering me father's bitterness for his remaining days became a price I could pay if it meant a warm home for ye during the winter instead of an uncertain fate against the elements. I knew at that moment the folly of me youth. The lesson landed hard on me. Yer mother wouldn't see it. The moment my father was gone, I would have afforded her every bit of respect due me wife. The rest of the Lindsey clan was no' harsh with her, for they knew I planned to wed her. Me father was dying. What sort of a son would I have been to leave him alone in the last months of his life?"

Colum suddenly felt every one of his years. His knees ached, and his back felt like it was impossible to straighten. He looked at his son and let out a soft grunt.

"Yer mother placed her hand on the altar and swore she'd never wed me because I wouldn't disrespect me father's will and run away with her that spring." Colum lowered himself onto a bench. "Those words gutted me, for I loved her, son. I still do."

Vychan wanted to argue. Colum could see the anger in his eyes. But there was something else there—maturity.

"My mother had a temper as red as her hair," Vychan admitted.

Colum felt the tightness in his chest easing as his son's lips twitched into a grin.

"But I did no' wed that Grant lass me father had me contracted to," Colum said. "I wrote to yer mother more than once after me father passed away. I laid me heart open to her, and she never replied. Ye were still on her breast when me father died. Ye would never have known ye were born a bastard, for I would have wed her. As laird, no man would have dared talked about the timing of it all. But yer mother was true to her word and kept ye from me."

Vychan looked down. He drew in a deep breath and reached into his jerkin. He pulled out a leather pouch.

"I did nae find these until after me mother died. She did receive yer letters."

Vychan unfolded the pouch so weathered parchment could be seen inside.

Colum flinched. "So ye know I waited for her, waited for her heart to overrule her wounded pride. Son, she was as drawn to me as I was to her. But I'm no making excuses. Being a man means thinking about the consequences of yer actions. Still, if I say to ye I regret giving into passion, then I am saying I wish ye were no' born, and that would be a lie."

"Aye." Vychan laid the pouch of letters down on the bench beside Colum. For a moment, he clasped his wide belt and stared at Colum. "It's the truth that I've cursed yer name more than once. But…" Vychan held up a finger to keep Colum from speaking. "But I realize now, me mother made her choices, and it's a solid fact that ye did no' wed until a full five years after yer father's death."

"I was waiting," Colum declared. "Waiting for her."

Vychan nodded. "I see the truth of it. So, I am here. That's my choice, to see ye and ask ye man to man about the matter." Vychan was still for a long moment. "I have no quarrel with ye."

Colum stood up, feeling stronger and taller than he had in years. His bones no longer ached. He placed his hand on Vychan's shoulder.

"This is me son!" Colum announced. Men who had been lingering nearby in case the laird needed protection, emerged from the shadows. Colum patted Vychan on the shoulder, grinning at the solid feeling beneath his palm. "Me wife is dead, and yer mother never wed," Colum said. "Follow me to the church, lad, I'm going to wed yer mother at long last and see ye legitimized."

If anyone thought the idea of wedding a dead woman was odd, none of them opened their mouths to voice concern. Instead, the crowd of people grew until the Lindsey castle was empty. They gathered around the church as the priest came forward to perform the ceremony.

Was it strange? The man of God might have thought so, but he began the blessing anyway. Life had far too many moments of disappointment and death, so it was important to celebrate the rare opportunities for them all to be happy. A clan without a clear successor was one headed for a bloody fight when Colum died.

One strange wedding seemed little cost to prevent so many deaths.

CHAPTER TWO

B UCHANAN'S STRONGHOLD WAS everything Rhedyn expected of a clan as powerful as the Mackenzies. It was a full castle. As they came around another endless bend in the road, the first of seven towers came into view. The horses picked up their pace, sensing an end to the journey. They'd traveled the entire night and on into the middle of the day. Ahead of them, the chimneys were letting out tapers of smoke, promising a hot meal.

Her mouth should have watered but instead, horror chilled her blood.

Thick walls ran between the towers. The entire structure was built up against a huge outcropping of solid stone. It looked a bit like the castle had grown from the stone itself. Escaping it would be impossible.

She shook her head. She had plenty of misfortune without allowing her mind to take flight. Tales of dragons and warriors needed to stay behind her in the winter evenings, where such stories belonged. She had enough trouble with the Mackenzies surrounding her without allowing herself to believe they were too powerful. They were strong; she knew that truth. But she wouldn't abandon hope.

Buchanan had to manage the same things any laird did.

Opinion.

She took hope from that idea. The Mackenzie laird had brought her home, but he really couldn't keep her too long.

He can and ye know it has happened before…

Rhedyn chided herself for thinking such a dreary thought. Since she'd always known she would marry with an alliance in mind, traveling to a strange place had also always been in her fate. She blinked and looked at the Makenzie stronghold again, this time making herself consider it through the eyes of a bride arriving.

Buchanan wasn't her groom.

At least he wasn't planning to bed her.

Rhedyn discovered herself recalling the way he'd recoiled from being labeled a villain. A trait worthy of respect.

You might just be desperate…

Rhedyn didn't bother to deny the charge. Did she dare to hope he might only hold her as his revenge? If so, she'd be grateful to him. Immeasurably so, for the men he rode with cast her looks which made it plain they cared not if she called them the blackest-hearted spawns of hell itself.

Where there was life, there was hope. Even Highland tempers cooled with time.

The bells set along the walls to help warn of impending attack started ringing. By the time they rode through the open front gates, the Mackenzies had gathered to celebrate the arrival of their laird and his men.

But they weren't cheerful. No, they'd known the reason their laird had ridden out. At first, the women counted the Retainers as they rode into the inner courtyard. Relief appeared on their faces after the last man arrived.

Which left only Rhedyn for them to shift their attention to. They aimed angry looks toward her and the strip of Lindsey plaid attached to her right shoulder and trailing down her back. Her airsaid was a practical garment because it might be used to cover her head when the chill of evening came. It also made clear what blood ran through her veins.

The Mackenzies snarled as she got close. More than one man

made a point of spitting in her path once she was off the horse and being pushed toward the stairs of the largest keep. Women leaned their heads together to whisper around her, while Graham finished his duties by releasing her at the top of the steps in front of the double doors which opened to show her a huge great hall.

"Laird Lindsey's daughter, by Christ."

"No' fit to scrub the steps Iain pissed on."

"Spilling her blood will be a pleasure…"

Buchanan wasn't deaf. He'd stopped to talk with a captain who had ventured out into the yard. The Mackenzie laird looked up, catching sight of her on the steps. His eyes narrowed before he was striding toward her. His gaze was filled with annoyance as he passed her.

"Follow me."

Assisting with her own abduction wasn't precisely what Rhedyn would have preferred to do.

But remaining among the Mackenzies and their growing outrage seemed far worse. She continued forward and heard several snickers behind her.

"I'll find ye, Lindsey bitch…" someone called after her. "Sleep light…"

At least the effort of keeping pace with Buchanan gave her little energy for thinking about the threat which rang in her ears.

"Tyree!" Buchanan called out as he strode across the great hall.

It was a grand place. Long trestle tables with benches were set out for the noon meal. The scent of roasting meat was thick in the air, making her mouth water. If there had been any food on the ride into Buchanan's territory, no one had bothered to share any with her.

Not that she had noticed her empty belly with all the tension around her.

Buchanan passed through the hall to the back of the keep where stone steps were. A huge man emerged from the passageway which would lead to the kitchens. He had too many scars on his face to count. His bonnet was pulled over his bald head. A huge set of keys dangled from the worn, leather belt he wore. Big ones and small alike, the Butler of the Mackenzie kitchen looked more than able to defend whatever stock was locked away to keep it from being pilfered.

"Keys," Buchanan demanded with his hand outstretched.

The Butler pulled the ring loose and handed it over. He eyed Rhedyn as his laird took the ring of keys with a jingle and mounted the stairs.

"Best ye get going lass," Tyree muttered as Rhedyn locked gazes with him.

"Ye'll follow or I'll leave ye to those waiting on the steps," Buchanan said from above her.

Her temper heated as she climbed up several flights of stairs, hiking her skirts so she might catch up to Buchanan. The great hall was left far below them as Buchanan kept going. At last he stopped and flipped through the keys. He fit one of them into a lock which was holding two ends of a chain together through a pair of wooden slats. One slat was on the wall, the other on a door. When the chain was free, it clattered as the end through the slat on the door was pulled free.

"Inside with ye," Buchanan ordered her gruffly.

No matter how ominous the sneers and threats below had been, Rhedyn still found her feet unwilling to move. Opening the door released air that was stale from how long the room had been closed. It was murky, as only fingers of sunlight made it through the edges of the window shutters. Those rays of light illuminated dust swirling up into the air.

No one visited this room.

And once locked inside, she would be easily forgotten.

Buchanan grunted and caught her upper arm. A moment later, she was skidding across the inside of the chamber, stirring up more dust.

She turned toward the door, unable to quell the urge to look for a way to escape.

Buchanan blocked the only exit.

"Ye are going to be a bloody lot of trouble, mistress," Buchanan accused.

He'd braced himself in the doorway, his arms across his chest and his feet shoulder-width apart, a combative stance.

"You don't want me," she said. "Ye hate my blood."

Buchanan's lips twitched. It was the unkindest grin she had ever seen.

"Me kin hate ye at this moment," Buchanan confirmed. "There is no honor in striking down an old man. I will have ye here to torment him."

His eyes narrowed, his expression bitter as though being too close to her turned his stomach. "Kill yerself, and I will return for yer sister."

Rhedyn gasped. "Bree is too young! Ye must not touch her."

Buchanan lifted his shoulder in a shrug. "I will see yer father bleed. He will know he could not protect his own daughter."

He cast a final look of loathing toward her before he was turning to give her his back. The longer pleats of his kilt swung out behind him as he sent the door shut. The chain made a chilling sound as it was looped back through the slats on the outside. It was a good thing no one had fed her, because her belly heaved as she heard the lock grinding.

Her sister's face rose from her memories, sweet and innocent, so oblivious to the hate filling so much of the world.

Rhedyn's stomach heaved again at the idea of Bree being where Buchanan might scare her.

Or worse…

The words cast her way from the Mackenzies made it clear their laird was hardly the worst of her concerns. Her true fears would become reality when she was without Buchanan's protection.

So, she would simply have to find the strength to endure. Lifting her arm, Rhedyn drew her sleeve across her face, wiping her tears away.

She would never cry again.

Not about Buchanan.

He wasn't worthy of her tears.

⟫⟫⟨⟨

BUCHANAN WAS DISGUSTED with himself. But Tyree was waiting just below the landing where the storeroom door was located. Several of his Retainers had followed them into the kitchen and stood waiting to hear what had been done with their captive. Iain was blood. Makenzie blood. And other men of the clan had been at his back when he'd died. The lust for revenge wouldn't burn out quickly or easily.

"No one," Buchanan stressed his order, "is to unlock that door without me telling them to."

Tyree nodded as he caught the ring of keys. Buchanan heard them jingle when the Butler attached them to his belt once more.

It was the best he might do...

That, though, further disgusted Buchanan as he climbed two floors to where his chamber was. The door was open as his Head-of-House directed a stream of lads inside with yokes over their shoulders. The sound of water being poured filled the chamber.

"Welcome home, Laird," Fenella greeted him. She was his Head-of-House, another ring of keys attached to her belt.

"I've told ye before," Buchanan admonished her softly, "Ye do nae need to prepare a bath in me chamber. I can use the bathhouse."

"It wouldn't be fitting now that ye are laird."

Fenella knew her art well. A maid was making sure a fire was crackling so that the length of linen she'd placed in front of it would be warm once Buchanan finished in the large tub. There was a splash as two more buckets of water were poured into it. The boy hauling the water reached up and tugged on the corner of his cap as he passed Buchanan on the way to the door. The maid used a handful of her skirt to grip the handle of a pot that was hanging over the fire. Steam rose from the water as she carried it to the tub and dumped it.

Fenella dipped her fingers into the tub to test the temperature. "Do ye care to have Innis remain to scrub yer back?"

The maid was waiting, but she wasn't looking at the floor submissively. Instead, she aimed a knowing look toward Buchanan, one which made it clear she was hoping to do more than wash his back. She leaned just a bit forward so her cleavage was in his view.

His father had made use of such invitations often, and he'd handed out rewards to his favorite members of the staff.

"I'll manage well on me own, Fenella."

She frowned. "Perhaps, Una? She has golden hair."

Buchanan shook his head and sat down to begin unlacing his boots. Innis was quick to move toward him, slipping to her knees to help work the leather lace free of the antler-horn buttons which ran on either side of the opening. It was caked with mud and grime from the road, but she applied herself to the chore with zeal. He struggled to hide his distaste. Was it too much to ask of fate for a woman to reach for him because she desired him freely and no his position as laird?

Rhedyn hadn't offered herself to him in leu of not being locked above the kitchen.

But how long would the lass's resolve last?

Buchanan was suddenly bone weary.

"I'll bathe by meself, Fenella. Go on with ye both now," Buchanan encouraged them.

Innis sat back on her haunches and sent a look toward Fenella.

"Do nae start thinking I don't have a taste for women," Buchanan admonished them both.

"I would no' dare think such a thing," Fenella defended herself quickly.

Too bloody quickly...

Buchanan finished with one lace and pulled the boot off his foot. "Me father has no' been in his grave for more than a season. A bit of decorum is called for. As it is, ye insisted I move into this chamber."

"It is the laird's chamber," Fenella stated firmly. "Every castle has its spies. We can nae have any talk about whether or not ye have been accepted as the new laird. If ye took yer bath behind the kitchens, everyone would say I don't accept ye as me laird."

Fenella snapped her fingers at Innis. They both lowered themselves before they left. Buchannan reached up and drew his hand down his face. There were moments when he wished himself the humblest of crofter sons.

Rhedyn likely felt similar at that moment.

That thought sobered him.

More like shamed ye....

He tossed his kilt aside and pulled his shirt over his shoulders. The tub was warm and inviting, but as he sank into the water, he wasn't feeling anything but disgust for his actions.

There were a great many things he'd known becoming laird would make him. But a kidnapper? There was something he'd not contemplated doing. At least not beyond a bit of well-meant ribbing over some ransom for a bride perhaps.

At least vengeance is no' leaving ye satisfied...

Perhaps there was some satisfaction in that idea. Buchanan ducked his head beneath the water and worked a lump of soap through the strands of his hair.

But he couldn't dismiss the guilt gnawing at his insides. His father had tried to explain it to him more than once. Buchanan felt the memories stirring as he rinsed the soap off.

Son, a laird must do what will cause the least suffering. Even when the path to that end is no' something you might have ever seen yourself taking.

Doing the wrong thing, for the right reason...

Buchanan understood it now. As he rose from the tub, he felt his teeth grinding. For certain, Rhedyn would like a bath, but he didn't dare order one taken to her. His clan wanted her blood, and if he wasn't going to appease that demand, then the Mackenzies certainly wanted to know their enemy's daughter was suffering discomfort.

She was a strong lass.

Alone, he might contemplate the strength she'd displayed. If she stood up to him in front of his clan, though, he'd have to crush her. But there was some solace in the fact that she was a woman. Even if he crushed her, she'd live, and in time, he'd find a way to send her back to her father.

It was an imperfect solution to a bad situation. But what mattered was the good which would come out of it. Even if Colum Lindsey had muttered the details of where Iain was riding, Buchanan wasn't fool enough to discount the fact that his half-brother had to bear part of the responsibility for his own death. Raiding by moonlight meant accepting the risk that those ye rode against might not allow ye to take what was theirs.

The problem lay in the men who had ridden at Iain's side. Good Mackenzies who could no more abandon their laird's brother than their own colors. Even if they'd been opposed to the actions of their leader, they'd have fought to the bitter end beside him.

And so, they'd died.

And now, Buchanan was tasked with keeping his Retainers from riding out to spill Lindsey blood in retaliation that would spawn a chain of bloodshed.

A crofter's son…

Well, he was the laird's son and now laird. Even a crofter's son could be tasked with no' being a coward and facing up to the challenges presented to him by life. Achievement wasn't at the end of the easy path. Rhedyn was a laird's daughter. She'd know it, too.

In any event, they were both stuck with their lots. And that was simply the end of it.

And they were stuck with each other, too.

That was the part Buchanan knew without a doubt was going to keep him awake.

⟫⟫⟩⟨⟨⟨

BUCHANAN HAD LOCKED her in a storeroom.

At least it had functioned as one at some point. Now, it was mostly empty. A thick layer of dust lay over the entire floor, affording Rhedyn a clear view of her own tracks. Her nose tickled as she turned in a slow circle to investigate her surroundings.

The shutters over the windows were weathered and dry. The wood had shrunk, allowing gaps between the two sides to appear. The stone wall marked where rain and snow had made its way inside to drip down to the floor. A dark trail of mold had grown almost to the floor.

The room was located all the way at the top of the largest tower in the castle. Above her head, she could see the rafters which held up the roof. No one came up to it because of the climb. The few bundles in the room were covered in dust as well, proving they'd been placed there and forgotten.

Was that Buchanan's intent?

To forget her?

The afternoon wind was making the shutters rattle. She could smell rain on the air and soon fat drops were splatting on the closed shutters. With the rain clouds came a gloom that cast the room into semidarkness. The lack of light spurred Rhedyn into investigating the few bundles resting on an old box. She'd be locked in darkness soon.

There was little in the bundles, just rabbit pelts. They'd been carefully stacked and wrapped to keep them fresh. She undid more than a hundred of them, likely the fruits of coffers paying their annual rents in

43

goods they could procure from the land. The fur was soft and warm, the hides cured so they could be sewn into hoods. Added to wool, the pelts would make a very nice cloak or over robe for the winter months.

The wind gusted again, filling the room with a chill.

She put the bundles aside and looked inside the wooden box. It was a large one, filled with carefully folded ends of wool fabric. Next to the fabric was a sewing box. She pulled out the contents, smiling at the way someone had thoughtfully stored the scissors and pins inside more wool to keep them from rusting. Small tails of thread lay on the bottom of the crate, proving someone had sat in the room and worked a needle through the pelts.

But whatever they had sat on was long gone. There was not so much as an end of a candle anywhere. Long cobwebs trailed down from the rafters, many of them dark with dust. The lonely room chilled her blood.

There were worse fates than death.

Left alive in the bare room, there were countless opportunities for suffering. She suddenly understood why a person might choose to end their own life. Starving took a very long time when compared to bleeding to death. Rhedyn looked at the small scissors in her hand.

"Kill yerself, and I will return for yer sister."

Buchanan's words rose from her memory. She listened to the shutters rattle and looked back at the pelts.

She'd have to make do. And keep her mind from running wild with crazy thoughts. Idleness gave her too much time to think.

She pulled one of the needles free and threaded it. Selecting two of the pelts, she began to tack them together. She wasn't going to shiver through the night hours when there was something she might do about it. Her dress was made only of linen, for she'd been bound to a wedding, not traveling. The afternoon rain was cutting through it easily, promising her a frigid night if she had naught else to shield her from the highland temperature. Later, the wool scrapes would make a fine partlet to protect her neck and chest.

The light was fading when she heard steps coming close. She set her blanket aside and stood. Someone fit the key into the lock and turned it. The chain was pulled free before the door opened. The yellow glow of a single flame spilled inside. Rhedyn bit her lip to contain the sound which wanted to escape her.

She'd never take a simple candle for granted again.

The pool of light cast by the flame was like the most treasured friend. Even if it was being carried by the huge Butler. Even his scarred, hairless head was a welcome sight.

He dropped a bucket on the inside of the chamber with a grunt. She thought she witnessed a glimmer of pity in his eyes, but he'd placed the candle down beside the bucket and closed the door before she was certain.

Not that it mattered. The sound of the chain being replaced made it clear Tyree was loyal to his laird's will.

But he'd brought her light.

The little, flickering flame was cheerful. She moved forward to investigate what the bucket contained. The wooden slats which made up the bucket were old and dry. It would no longer hold milk or water. The Butler had used it to carry up several items. The largest was a chamber pot. Her temper flared over feeling thankful for such an item, but she had to be practical as well.

Her belly rumbled as she lifted a bowl from on top of the chamber pot. The scent of warm stew filled her nose, making her mouth water. She sat down and unfolded the length of linen wrapped around the bowl. A spoon was tucked into the bucket, along with a pottery jug with a piece of waxed rope into its neck. Once she removed the stopper, she found the jug filled with fresh water. The last thing in the bucket was a simple wooden comb. She stared at it as she chewed on a piece of meat from the stew. She wouldn't have thought Tyree would think of such a comfort, and she discovered herself feeling warmed by his foresight.

Do nae see more in his actions than a man obeying his laird...

Tyree had heard Buchanan tell her not to kill herself. Aye, the supper was to ensure she lived.

But the comb?

Rhedyn shook her head as she tipped the bowl up to drink more. It was humbling to discover herself so grateful for something as basic as a comb. She hadn't been properly thankful for the life she lived.

With her belly full, she pulled the fur blanket close and sipped at the water. The wind made the flame dance. She hummed softly in response. Somehow, she'd get out of the room.

Somehow.

>>><<<

BUCHANAN PAUSED OUTSIDE the door.

Humming?

He listened to the soft, feminine sound and felt his emotions stir. Crying he might have understood, but the lyrical melody stunned him. He stood for a long moment, his lips curving up. But a tingle on his nape made him turn.

Tyree was watching him from the stairs. The Butler had one of his massive hands clasped around his ring of keys to keep them from jingling. Buchanan felt the man's presence like a noose around his neck. The grin was gone from his lips along with any outward show of his emotions.

"Ye fed her?" Buchanan asked as he moved toward the stairs.

Tyree nodded. "Seeing ye told her no' to kill herself or ye'd go after the younger daughter. Seems a waste of a trip to Lindsey land to find her sister. I'm thinking of the horses, mind ye."

"It would be a waste," Buchanan agreed.

His tone was gruff. He passed Tyree as he tried to decide why he was so irritated. The answer Buchanan arrived at didn't settle his mood. He grunted as he walked by Fenella, never seeing the calculating look the Head-of-House sent his way.

The reason for his mood was simple enough. As much as he hadn't wanted a hostage to deal with, what he needed even less was a distraction. His father had only been dead for six months. Securing and maintaining the position of laird required all of Buchanan's attention. Highlanders didn't follow a weakling.

Aye, that's how ye ended up with a hostage, laddie…

He wasn't regretting it. Not when the alternative was to have carried back the knowledge that he'd run Colum Lindsey through.

She'd likely be crying if he'd killed her father.

At least in private. It was the truth that Rhedyn Lindsey had a solid spine, and it was the sort of compliment he didn't often get to pay to a female. She'd spit in his eye, sure enough, if he earned her disapproval. Something new stirred inside him. A 'something' he got the feeling he'd be better off not naming. At least so far as it went with his captive.

Buchanan stopped, pausing in the passageway between the kitchens and the great hall. A few candles flickered in holders along the walls, but they could only chew back a portion of the darkness. It suited his mood as he contemplated the way being the laird meant he was going to live a life of always trying to decide which evil action was the lesser one.

"Ye look in need of some comfort, Laird."

Buchanan snapped his head around to see Innis emerging from the kitchens. There was a sweet smile on her lips and a gleam in her eyes.

"I told ye abovestairs, lass, I am no' interested."

Innis fluttered her eyelashes, appearing just a bit disappointed as she lifted the tray in her hands up to gain his notice. "Fenella instructed me to serve ye, and I dare not refuse. She might put me out of the kitchens if I am disobedient. I need me place, for me parents are both gone. Surely ye do nae begrudge me a small place here?"

The tray held a goblet.

His Retainers would require cunning to handle, but Buchanan realized his household would take just as much forethought. Fenella watched him closely, and her staff was very good at reporting his every move. Innis came forward, offering the tray. As Buchanan lifted the goblet, he recognized the scent of the cider.

It was one of his favorites.

He'd thought he'd snuck more than a pitcher or two of it out of the kitchens beneath Fenella's notice, but he realized it wasn't likely so. Fenella's duties went beyond just knowing how much flour was needed to see the Retainers fed through the winter. She needed to understand how to please her laird.

"Thank Fenella for me."

Innis lowered herself, but her eyes offered him a blazing look of spiritedness if he was in the mind to partake of more than just cider. When he continued to turn away, the maid let out a sound of frustration.

"Fenella is burying herself in work…to forget the loss of her son."

Buchanan stopped and turned toward Innis. There was a flash of victory in her eyes that she didn't allow to show on her face.

"Iain should have had more care for his actions," Buchanan began carefully. "He condemned the men who rode with him to death with his recklessness. Raiding by moonlight is best left to fireside tales, for the reality is no' so grand."

"It was no' Iain's fault that he was betrayed by the bastard Lindseys," Innis declared passionately.

"A man must take responsibility for his actions, Innis." Buchannan stepped closer to her to keep their conversation from traveling down the hallways and into the ears of anyone who might be hiding in the shadows.

She stepped forward, making Buchanan stop short. He had a clear view of her ample cleavage.

"I know ye are a man who does nae shirk from his responsibilities," she whispered heatedly.

Buchanan shook his head, and her eyes narrowed.

"Better to let me help ye find a husband, Innis, a man of yer own."

She took the last step between them. "I'd forgive ye a wife."

Buchanan retreated from her. Frustration showed on her face for a moment. "I can be very helpful to ye. A girl like me may no' have anything much to her name, but I've heard plenty in me time serving. I know what's being said and by who. A girl like me can help ye avoid making mistakes."

Her threat wasn't lost on him. Buchanan's visit to the storeroom had been noted by his staff. Perhaps in an English castle the servants might keep to their places, but every person serving in the kitchens was a member of the clan as well.

Another lesson his father had made sure to teach Buchanan.

Damn Iain and his foolishness!

Buchanan felt his half-brother reaching back from the grave. Iain had always been more rebellious to their father's rules. His mother had followed her heart and defied the wishes of her family to love Buchanan's father. Her son had inherited that trait and never mastered self-control.

"Thank ye for the offer, Innis."

He left before she might come up with another argument. But he doubted she was finished attempting to secure a place in his bed. Buchanan rubbed his forehead once he'd reached the sanctuary of his chamber. It was the only place he was completely at ease now.

He suddenly understood why Rhedyn was humming inside the storeroom. She was alone there, with no one to judge her. It was a pleasant thought indeed. Even if it surprised him to discover himself contemplating how alike their circumstances were.

Captor or captive. There appeared to be little difference.

➤➤➤≪≪≪

Edinburgh...

"YE ARE DISPLEASED with me," Vychan stated what was obvious.

Colum grunted. "Me daughter is in the hands of the Mackenzie, and we are riding south."

"We will no' be able to help her if we are dead on the border of their land," Vychan informed his sire. "The Makenzies are powerful."

"I know it well."

"Me mother was a McLeod, sister of the laird," Vychan said. "Once I'm legitimate and yer heir, Cedric McLeod will have a stake in this matter. Even the Mackenzie will no' want to face so many clans united against them."

"A sound enough plan," Column agreed. "Except why are we sitting here?"

The town house was a fine one. Servants were hurrying to pull lengths of cloth off the furniture and open wide the window shutters. They'd arrived without warning, but it wasn't an uncommon occurrence. The servants who kept the Edinburgh residence of the Lindsey clan were adapt at springing into action when their master appeared suddenly.

"I'm going to see the Arch Bishop," Vychan replied. "It's one thing to wed me mother on yer land. Another thing altogether if we want the other clans to recognize me as yer son. For that, we'll need the blessing of the church. The Makenzie might release Rhedyn if they hear we have the church on our side as well, but I have to be acknowledged as yer son and heir before I can stand in front of Buchanan and tell him to hand over me sister. As a bastard, I do nae have much respect. The other clans will no' likely stand with me if the church does nae accept yer union."

"Aye, aye," Colum grumbled as he accepted a mug of ale from a servant. "I've done ye wrong in this life son, and it would seem I am still no better at making judgements using me brain instead of me emotions. The Mackenzies will no' give up Rhedyn easily."

Vychan watched Colum settled into a large chair near a hearth. A fire was just beginning to get going, crackling and cutting through the chill in the room.

His father.

Vychan had spent more than a few hours thinking about the moment when he'd be in the same room as Colum Lindsey. The shameful truth was that most of those times he'd enjoyed the idea of what insults he'd unleash on the man who had left him bastard born and his mother shamed by her lack of husband.

Reality was surprisingly better than his dark ideas.

For now, he faced a future with his father. It was the honest truth he'd never thought such a thing was possible until he'd found his mother's letters.

There really were always two sides to an issue.

Vychan felt that knowledge sober him. He'd longed for a future with his father. Been envious of other boys who had fathers in their lives when he was called bastard for something he'd had no control over. But he'd still fought and bled when one of those boys had called his mother a lightskirt. Even when he knew he'd go home to her bleeding.

She was all he'd ever had until now. It was hard to understand why she'd chosen a life as a shamed woman over going to a man who loved her.

Pride was a burden.

But Vychan acknowledged he had it in spades. Why else would he fight against the truth being spoken? He was born bastard. Maybe he should be thankful, for he'd grown up strong and knowing what it was like to have naught but the people in his family.

Buchanan Mackenzie had unwittingly made himself Vychan's

enemy. For Rhedyn was his sister. She was family. And Vychan would always fight for his blood.

><<<

Makenzie land…

TIME CREPT BY.

Rhedyn found the days growing longer and longer. Tyree came only once a day. She was grateful for his visit, and yet mortified to have him carrying away her chamber pot.

Still, the Butler was her only source of companionship. Sometimes he brought her something new. Such as a bucket of water and a sliver of soap. She found herself excited as she approached the bucket, peeking over the chipped edge to see what wonders it held.

By the end of the week, though, she suddenly realized the sound of the chain slipping through the slats was truly beginning to wear away at her sanity.

She covered her ears to block it out, backing away from the bucket.

Turning around, she opened one of the sets of shutters. A gust of evening air blew in. It raised goosebumps along her limbs, but she sucked in a deep breath and closed her eyes. She was not dead! And she wouldn't accept that she would never be free again.

She could smell the heather beginning to bloom.

And there was the scent of newly-turned earth.

And…a hint of the smell of horses.

The wind gusted again, and she drew in a deeper breath. She squeezed her eyes shut, allowing her sense of smell to take over. The candle blew out, but she didn't care, she sunk down and lay on the floor where she might look up at the stars. Pulling the blanket close, she huddled inside it as she returned to trying to identify the scents on the wind.

But the sound of the chain came again. She turned to stare at the door.

Tyree opened it and looked at the bucket where he'd left it. He held another candle in his hand. Lowering it toward the one he'd left by the bucket, he relit it.

"Best close the shutters," he instructed. "I felt the chill all the way in the kitchens."

A gust of wind blew in and went down the stairs. It made a whistling sound but drew more scents from the outside world. Rhedyn turned toward the open window and smiled. She wouldn't be deprived of her only link with life, for it was her only way to hold onto her sanity.

"It's fine and fair and suits me well," she told Tyree before ignoring him in favor of discovering what other scents the next gust might deliver to her.

The air chilled her nose, but she liked it. At least with her eyes closed and her mind keenly focused on deciphering scents, she wasn't aware of time creeping by.

"Why are ye not eating?"

Rhedyn jumped. Somehow, Buchanan had appeared. She rolled onto her back and came to rest on her bottom. Her legs were sticking out from her tangled skirt as she blinked.

"Mistress, I will have an answer from ye," he demanded after she remained silent.

Her temper suddenly flickered. Rhedyn enjoyed the surge of anger because it burned through the melancholy which had taken hold of her. She got to her feet, suddenly realizing that her head only came to Buchanan's shoulder.

He was a brute. His eyes narrowed as she remained silent. He pointed at the bucket.

"Me Butler took the time to see to yer needs, and yet ye leave it there? Do ye expect Tyree to cater to yer likes and dislikes, then?"

The Mackenzie laird's frustration struck her as amusing. But in that way that a good fit of temper found things entertaining. His arrogance certainly knew no bounds! Was it the captive's place to please the brute who had locked her abovestairs for too many days to count?

Ha. He'd grow impatient waiting for her to voice such a thing.

He grunted and braced his hands on his hips. "Let's hear it, madam," he pressed. "What is it ye are expecting?"

"Naught," she replied tightly.

He raised an eyebrow at her tartness.

"Naught," she repeated more firmly. "I expect nothing from ye. Certainly no' this display of concern over me missing a meal. Leave if all ye seek is me crying to ye, for I won't be asking anything of ye, Laird Mackenzie."

Aye, it was her pride leading her, but she refused to look to him for affection.

But Buchanan remained where he was. Contemplating her.

"Since it is the only meal ye have been afforded this day, it is necessary for ye to consume it."

Her lips twitched, and she didn't quell the urge to smile. The look of confusion on Buchanan's face was certainly worth having her feelings seen by him.

"Sitting in this room all day simply does nae build an appetite, Laird Mackenzie."

Her circumstance could be worse, but she wouldn't crumple at his feet like some dog.

Instead, she stared straight at him, noting the warm, brown color of his eyes. They went well with his dark blonde hair, she supposed. If she were of the mind to find anything about him favorable.

"Ye're being stubborn, woman."

"I do nae deny it," Rhedyn confirmed. "How else am I to survive this visit to the Mackenzie stronghold? As ye've threatened me with me sister's well-being, it seems I need to gather my strength lest I be responsible for Bree falling into yer keeping."

Buchanan slowly nodded. For a moment, something flickered in his eyes. She should have been more wary of it, of prodding him. But she simply wasn't, for time was a far crueler adversary.

So, she stared back at him, even when she suspected meekness might have been the wiser choice of action. Buchanan Mackenzie wasn't a man who refused to take a challenge, and the way his eyes narrowed, warned her he was plotting to win the battle she had started.

She'd not back down.

"No appetite is it?" he asked softly.

His tone was menacing really, but her pride refused to allow her to bend. The man already hated her. Perhaps when she had first arrived, she feared being put to the sword, but after endless days of being locked away, she realized a quick death really was a mercy.

"I see, lass." There was a hint of enjoyment in his tone now, the sort a man used on a mare he was intent on slipping a bridle onto.

A sense of foreboding tingled through her. A moment later, Buchanan reached out and clasped her upper arm. He was turning her toward the open door as Tyree cleared out of the way. Buchanan pulled her down the stairs quickly, before she had time to realize what he was doing. She barely got a look at the kitchens while he tugged her across their length. And then there was another passageway before she heard the buzz of conversation and they entered the great hall. He spun her free.

"Dance."

Rhedyn skidded to a stop. Her skirts kept going before falling back down to cover her legs. The hall was full of Mackenzie Retainers enjoying the last meal of the day. Long tables filled the space, and they were piled with bread, cheese, and meat. Men stopped talking, turning to glare at her, like a rat had suddenly crawled up and onto the supper table. In their eyes, she could see them contemplating the best method to dispatch her and rid their home of vermin.

Rhedyn straightened her back. She'd not shirk. They might call her many things, but she refused to allow them to turn her into a coward. If they didn't like her being there, well, they could bloody well take the matter to their laird. He was the one who had drug her into their midst.

"Is there something wrong with yer hearing? Build yer appetite," Buchanan demanded. He'd left her standing on the main floor while he climbed up several steps to a raised platform at the end of the great hall. He sat down and contemplated her like a rabbit he was toying with before he snapped its neck.

But it suited her mood. She was drunk on her own temper. Ready to dig her heels in and defy him, for the sake of opposing him. The flare of temper warmed her insides.

There was a rumble of amusement from his men. Her eyes narrowed as she caught more than one of them leering at her. Her temper flared and she crossed her arms over her chest in defiance.

"I'll dance with you."

The men had started to clap and stomp their feet in a crude rhythm. The young voice was hard to separate from the men who wanted to make a mockery of her. But a girl came through the tables, looking at Rhedyn. She wasn't overly young, but she wore an expression that suggested she was still innocent. Whatever the truth of her age, the Mackenzies froze, suddenly mindful of their jeering. A few even looked away, as though shamed by their behavior.

"We're unmarried," the girl continued as she took the time to lower herself in a practiced motion. There was a hint of mocking in her motions though. In that way in which a respectable daughter showed up and her kin were none too pleased to have her see them doing things they had forbidden her to do.

"So, we can dance together." Her voice bounced between the

walls of the hall which had gone as silent as a tavern when the priest arrived unexpectedly.

"Cora…"

Rhedyn turned toward the high ground. It seemed Buchanan did in fact have a tone of voice other than mocking. He was sitting forward now, his eyes narrowed.

Wonders truly never ceased…

Rhedyn wanted to enjoy the gray pallor which had taken over his face, but shame suddenly rose up to smother her temper. The girl was clearly his sister.

His *younger* sister.

And he cared how Cora saw him behaving.

So, he did have decency buried down inside him…

"Are we to dance, brother?" Cora asked. She turned and sent a look toward the high ground. "Did I mishear yer command?"

Off to the side of the platform where the laird's table stood were four musicians. One of them lifted his instrument and began to play in response. The melody was joined by the other three as Cora smiled and began to dance.

Rhedyn discovered herself loath to continue acting like a shrew. In a way, it was a moment of happiness to discover a Mackenzie who didn't hate her. Cora had a sweet smile on her lips, but there was also a glitter of something in her eyes, which hinted at the girl knowing she was taunting the intent of her clansmen.

Rhedyn clapped her hands and smiled back at Cora. They kept time with one another until a small flood of other Mackenzie women separated them. They surrounded her, pushing in so that Rhedyn could no longer see her.

The music kept playing as Rhedyn was shoved back to where the passageway joined the kitchens to the great hall. She went willingly enough, for the harsh looks were like sword points, pricking her and reminding her that she was no longer in her father's house. Cora might toy with her brother, but she was a Mackenzie.

But Rhedyn smiled anyway. Her victory was small but hers none the less.

"My sister shamed me. And rightfully so."

Rhedyn turned to see Buchanan standing nearby. He had a grim look on his face. Seeing it should have pleased her, yet Rhedyn suddenly had no stomach for hate.

"And me as well. I am past the age of having temper fits in public, no matter the provocation," Rhedyn muttered. Perhaps she shouldn't have confessed to him. For certain, her father's Retainers would likely remind her that Mackenzies were the enemy and must always be treated with disdain.

It felt so very pointless at that moment.

"Yer sister is wise," Rhedyn said.

"Wiser than myself?" he asked. "Is that what ye want me to notice, Rhedyn Lindsey?"

His expression had hardened as he faced off with her. Behind him, there was a jingle as Tyree moved closer in response to his laird's voice.

"Ye seem to have taken little enough notice of me since ye insisted on bringing me here, Laird Mackenzie," Rhedyn said. "It suits me quite well. As for yer sister, well, she seems to think humiliating me for sport is no decent behavior. Me own kin taught me the same. However, go and correct her if ye disagree. Ye are laird here."

She lowered herself in reverence before she turned and marched straight past the Butler. At least that was her intention. But Tyree stuck his arm out before she made it past him. Unshed tears born of frustration burned her eyes. She fought against them before turning around.

"Tell yer man to let me leave."

"Ye prefer the tower room?" Buchanan asked.

"Aye!" Rhedyn declared. "Ye brought me down here to make a mockery of me for the sake of yer pride."

Something crossed his face. Later, she might even realize it was shame, but Rhedyn forbid herself to do anything but turn her back on him. The shutters in the storeroom must still be open, for the wind whistled down the stairs as she climbed up them.

It kept the tears from falling from her eyes.

She heard Tyree following her, his keys jingling to announce each of his steps. So, she closed the door and left the bucket nearby as she went over to sit beneath the open shutters.

She'd not be worried about displeasing Buchanan Mackenzie.

On the other side of the door, the chain rattled and the key turned in the lock. The wind gusted, making her rise to close the shutters because she didn't need to suffer the night chill.

At least her memory offered up the sound of music. Alone in the dark room, she heard every note just as crisp and bold as it had been played while she danced with Cora. It followed her into her slumber as she huddled beneath the blanket.

⇢⇥⇤⇠

BUCHANAN REMAINED IN place for a long time.

"Ye brought me down here to make a mockery of me for the sake of yer pride."

It was a solid truth. One which shamed him. And left him staring at a dark stairwell long after Rhedyn had disappeared into the shadows. She was helpless and yet, not without the means to stop him in his tracks. A formidable woman to be sure.

Ye needed to be stopped laddie...

His childhood was full of times when his father had tried to impress the importance of controlling his impulses. A laird had to always be mindful of his actions. Those around him would act upon what they perceived as the lairds will. He also had to be the voice of reason.

His men would kill Rhedyn if he gave them any hint that he'd consider it fitting. Her fate was completely in his hands.

>>>><<<<

INNIS KNEW HOW to go unnoticed.

Highlanders liked to believe they were great warriors, and she wasn't arguing that the men of the Mackenzie clan were anything less than the best.

But they knew it, and along with confidence went arrogance.

Buchanan was no different.

The new laird had a frame thick with muscle and a fine, educated mind. Still, he was a man who forgot from time to time that the castle housed a great many women. Innis watched the way he stood at the base of the back stairs. The look on his face was unguarded, showing her plainly that he was fighting the urge to follow Rhedyn Lindsey.

Innis couldn't allow him to do something like that. Oh, she was no fool when it came to men's natures. For a girl such as herself, she had to make her own opportunities. Fenella would parade the prettiest kitchen maids past the new laird until one of them caught his eye. The Head-of-House was only thinking to advance her own reputation by getting the laird what he fancied.

Which was why Innis had to look out for her own interests.

Buchanan was looking up the stairs. She could see the indecision on his face. What she mustn't allow to happen was for the laird to go abovestairs where his pity would lead him straight into Rhedyn's embrace.

Lindsey women couldn't be so very different from Mackenzie women after all. Being born female meant you'd better be clever enough to trap a man before another woman succeeded. That was the way to ensuring a good place in life. It was just as deadly as any fight between men with swords. Innis contemplated Buchannan. She intended to have him as her prize.

"My laird," she greeted Buchanan as she passed.

The laird jerked, clearly taken by surprise. She hid her expression and lowered herself prettily.

Then she placed a bucket at the base of the steps.

"What are ye about, mistress?" the laird asked.

"I'm tasked with cleaning these steps," she replied as she dunked a cloth into the water and carried it to the first step. It made a wet plop as it landed on the stone.

Buchanan stared at her for a long moment before he strode away.

She slowly washed the first step, lingering over it while she made sure the laird wasn't planning to return. She peeked into the hall later and discovered Buchanan had gone to his chambers.

She smiled with victory. The chill in her fingers was worth being able to keep the laird from going up the stairs. He couldn't form an attachment if he wasn't alone with the Lindsey girl. Of course, that was only one part of succeeding. The Lindsey girl didn't seem to hate the Mackenzie in spite of him taking her hostage.

So, Innis would have to make sure Rhedyn had a reason to hate Buchanan.

⇥⟫⟫⟩⟨⟨⟨⇤

"HERE NOW," INNIS said sweetly the next evening. "That is no' a task for a man."

Tyree angled his head so he could peer at her. The Butler was trying to decide just what she meant.

Innis fluttered her eyelashes and scooped up the bucket dangling from his fingers. "A maid should see to delivering this abovestairs. Ye have more important matters to attend to."

"I hold the keys," Tyree said.

Innis played her part well. She looked at the Butler and blinked as though she hadn't considered that fact.

"Oh...yes," she muttered. "Still, it is the duty of a maid to be carry-ing meals and chamber pots." She suddenly flashed him a smile. "I'll follow ye up and take the chamber pot away while ye see to the matter of holding the keys."

Innis knew there were plenty listening to her. But the other maids never allowed Tyree to see them watching. Instead, they continued to work as though they were oblivious. They weren't. Innis knew they were absorbing every word, because just like her, they all knew information was valuable.

"Well then…" She didn't want the Butler to ponder the matter too long. Tyree wasn't the sharpest man, but he didn't lack all sense.

"Aye," Tyree spoke. "I won't be arguing over the task of emptying a chamber pot."

He turned with a jingle of his keys. Innis caught one of the maids sending her a raised eyebrow, but Innis only scooped up the bucket from the table and followed Tyree. There would be a price to pay to the other girls, because silence wasn't free, but Innis wouldn't think about that at the moment. She needed to find a way to cultivate hate in Rhedyn. She couldn't do anything if the Lindsey girl was locked away. Emptying a chamber pot was a small price to pay for the opportunity to ensure the next time Rhedyn had a choice on how to behave, she lashed out at her captors. A nice, neat wedge between the laird and her would serve Innis's purpose well.

Tyree opened the lock and pulled the chain loose. Innis walked through the door once the Butler opened it wide for her and made certain Rhedyn was standing in one of the far corners. The storeroom wasn't an unfamiliar place to Innis. She controlled the urge to smile because she knew the storeroom had often been used for trysts.

And by whom.

She looked across the expanse of the bare floor, expecting to see the bundles of pelts a couple of the Retainers had left there for pillows when they decided to attempt to lure one of the maids up for a liaison.

But the bundles were gone. Their location wasn't a mystery, for she saw the blanket. The chore of seeing to the chamber pot was suddenly unimportant. She hummed on her way down the steps, anticipation filling her.

Was it unkind of her?

To be so focused on making sure the Lindsey girl suffered? It wasn't as though Innis planned to bully the girl for the long term. No. She simply needed to make certain Buchanan received a cold shoulder from his hostage. The laird wouldn't question such a response all that much, not when he'd taken the girl from her home.

As a maid, Innis was ignored for the most part. She might have taken to feeling pity for her plight, but instead, she'd chosen to use her less-than-important position in life to gain the things she craved. Information, well, there was something which held value. The trick was to discover who would pay the most for a bit of secret knowledge while doing her best to remain unnoticed.

And she wouldn't be shamed for it either. Was her business any different than those who had more money and higher positions? No, she was increasing her holdings, one silver penny at a time.

Innis was only looking out for herself. After all, no one else would.

⟫⟫⟫⟩⟨⟪⟪⟪

"WHY DOES MISTRESS Lindsey no' sit at supper with us?"

Buchanan flinched as his sister asked the question. Her voice was so innocent. Falsely so, for Cora wasn't that tender in years. But she was illuminating something everyone sitting at the high table would likely rather never discuss with her. His captains might consider it fair what they were doing to Rhedyn, but they also knew it was foul business.

His sister was his father's child all the way to her toenails, by Christ.

His captain, Graham, looked up with a scowl but froze once he realized who had voiced the name of their hostage. Buchanan had to suppress a grin as his captain swallowed and remained silent instead of answering.

Cora turned her blue eyes toward Buchanan. "Did I ask a rude question?"

Buchanan had reached up to rub the side of his face in order to avoid grinning. "Nae, ye did no'."

Cora wasn't finished though. She turned and looked down the length of the head table. His captains had all gone silent. They sat staring at him. As his sister returned her attention to them, they jumped and tried to school their expressions.

But too late.

Cora snapped her attention back to her brother. There was a frown on her lips and a spark of irritation in her young eyes. "Ye told me we do not make war on women. Mackenzie honor."

Buchanan stared straight back at his sister. His neck tightened because he felt the attention of his men being aimed at him. Even the maids were slowing down so they might catch his words. Every word that crossed his lips might become a weapon in someone's hands.

"I do not make war on women, Cora," Buchanan answered firmly.

She lifted her fork to her mouth but paused before taking the food. "Then...is Mistress Lindsey to be yer bride, brother? To form an alliance with the Lindsey?" His sister beamed brightly. "I think she would be a very nice sister-in-law. I hope she will accept the arrangement soon and be able to join us at high table. May I visit her?"

One of his captains made a strangling sound. Buchanan resisted the urge to shoot a glare past his sister. Cora was currently watching him. But what she was really doing was using her gender as a shield, and there wasn't a captain sitting behind her who dared to disagree with her.

"Cora...." Buchanan began.

But his sister turned and caught his men glowering. Several of them jumped or fumbled their cutlery when faced with her direct attention. Cora turned back toward him.

"So, it isn't as ye told me," Cora declared in a low tone to try and keep her outburst from those listening. "An alliance bride isn't treasured. She is hated for her blood and never accepted. Yet, ye all can nae stop telling me how grand my own marriage will be. Naught but empty words."

Cora pressed her hands against the edge of the table and shoved with all her might. Her chair skidded back with a grinding sound before she jumped up. Her feet made hard sounds as she left the hall.

Buchanan pounded the top of the table with his fist. Plates bounced and clattered in response. "The lot of ye could no' keep control of yerselves for but a single meal?"

"When it comes to the matter of that Lindsey whore..." Arlo began as he pointed his knife at Buchanan.

"Whore?" Buchanan hit the table again. His temper was flaring.

Graham sent his elbow into Arlo. "Whore is a harsh word, man."

Arlo rolled his eyes.

"One not fit for the supper table," Buchanan warned.

"Does Iain's death deserve kind words?" Cedric asked from where he sat at the end of the head table.

Buchanan drew in a deep breath. "Iain's death will be a matter between men. As I have warned ye already."

"Yet the Lindsey girl is here," Arlo reminded him.

Buchanan let out a grunt. "Aye, and the lot of ye know I took her to avoid running an old man through. But she'll no' be called whore." He held up a finger to silence his captains. "For Christ's sake, the lot of ye seem to no' understand the difference between eating on the road and sitting at a high table where wives and daughters hear yer words."

There was a rumble of agreement from the lower tables.

"As for our Lindsey guest," Buchanan continued, "Cora does no' need to be worried about being received by the Grants poorly. The contract was made by me father. It would no' reflect well on us if I break the betrothal or send a weeping bride because me sister sees the way the lot of ye are treating Rhedyn Lindsey and thinks it will be her lot as well when she goes to the Grants. She shamed ye rightly so."

Buchanan watched as his captains nodded with understanding. Conversation began to flow once more as the meal continued. Buchanan found his appetite gone.

His father had once told him a laird shouldered the guilt for the good of his people. Tonight, he felt it pressing down on him.

The wrong thing, for the right reason...

≫≫≪≪

CORA STOOD FOR a moment in the passageway outside the great hall. She smiled as she heard her brother's words, but her enjoyment was short lived.

She was betrothed to a Grant.

And she didn't really bother with his first name. After all, he'd never even sent her a single letter in spite of the ones she was required to write to him.

Her duty.

Oh yes. As far back as she might recall her position in the clan had been impressed upon her. She was to wed the man who would bring an alliance to the Makenzie, and she must never, ever venture away from her father's Retainers lest she be kidnapped and used against her kin.

Men were two-faced.

The very captains sitting with her brother would have her behave perfectly, ignoring her impulses, while they, themselves, gave into temper. It turned her stomach. But mostly, it irritated her nearly beyond her endurance. Which left her realizing just how much she and Rhedyn Lindsey had in common.

〉〉〉〉＜＜＜＜

"WHAT GAME ARE ye playing, Innis?"

Fenella was quick to prove how sharp her eyes were when it came to watching the kitchens. She was waiting for Innis when she made it to the bottom of the steps with the chamber pot.

"I did no' set ye the task of seeing to the tower room."

Tyree was hovering in the stairwell, his huge frame bent slightly over.

Innis knew that Fenella expected to have complete authority over those working in the kitchens. It was a fine position to have in the castle. One which came with plenty of food and a warm place to sleep in the winter. For a girl like Innis, one without parents or brothers to arrange a match for her, pledging obedience to the Head-of-House was her only way to secure a brighter future.

Innis lowered herself quickly. "I thought to bring down the bundles of pelts stored abovestairs. Seeing as how they were given as rent."

"Pelts?" Fenella questioned.

Innis looked at the Head-of-House. She contemplated her for a long moment before she offered Innis a flick of her fingers.

Innis straightened up. "Aye, Mistress. Rabbit pelts. There were a pair of bundles in the tower chamber."

Fenella's eyes narrowed. Her mind was quick to offer up just why the bundles would have been moved without her direction. Every maid in the kitchen was suddenly absorbed in her duties, making not a sound as they toiled.

"The Lindsey girl has sewn them into a blanket," Innis said quickly.

Fenella's lips thinned. There was a flash of temper in her eyes, but Innis wasn't worried about it. No, the hatred was for the Lindsey girl. Fenella looked at Tyree.

"Bring those pelts down, and that bitch!"

"The laird said no one was to go into the tower chamber without him telling me so," Tyree said.

Fenella propped her hands onto her ample hips. "Well now, I do nae see any difficulty. For I told ye to bring her down, no' allow me into the chamber."

She snapped her fingers at the Butler. "When it comes to the matter of running this kitchen, I hold the keys!"

Fenella grasped the ring of keys secured to the front of her belt. Food meant the difference between living and dying. Next to the defense of the outer walls, there was nothing in the castle more valuable. As Head-of-House, Fenella was responsible for controlling all the resources to ensure the harvest lasted through the winter months. It was also her duty to safeguard against the laird being poisoned. She chose every maid herself, and would answer if even the lowest of them sold out the laird.

Tyree was still for a long moment. Fenella maintained her stance as well, glaring at the him as intently as she might the lowest servant.

"Aye," Tyree bent. There was a scuff as he turned around, his shoulders brushing the side of the stairwell.

"Finish that chore." Fenella proved she'd not forgotten Innis. "And scrub yer hands before ye return to the kitchen. If ye'd rather be a chambermaid, so be it."

"I like the kitchens full well," Innis was quick to assure Fenella.

"Then do nae stray from yer assigned duties again."

Innis nodded on her way out of the back doors. The night was still bitter. If her duty hadn't been one best finished quickly, she'd have hurried to finish just because of the chill. She stopped diligently outside where a bucket of fresh well water sat beside a stone washing basin. She dipped up a ladle full of it and dumped it over her hands before reaching into a chipped pottery jar to scoop up some soft soap. It stung slightly as she scrubbed it across her palms and over the back of her hands. She didn't rush though, for Fenella was known to dismiss those who didn't keep their hands clean.

Innis dashed back into the kitchen the moment she rinsed the soap from her hands. She was drying them on her apron as the Butler came down the stairway.

>>><<<

RHEDYN STOPPED CHEWING as she heard the chain being pulled free.

Her heart accelerated in response. She would have liked to quell the nervousness rising inside her, but the truth was, she really didn't see the point in squandering the moment. Whatever was happening, it was better than waiting for the night and day to pass before supper arrived once more.

Tyree looked in, his attention on the blanket she'd unfolded as the night became darker and colder.

"The Head-of-House wants to see ye."

Would the woman put her to work? Rhedyn hoped so.

She stood quickly and folded the blanket. No Head-of-House worth her pay would abide idleness. Running a castle the size of the Mackenzie stronghold would take as many pairs of hands as possible. Perhaps something would be sent back up with Rhedyn to be done during the long hours of the day.

She didn't much care how lowly the task might be. No, all that mattered was that she walked toward the door of the chamber and passed through it.

Something to do.

Anything to do...

Rhedyn felt light as a feather. Her shoes made little tapping sounds on the stone steps as she all but danced down them. She stopped at the last few, gathering her composure before descending to the kitchen floor.

"Ye wish to see me?" She offered a courtesy out of respect.

The Head-of-House was waiting on her. She had her hair concealed beneath a cap, but several wisps had worked free with her labors. The dark brown was streaked with gray. The apron she had tucked into her belt was splattered and stained, proving she kept her eyes on everything under her authority.

"Aye, I do, indeed." The woman looked toward Tyree.

The Butler had followed close on Rhedyn's heels.

"It's here, as Innis said." Tyree moved past Rhedyn, the pelt blanket draped over his arm.

The Head-of-House took it and held it up. Every maid in the kitchen strained to gain a glimpse of it. A moment later, more than one of them was sending a smirk toward Rhedyn. A tingle of foreboding touched her nape, for there was something far too gleeful in the looks of the maids. They were clearly anticipating some bit of sport, and Rhedyn got the feeling she would be the one at the center of it.

"I am Fenella, the Head-of-House."

Rhedyn clasped her hands in front of her and lowered her chin respectfully.

Fenella placed the blanket on the table which ran the length of the kitchens. She tapped it with her finger. "Who gave ye permission to use these pelts?"

Rhedyn felt her stomach clench, but it was nothing compared to the way her temper flared. So, Fenella wanted to deny her even protection from the chill of night? The growing excitement in the expressions of the maids truly sickened her. Yet, it flooded her with courage, for she'd not tremble in front of them.

"No one did."

Fenella let out a grunt. She propped her hands on her hips, and her hard gaze raked Rhedyn from head to toe.

"I do not find it hard to believe the bitch daughter of the Lindsey would have no shame over stealing from others," Fenella declared.

She raised her voice so everyone could hear her.

"I am no' a thief," Rhedyn said.

Fenella lifted one hand into the air. "Ye have already admitted to using these pelts for yerself."

"Is it not customary to take comfort in a chamber?" Rhedyn asked. "In my father's castle, no one is left to shiver through the night."

"Ye are no' in yer father's castle anymore," Fenella cut back. "Here, I am the Head-of-House. I did no' give ye leave to use the pelts. They were given as rent. Ye have pilfered."

It was a common enough thing, for many crofters paid their due to the laird in goods. Much of the grain used to produce the bread in the kitchens was from rent payments. Everything from chickens to pelts. The common people offered a percentage of their yearly toil to the laird, who, in turn, maintained Retainers who would protect those living on his land.

"I'll show ye what happens to those who steal from the Mackenzie." Fenella sent Rhedyn a scathing look.

The rest of the kitchen staff abandoned their work.

Clearly, they understood Fenella. A few appeared reserved about watching whatever was to come, but they hid behind the ones who pushed forward to make certain they had an unobstructed view.

"Put her across the table, Tyree." Fenella turned and went toward a wall.

She held up a long rod as the Butler grabbed Rhedyn by the wrists and stretched her across the work table. Rhedyn barely had time to wrinkle her nose at being forced face-down on the remains of the meat which someone had been cutting on that table before Fenella unleashed a blow that landed across her arms.

The pain was sharp and excruciating.

Rhedyn struggled to draw in a breath as the rod came down again.

"Ye'll no touch a single thing which has no' been given to ye so long as I am in charge of this house!" Fenella declared between blows.

Tears streamed down Rhedyn's face as she struggled against the hold on her wrists. But the Butler was strong, pulling until she felt like her wrists were going to be ripped clean off her arms. She was helpless.

"That's ten now," Tyree surprised Rhedyn by speaking.

The Butler started to release her, but Fenella gasped.

"Ye'll be next if ye let her loose!" she declared. "This Lindsey needs to learn her place."

The rod came down again. Fenella was peppering the blows up and down Rhedyn's arms. The Head-of-House was breathing hard as she wielded the rod without mercy.

"She'll get ten across the back as well!" Fenella informed those watching. The rod descended several more times.

The snickers of the maids watching horrified Rhedyn more than the pain. Turning her head, she gazed at Fenella. There was a sick look of satisfaction on the woman's face as she lifted the rod and brought it down again. This time, she struck Rhedyn across the shoulders. The impact sent the breath out of her.

She'd lost count of the blows, and her vision began to waver. She felt blackness approaching and welcomed it. What was the point of enduring when all there was to experience was more pain? Her pride wasn't going to grant her relief from the agony being inflicted on her body.

She sunk down into the welcoming fold of unconsciousness only to be awakened by a splash of cold water. Rhedyn was laying across the table top still, water soaking into her hair and back.

"Think ye'll be escaping by fainting? Ye'll feel every last blow," Fenella declared ominously. "Hold her, Tyree."

"Enough now, mistress," the Butler argued. "Ye've given her near to twenty blows. Take it to the laird if ye feel she needs more punishment."

"I am the Head-of-House." Her tone was edged with grief and fury. "Me only son was cut down with Iain! I'll not suffer this Lindsey thief!"

"Hold!"

Fenella hesitated but seemed too far gone in her anger to heed the command. The rod landed again, this time making a wet sound as it hit her drenched clothing. But the Butler was no longer holding her down. Rhedyn rolled across the table in a tangle of skirts and hair. Her body was pulsing with pain, every twist and turn releasing new points of agony.

She wouldn't whimper.

The pain fed her determination. She kept going until she went over the side of the table and landed on her feet. Straightening up took more resolve as her back protested. But she suffered the hurt, lifting her head in case Fenella was intent on continuing.

By Christ, Rhedyn would show her how much grit a Lindsey had.

But Fenella was standing still, her expression sullen like a child who was being denied a treat.

"Laird," Fenella said.

"Fenella," Buchanan answered as he stepped closer.

The kitchen was silent. The air was so still, when the fire popped, Rhedyn was certain she felt it.

"Yer service to this house is greatly appreciated," Buchanan stated. "However, ye would have leave to mourn yer son, I gladly grant it."

"I do nae need to be sitting around," Fenella said. "I never would have risen to be Head-of-House if idleness was something I favored." She drew herself up, the expression on her face easing as she regained her confidence. She pointed the rod toward Rhedyn. "This Lindsey ye saddled me with keeping made free use of rabbit pelts which she was no' granted permission to make her own."

"Ye care not if I shiver with naught but a spring linen dress on me back?" Rhedyn lost the battle to bite her lip.

"The pelts were given as rent." The Head-of-House looked at her laird. "I can nae have such a matter going unpunished. Every maid under me will know she is not to make free with the stores in the storage rooms. That will get us naught but fat bellies in the autumn, and naught to sustain us when the snow has us trapped inside."

The silence returned as the staff waited to hear what Buchanan would say. No one was so dense as to miss the fact that Fenella had overstepped her duties. But Buchanan didn't dare dismiss the woman, not unless he wanted a hall full of hungry Retainers and no supper to lay on the tables. A competent Head-of-House could demand a hefty ransom in the highlands.

Buchanan looked at the blanket. His expression gave little away, but he appeared to be weighing his next words carefully. In spite of the pain coursing through her body, Rhedyn clasped her hands together and held her silence. Hurling insults at one another wasn't going to do anything but incite a mob which would likely hang her in retribution for the men lost with Iain Mackenzie.

"Being Head-of-House is demanding," Buchanan said. "Forgive me for leaving another task to add to yer burden. I will settle Mistress Lindsey in the north tower."

The kitchens were silent. Buchanan stood firm, suffering the glowering coming from his clanswomen. He was making a public stand for her, making it clear that he'd not allow her to be at Fenella's mercy. It was a risky move, for the need for vengeance was running high among the women who had suffered losses.

Buchanan reached over and clasped her gently around the upper arm. "Ye shall no' have to deal with Mistress Lindsey again."

Now there were gasps. Several of the maids were unable to contain their astonishment. Buchanan sent them all a final look which had Rhedyn nervous.

He was standing up for her?

Or at least between her and his people.

She'd had some wild thoughts abovestairs but never had she imagined the Makenzie laird might shelter her against his own kin. It was a bold move. Many would say a foolish one, for if Buchanan had a half-brother, there were likely other close blood kin as well. Siding with the daughter of an enemy could see him stripped of the lairdship and hanged right along beside her.

But he didn't hesitate. Buchanan turned her around and sent her out of the doorway of the kitchen as he placed his back to the people who would likely cheer as she was fitted with a noose.

CHAPTER THREE

A CHAMBER.

There was a bed with a thick comforter and a chair by the window.

And...

And...so many comforts that Rhedyn stopped just inside the doorway because she wanted to look at it all and savor what she had always taken for granted.

"If ye'd yelled..." Buchanan began behind her. "Someone might have heard ye."

She turned and shot him a disgruntled look. "I can endure quite well. Ye will no' have the pleasure of hearing me cry."

She'd never realized there could be so much agony in her body all at the same time. The simple act of walking and climbing stairs seemed to have left her hurting even more. The sight of the bed was a torment, for she desperately wanted the comfort of it and yet, climbing up on it was something she didn't believe she might accomplish without crying out.

Buchanan was still in the chamber, his keen, amber eyes focused on her. Like a raptor contemplating prey.

She'd offer him nothing to indicate how much she suffered. But she was shaking. Her body wasn't obedient to her pride. Instead, the walk from the kitchens to the north tower had cost her almost all of her strength. A chill made her think her toes were frozen. She had her hands buried in the folds of her skirt.

The bed offered sanctuary. A haven where she could find relief from at least part of her suffering. She'd not climb into it until she was alone.

"What are ye waiting for, Laird Mackenzie?"

His eyes narrowed. "I want yer promise that ye will tell me if there is abuse being done to ye."

"Did ye no' bring me here to extract vengeance?"

His face darkened. "Did ye no' implore me to spare yer father when he made to face me in combat?"

She had. Rhedyn looked away from him. But he caught her chin. He used just two fingers and his thumb, but the contact was jarring. She felt it all the way to her toes.

"Ye are not simple minded Rhedyn. Ye have been raised as I was. To think before ye act and to understand the weight which is on yer shoulders. Hamish and his men were looking for blood. Yer father's blood. I took ye to avoid giving it to them. Such makes ye a target for me kin. I locked ye away to protect ye from them."

Rhedyn stepped back to break his grip. "I understand well enough."

"Do ye?" Buchanan demanded softly. "I have me doubts."

"Because I would nae please yer Head-of-House by screaming?" Rhedyn lifted her chin in defiance. "Ye'd no' have muttered a sound if ye were locked in the Lindsey dungeon, Buchanan Mackenzie."

His lips twitched. "I am no' a lass."

Rhedyn shot him a fuming look. "I…"

Buchanan smothered her argument with his hand. He reached down and caught a handful of her skirt to keep her from stepping back again.

"What ye are is me responsibility, Rhedyn Lindsey. I took ye because there was no other means of keeping the peace."

He suddenly shook his head and backed away from her. There was a flicker of disgust in his eyes, and she realized it was directed at himself. He let out a sound of frustration.

"Ye'll tell me everything," he began sternly. "Ye will no' suffer abuse silently. Do ye understand me? Taking ye is enough guilt for me to shoulder."

She nodded, still stunned. Her mind was truly having difficulty processing the way he seemed determined to shelter her from his staff. "I see ye are serious."

Her response didn't please him.

"I suppose I should expect ye would no' trust in me sincerity," he said. "Still..." He looked around the chamber before he nodded. "Fenella's disobedience affords me the chance to place ye here. Do nae be unwise, lass. Me kin is still angry, and some of them unwilling to not vent their temper on ye. Mind where ye go. Please." Buchanan stared at her for a long moment before he turned and left. The door closed, but there was no sound of a chain.

Please...

Rhedyn felt her knees weakening. It was her resolve as well, for she truly was at a loss as to how to see Buchanan now.

He was her captor.

Yet now, he'd become her protector.

Oh, for certain her pride wanted to baulk and declare that she didn't need his help, but the pain in her back and arms was all too real a reminder of just how dire her fate might be if Buchanan didn't care about her suffering.

So now what?

Buchanan would have her turn to him for help. The concept was daunting. And too much to contemplate while standing.

Rhedyn turned and made her way to the bed. It was a large one, made for two people.

Or an esteemed guest.

She smiled at the idea of Fenella hearing that she, the Lindsey bitch, was sleeping in so grand a chamber. Surely the lord wouldn't begrudge her a bit of pleasure over such a thought. Not when her arms and back still felt like they were on fire from the blows the Head-of-House had rained down on her.

As far as sins went, it had to be minuscule.

She stopped at the side of the bed and tried to give herself that little bit of a jump to get onto the mattress.

But she failed.

A sound of anguish got past her lips, and Rhedyn found herself sagging against the side of the bed, because it seemed the only thing she had the strength left to do.

Apparently, there was something worse than the chamber above the kitchens with naught but a blanket of pelts against the chill of the night.

⫸⫷

BUCHANAN STOOD IN the passageway.

Rhedyn had kept silent.

Of course she had. The lass had strength. It wasn't the first time he'd noted the trait but now, his awareness of it was far stronger. No one used the north tower during the winter. The stone walls took the brunt of the winter winds.

"Ye'd no' have muttered a sound if ye were locked in the Lindsey dungeon, Buchanan Makenzie."

Was that the first time Rhedyn had used his name?

The sensation the thought sent through him was odd. He remained in place for a long time, attempting to decipher the way his emotions seemed to be reacting to her voice echoing inside his skull.

So formal.

Proper.

Neither of those ideas should have surprised him and yet, Buchanan discovered himself feeling as though she'd pushed him back.

Can ye blame her, lad?

He felt guilt slicing at him once again. No, by right, Rhedyn should spit on him at the least.

But what he was certain of in that moment was that he didn't like it. Not one bit. The animosity between them was something he had a sudden urge to tear down. The problem was, he wasn't sure of how to even begin such a process. Fate had placed them both so firmly on opposing sides.

A muffled sound came through the door. He was turning around and pushing it open before he thought the matter through.

"Christ, woman," he exclaimed as he spied her clinging to the side of the bed. He was across the space between them in a few strides, scooping her up in his arms. But the bedding was tucked up to the headboard beneath the pillows, so he stood for a moment with her cradled against his chest. It was among one of the longest moments in his life. Time seemed to have slowed down, just so he might notice the way she fit in his arms so perfectly.

"A moment, Laird."

A smooth voice issued the comment from the doorway. Buchanan turned his head to see Shona, the mistress of the towers, entering the chamber. She set a small tray down on the table beside the chair in front of the hearth before she was hurrying around the bed to the other side where she tugged at the bedding.

"Put me down," Rhedyn whispered.

Buchanan looked back at her, but only for a moment before she tucked her chin and averted her eyes. She drew in a breath, shuddering. Something inside him responded to that involuntary motion. A feeling he'd never experienced before. Naming it seemed impossible, but he stood in place, unwilling to let her go before he understood the strange reaction to her.

"Laird?" Shona patted the sheet.

It made no sense.

None at all.

Yet the impulse was there, a surge of determination to maintain his hold on her. Rhedyn looked back at him, her startled gaze offering him an unexpected glimpse of appreciation in the strange moment. Something passed between them, the intensity of which shocked him with just how deep it ran.

But she was pushing against his chest. Pain flickered in her eyes as she stiffened. His own impulse was to hold onto her and show her that she wasn't the only one with resolve.

"Me guest is wet," Buchanan informed Shona. He lowered her to a chair as Shona went toward a wardrobe and pulled the doors open. "I will wait," Buchanan announced before he turned and headed back toward the door.

"There is no need," Rhedyn responded tartly. Her cheeks were blazing with a blush which was completely misplaced.

Buchanan turned and shot her a look. "I'll see ye settled into bed."

If her face hadn't already felt like it was on fire, it did after his words sunk in. The knowing look on Shona's face as she helped Rhedyn from her clothing only intensified everything.

Why was she blushing for Buchanan Makenzie? Rolfe Munro had spent several hours in an attempt to grant her time to become accustomed to him. He had displayed kindness and...and...she was blushing for Buchanan!

Shona peeled away the layers of her springtime dress. Doing it with expertise until Rhedyn was dressed in a fresh smock and a dressing robe.

"I can manage," Rhedyn declared as she stood.

But where her mind was willing, her strength couldn't be found. Her knees were weak, too much so to support her. Too many days of little food and cold had taken their toll.

She would have preferred the floor to the way Buchanan reappeared and scooped her up.

Foolish...

"Settle her carefully, Laird," Shona muttered. "Fenella was putting her back into those blows."

"I am quite well, I assure ye." Rhedyn sat straight, pushing Buchanan back as the new woman adjusted the pillows behind her.

There was no hiding the way relief surged through her as she felt the bed give just the right amount beneath her weight. There was a slight groan from the bed ropes and the scent of rosemary from the bedding as it was tucked up to her chest.

Whatever else Rhedyn might have thought about, it all evaporated as Shona tucked the bedding up to her chin. Truly warm for the first time in too many days to count, Rhedyn slipped away into sleep.

⟫⟫⟫⟪⟪⟪

Edinburgh…

"YER GRACE…"

The arch bishop held up his hand. His subordinate closed his mouth, even if he commenced with glowering after he obeyed his superior.

"Our Lord was the Prince of Peace," the Archbishop stated. "Colum Lindsey claims he declared to Heaven and God that he took Brenna McLeod as his wife. We will acknowledge it."

The other Bishop didn't agree.

Vychan didn't care.

He lowered himself before the Archbishop before leaving the room as quickly as Colum was able. Once they were outside, Colum shared a look with his captain, Rory.

"How much did it cost ye?" Vychan asked his sire. "How much does one need to bribe an Archbishop?"

"It was only a matter of convincing the man of the good which might be accomplished if I were his friend."

"A donation to the hospital in remembrance of yer mother," Rory filled in the details.

"So, all in all," Colum continued, "a good ending for everyone."

Colum indulged in another moment of satisfaction before his expression tightened. "Now, lads. Me daughter has been in the hands of Buchanan Makenzie for too long."

The assembled Retainers nodded gruffly. They checked their saddle straps before they mounted, for they were going to ride hard. Every man among them understood the peril they were heading into.

And not a one of them hesitated.

⇥⤜

"CORA." BUCHANAN CAUGHT his sister hovering in the passageway at the base of the steps which lead up to the chambers in the North Tower.

His sister turned and lowered herself briefly.

Buchanan finished descending the steps. "I suppose the matter is spread all over the stronghold by now."

"And likely into the stables," Cora confirmed. "Fenella is sputtering in rage. And I am feeling no' less incensed toward our Head-of-House."

"She lost her son," Buchanan argued.

"Because of Iain's recklessness," Cora spat back. "Why is it always a woman's burden to suffer what men do in the name of glory? Fenella should know better at her age. To vent her rage on Rhedyn is...is..."

"I will no' allow the lass to suffer." His sister paused. Buchanan pointed behind him. "Shona has care of her now. Fenella has given me the chance to remove our guest from her reach."

Cora looked both ways before she moved close and lowered her voice. "It would be better if she were gone from Mackenzie land."

"If she is gone, the men will demand I seek out her father for recompense. The matter is still too fresh in everyone's minds."

"Colum Lindsey is a long way from here," Cora replied. "Secure in his own stronghold. If he has his daughter back, he will have no reason to venture outside his walls. Much less fight with ye."

"It is no' so simple as that, Cora." Buchanan shook his head. "It's spring now. The men will want to raid if Colum does no' accept me challenge."

"Ye'll think of something to dissuade them," Cora said adamantly.

"Aye, well, while I'm thinking, ye should be learning how to manage the house."

Cora propped her hands on her hips. "I will sit with Rhedyn and make certain no one trifles with her."

"She's had enough Mackenzies for one day," Buchanan said. He held up his hand when his sister made to argue. "How can she not see ye as a Mackenzie? Ye are me sister, Cora. Ye can no more go against the clan than I can. Make a fuss and the hall will be full of conversation about ye no' knowing yer place which will lead to talk of setting the date for yer wedding so yer groom can take ye in hand. I will nae start such a conversation, but ye know very well I can no' ignore it if it begins."

Cora narrowed her eyes. "Perhaps she's had enough of the sort of Mackenzie ye appear to be, brother. Do nae count me among the number who can nae see there is likely more to the tale of the evening at Sow's Troth. Because I know full well the tavern is where men find courtesans."

His sister sent him a final fuming look before she turned and left. Her words rung in his ears, for he suddenly realized just how much Cora and Rhedyn had in common.

He detested the idea of thinking of Cora arriving to a place full of animosity toward her blood. He was helpless to do anything about the reception she'd receive, and that bit of knowledge felt like a knot in his gut. It persisted, driving his desire to manage the situation. He could not even voice his demand that his sister be treated kindly when it would be all too simple for the Grants to point to his taking Rhedyn as a captive.

So maybe he should lead by example.

Buchanan looked back up the stairs.

Aye. Perhaps he'd do exactly that and just see what his Lindsey guest made of his overtures.

➤➤➤◄◄◄

HER BELLY GRUMBLED.

Rhedyn was still tired but hunger was gnawing at her insides. She shifted in the bedding and realized the scent of hot food was drifting in the air. Sleep was suddenly the last thing she craved.

Had she missed the sound of the chain?

She opened her eyes and sat up. Pain shot across her back, recalling her memories instantly.

"I am Shona."

Shona lowered herself in a simple motion before she was moving around the foot of the bed. Her steps barely made any sound at all. The dress she wore was a gray-green wool. Her over sleeves were tied behind her back. Unlike the maids in the kitchens, Shona wore a narrow-brimmed cap. It was tilted to one side, giving her a playful appearance.

"Yes, I remember," Rhedyn responded.

Shona folded the bedding down. Rhedyn's belly grumbled long and low.

"Ye slept the day away, but I knew ye'd need some supper or ye'd wake in the wee dark hours," Shona said.

A pair of slippers were waiting for Rhedyn to slip her feet into before she moved across the room to where a tray was placed on a small table. The scent of food made her mouth water, but Shona took a brush to her hair first. Rhedyn sat still until the woman decided she was neat enough.

"Thank ye," Rhedyn said before she reached for a ceramic lid atop a bowl. Steam rose up in a little puff as she leaned forward to see what supper there was. She smiled before she picked up a spoon and dug into the hearty stew.

"Shona attends to the chambers and guests," Buchanan spoke as he came into the chamber.

Rhedyn swallowed and pulled the spoon out of her mouth while the Makenzie laird made his way across the floor to a chair opposite her.

Rhedyn was only wearing a dressing robe.

Captors don't follow the rules of etiquette...

Of course they didn't, but Rhedyn still couldn't quite dispel her surprise.

Shona walked over to the small table by the chair. She retrieved the tray and brought it over to Buchanan. His eyes narrowed, but only for a moment before he was lifting the bottle from the tray and pulling the waxed rope stopper from it. The scent of strong whiskey teased Rhedyn's nose. He poured two glasses, placing one back on the tray, which Shona carried over and placed in front of Rhedyn.

"I do not partake of strong spirits," she informed him.

"Thank ye, Shona." Buchanan ignored Rhedyn.

Shona inclined her head before striding out of the chamber. It left Rhedyn alone with Buchanan and the odd way his presence affected her.

"I do nae expect ye are accustomed to strong spirits. But I have no taste for French wine, so there is none in the cellar, or Shona would have brought it. Whiskey will have to do until I can fetch something more appropriate for a lady."

He lifted the glass to her in a toast. Rhedyn was frozen, her mind refusing to process his words.

"Do ye suspect me of attempting to undermine yer wits, lass?" he asked when she left her glass on the table.

Rhedyn scoffed at him but picked up the glass because she refused to allow him to think he'd intimidated her. "I've been here long enough if ye cared to ruin me."

The topic was forbidden, or unseemly at best. Still, for the moment, Rhedyn discovered herself too lacking in strength to do anything except speak plainly. If he didn't care for it, he knew where the door was. Her response left him contemplating her with a questioning look as she sniffed at the whiskey.

"Ye are a fine enough looking lass, Rhedyn," Buchanan remarked as he sipped at the whiskey.

The compliment caused her to choke on the second sip of whiskey. One side of his mouth rose in response.

"The idea of ye sending any of yer people to fetch something for me was what gave me pause," Rhedyn said as the strong drink stung her throat. But it also cleaned her teeth and mouth, so she took another sip. "As if ye'd bother on me account. Why are ye still here?"

"There is only one way ye will understand I am sincere," he said.

Rhedyn looked up from the glass to find him watching her with an honest expression. One she discovered she liked far too much, for it lacked the icy chill she'd come to expect.

"And what precisely is that?"

Buchanan flashed her a grin. "To tell the truth, I do nae know but—most negotiations start with having a drink together. So...let's have a drink."

So, this was the man beneath the laird. Meeting him was a bit unsettling.

A shiver went down her back. Only, it was a different sort of sensation. It raised gooseflesh along her limbs, but it had nothing in common with the way Fenella had chilled her blood. Buchanan drained his glass and refilled it.

"I crossed Fenella a few times in me youth and gained a taste of that rod of hers," Buchanan told her. "Drink up. There is no reason to suffer."

"Oh," Rhedyn muttered after another few sips. "I do nae know how I might have come to any other conclusion."

Buchanan frowned. "Ye know well I have no liking for being called a villain."

He was explaining himself to her. Rhedyn tossed the remaining liquid into her mouth and drew in a deep breath as it felt like it set fire to her tongue. It was surprise that made her do it so quickly. Never could she have imagined Laird Mackenzie attempting to make amends with her.

"It is me failing that Fenella was able to vent her grief upon ye." Buchanan stood and moved toward her. He refilled her glass before locking gazes with her. "I apologize, lass. Sincerely."

There was a gleam of self-reproach in his eyes. He gave her only a moment to see it before he was returning to the chair by the hearth. For a brief moment, she watched the longer pleats of his kilt sway with his steps before he turned and gave her a glimpse of his knees and bare thighs.

There wasn't a spare bit of flesh on him. He wasn't a laird in title first and foremost. No, Buchanan was earning his respect by working as hard as any of his men.

"No retort?" he inquired from the chair.

"I am no' a harpy. Or a child to no' see the value of yer apology." She felt the warmth of the liquor spreading through her body. It burned away the pain, leaving her happy to indulge in more drink.

"No, ye are a woman. Yer father should be pleased with ye, lass. Ye have done the Lindsey name proud."

"Ye did nae insist on fighting me father." Rhedyn wasn't certain when she decided to speak. But the words were across her lips before she thought to quell the urge. "It would likely have been better for ye if ye had. Yer men are not pleased with yer restraint."

"Some are," Buchanan replied. "Others, well, taking ye affords me the opportunity to let evidence surface to clear yer father's name."

"It was a tavern," Rhedyn defended her father. "If yer brother was talking in a common room more than one man would have heard him. Naught but pure nonsense for anyone to point solely at me father as the culprit."

Rhedyn drew in a stiff breath. Her heart was beating hard, but she felt better than she had in days for being able to speak her mind. She reached for the soup and ate the rest of it before placing the bowl down with a little sound of victory. Buchanan was still contemplating her. He suddenly put his glass down and left the chair.

She gasped, for the man moved quickly and with a fluidness that spoke of just how lethal his body might be. She was suddenly frozen like a rabbit that had spied a predator. Buchanan kept coming until he was only a pace from her. She tipped back her head, keeping their gazes fused.

"Which is why I acted like a villain and stole ye."

His tone was edged with remorse. Rhedyn might have contemplated his expression, but with her second glass drained, she found herself far more interested in enjoying his admission.

He suddenly leaned down and scooped her up. She gasped, amazed by the strength he had. He cradled her against his chest, turning and carrying her toward the bed.

Strange how she noticed the scent on his skin.

Clean.

Healthy.

Strong.

So many of her father's men were the same and yet, completely different than the Mackenzie laird. As he lowered her to the bed, she stared into his eyes, fascinated by the topaz color.

"An innocent is what ye are, Rhedyn," he muttered again as he leaned forward and stroked some hair back from where it had fallen across her face.

She let out a little sound of surprise, for the contact between their skin was astounding. And she wasn't the only one who felt it. He went still, hovering over her before he deliberately stroked the side of her face. Something sparked in his eyes.

Something that sent a warning through her.

But her eyelids were too heavy. They lowered, and Rhedyn didn't have the strength to lift them again. Instead, she felt Buchanan stroke her face once more, his touch penetrating deep now that she didn't have her sight to distract her. Another little sound escaped her lips before she drifted into slumber.

⟫⟪

HE WAS PLEASED.

Buchanan forced himself to straighten up. Pulling his hand away from Rhedyn seemed by far one of the greatest acts of self-discipline he'd ever demanded of himself.

It was likely a misplaced emotion but for the moment, he was alone. So, he contemplated Rhedyn while he tried to decipher the emotions welling up inside him.

The dark bruises on her arms enraged him. But it was completely self-directed. He'd left her open to attack.

It wouldn't happen again.

Buchanan felt like he was making a solemn oath, and just possibly he was. Long moments passed by as he watched the way she slept. There was something innately satisfying about watching her resting so deeply. But right on the heels of that feeling was guilt. Sharp-edged reproach for the way he'd left her in the chamber above the kitchen with naught but rabbit pelts.

The truth was, he'd never thought his staff would be so petty.

Well ye know it now, laddie...

Buchanan nodded.

He tucked the blankets up to her chin before departing the chamber. Shona was at the end of the passageway, her eyes on a small, leather-bound book she seemed to always have tucked into a pocket on her skirt. She knew he was there, but waited until he closed the chamber door before she glanced up at him.

"I entrust our guest to ye, Shona."

"Guest?" she inquired. Her intent was to make certain she understood clearly what Rhedyn's position was.

"Aye," Buchanan said. "One who does nae have the liberty to leave the tower without escort."

Shona inclined her head. Buchanan held up his finger.

"Tell yer staff that I will be deeply displeased if there is any further abuse. Rhedyn Lindsey is me personal guest. If they have an argument about it, they can see me."

Shona was in her position because she was smart. She fluttered her eyelashes before her lips lifted into a grin. "I will make certain of it, Laird."

Fenella was the Head-of-House, but when it came to the upper tower chambers, Shona held the authority. In a castle as large as the Mackenzie stronghold, such an arrangement was necessary.

The look on Shona's face granted him the peace of mind to turn and walk away. But he wasn't fully at ease. There were plenty in the castle who would happily take their anger out on Rhedyn.

He was responsible for her.

Buchanan felt the muscles between his shoulder blades tightening. Aye, he'd taken her, and he'd have to find a way to prove the issue one way or the other else there would never be any peace.

And if Colum Lindsey is innocent?

Buchanan didn't shy away from the question. His father had done a good job of raising him to be laird. There was no shirking his actions. He'd answer for taking Rhedyn if need be. For the moment though, he sat at his desk and began to draft a letter. He didn't crawl into his own bed until late into the night as he wrote out several messages meant to accumulate information from several sources. Perhaps in a castle there might be loyalty, but a tavern, well, that was another matter altogether.

But will ye send her home, laddie?

That question came as he was lying in his bed and thinking about the way Rhedyn had looked while sleeping.

She stirred the oddest sensation in him.

Alone in the dark, he could be honest with himself. Well, it was a bit more of being unable to stop his mind from going where it would. Rhedyn drew his interest in a manner he'd never encountered in a female before.

Cradling her had pleased him.

Her weight, her scent, were details branded into his mind for some strange reason. It defied rational thinking the way he recalled tiny details about her pretty face. From the exact color of her hair to the way her hazel eyes were greener than anything else. She was mesmerizing, even now when fatigue was clawing at him and sleep remained elusive.

The only idea he wanted to entertain was one which included finding a reason to see her again. Sending her home made him bristle. It made no sense, but his fickle emotions weren't interested in logic.

Just his impulses.

⟫⟫⟫⟪⟪⟪

Munro land...

ROLFE MUNRO FLATTENED his hands on the table in his study and eyed the Retainer in front of him.

"The Church allowed Colum Lindsey to wed a dead woman?" he demanded.

"Aye," the man answered. "Vychan has been acknowledged and legitimized."

Rolfe let out a low whistle.

There was a cough from near the hearth. Rolfe's father sat hunched over, his shoulders draped with a thick blanket in spite of the flames dancing away just a few feet from him. His face was thin and pinched, age taking a vicious toll on him. Yet, there was life in his eyes still.

"Ye should have wed that Lindsey girl last season....as I told ye to."

Rolfe sent his sire a hard look. The old man coughed again and lifted a trembling hand so he could point a finger toward his son. "Age will take me from this world soon enough, lad. Ye do nae need to send me a look which implies ye'll snap me neck." His father chuckled. It was a rattle in his chest now.

Rolfe ended up shrugging. "I tried, but her father would no' have it without her consent," Rolfe muttered. "One more season and she'd have been mine. Now Colum has managed to find himself a son. A fully grown one at that."

"Vychan *is* his son," Laird Munro spoke clearly. "I know that story well. Everyone wanted a taste of that redhead who bore him. Tried me luck with her, but she only had eyes for Colum. If you'd wed that lass, the dowry would be in our coffers where no newly recognized son could touch it. Ye won't be getting as much now that Vychan has come to take his place."

"It would still be a useful alliance," Rolfe insisted. "I'll get Rhedyn wed and see to the matter of her new brother. He'll bring a connection to the McLeod. That will be worth the decrease in dowry."

"Laird Mackenzie took Rhedyn," the Retainer informed them.

"What?" Rolfe demanded. "Colum agreed to another suit? He promised her to me!"

The Retainer shook his head. "Hamish Mackenzie accused Colum Lindsey of betraying Iain. Buchanan took the girl in payment for losing his only brother."

For a long moment, only the crackling of the fire was heard. Laird

Munro choked and sputtered first. Rolfe sat down.

"Looks like ye made a mess of it all, boy," Laird Munro informed his son. "Ye'll no be getting that lass back from Buchanan Mackenzie."

Rolfe glared at his father. "Can ye no spare a thought for the fact that the lass suffers for a deed I committed?"

Laird Munro raised an eyebrow and pointed at the bandage around Rolfe's shoulder. "Killing Iain cost ye blood, yer own blood, and eleven of our men. I admit, ye did well there, boy. But Buchanan is no' like Iain. He's no one to ride into the night like an untried lad seeking glory found only in the verse of song."

Rolfe grunted. "I'm surprised to hear Buchanan is being so easily led. Iain… well, he lacked sense, but Buchanan never struck me as the sort to follow gossip so quickly. I understand why Vychan met with his father at long last. With Rhedyn in the Mackenzie stronghold, the Lindsey clan is ripe for a bastard son to claim."

"Buchanan is no fool, even if he failed to control Iain," Liard Munro agreed. "Likely, he knows what value Rhedyn has. With his father newly in his grave, it's time for Buchanan to wed. He made use of the opportunity to take the girl without her father's agreement. Something ye could not do."

"But if his clan believes Colum was responsible for Iain's death, I doubt Buchanan will wed Rhedyn straight away. There might yet be time to reclaim her." Rolfe flattened his hand on the table top. "It looks like me spy in the Mackenzie stronghold still has a use."

"So ye are no' planning to clear Colum's name?"

Rolfe locked gazes with his father. "If I did that, Buchanan wouldn't have to think of wedding Rhedyn. Buchanan is nae like his half-brother. He'll not hurt Rhedyn."

"Being locked away might just make her more receptive to yer suit." Rolfe saw the gleam in his eyes as he smiled and stroked his beard. "She'll likely be thinking more kindly toward ye for courting her now that she's had a taste of rough wooing."

"I'm more concerned that the Makenzies will see her as a target for their rage once they know I killed Iain and planned to make Rhedyn me wife," Rolfe explained to his father.

Rolfe dipped a quill into a small ink well and began to pen a letter. He felt a tug on his conscious but couldn't act upon it. Not right away. Clearing Colum's name was something he'd do. He'd take the blame for the deeds he'd done, but not while Rhedyn was in the Mackenzie stronghold. He didn't know Buchanan well enough to trust in his ability to safeguard the lass. Once it was dry, he folded it, but didn't seal it. Instead, he handed it over to the Retainer.

"Ye know what to do with that."

The Retainer reached up and tugged on the corner of his cap. "Aye, Laird."

There was a scoff from the hearth. The Retainer hesitated, looking between Rolfe and the old laird. Rolfe waved him toward the door.

"He meant no disrespect," Rolfe assured his father once the man was gone from the room.

"Men need a strong leader," Laird Munro said. "I'm blessed to have ye to carry on the family line."

Rolfe moved toward his father and poured him a measure of whiskey. He held it for his sire, lifting it to his lips so he might sip it down. Not too long after, his father was snoring softly. The wound in Rolfe's shoulder ached, but he didn't indulge in any of the liquor.

He had work to do. His father was correct; men needed a strong leader. He would prove his worth to the Munro. Iain Mackenzie was no innocent. The man had raided up and down the length of Munro land for several seasons. Rolfe wouldn't be suffering any guilt for ridding his father's land of the menace.

Iain might have been sired by a laird, but the blood of his common-born mother had left its mark on him. He'd been tainted by a lack of self-discipline and low morals. Just like the mother who had taken a lover instead of wedding a man her family had contracted for her.

Rolfe had no quarrel with Buchanan, or at least he hadn't until the Mackenzie laird had taken Rhedyn.

Now Rolfe was going to retrieve his bride. Buchanan would be wise to let her go.

⇟⇟⇟⇟⟪⟪⟪

Mackenzie land...

THERE WAS A knock on the chamber door the next morning. Rhedyn looked toward it as she blinked and tried to manage to think. The pain in her arms sobered her quick enough. She sucked in her breath as she felt the effects of Fenella's handiwork.

Whoever it was knocked a second time. This time louder and with more repetitions.

"Yes?" Rhedyn asked.

The door opened. Shona was there, looking in first. She held her hand up once she ensured that Rhedyn was fit for company.

"Good morning to ye, mistress," Shona said once she was in the center of the room. The word 'mistress' was spoken firmly and directed toward the maids following her. The first one hesitated, causing the girl following her to bump into her.

"To the table by the hearth," Shona instructed them firmly.

Two of the girls shared a glance, but it appeared no one was willing to challenge Shona. They set their trays down as one of the last girls in line came to the bedside and folded the bedding down so Rhedyn might get up.

"The dressing robe, Una," Shona directed her.

There was a tapping of shoes against the wooden floor as one of the maids hurried over to a wardrobe to fetch the garment. Shona stood still, her position of authority clear. Her eyes were bright as she watched her staff.

"After ye have broken yer fast, I will take ye to the bathhouse, mistress," Shona continued.

One of the maids was standing behind the chair Buchanan had sat in the night before. Rhedyn made her way to it as two of the girls set to making up the bed. She'd grown up with such attention, but today it was as though it was brand new.

Her time with Buchanan had changed her.

Rhedyn took a bowl from the maid who had stayed near her. It was warm from the porridge inside it. She couldn't help but let out a little sound of enjoyment as the chill of the night was chased from her fingers. Every movement sent pain through her arms and back, but it was lessened by the memory of having only one meal a day. Tyree had delivered it late, too. Likely so she'd not have a rumbling belly in the dark hours of the night to keep her awake. However, it meant mornings were long as she waited for more sustenance.

So many little comforts... She'd not forget to notice them again.

"Did ye say bath?" Rhedyn finally realized what Shona had meant.

"Aye." Shona grinned. "The water is already over the fire. I imagine ye will want to go straight away."

In spite of her resolve to savor every moment, Rhedyn suddenly hurried to finish her meal. Her skin began to itch with just the mention of being able to clean herself. As soon as she finished the porridge, she stood, convinced she could smell herself.

"Please show me the way, Shona."

Shona lowered herself again. "The laird has instructed me to make certain ye are treated as his personal guest."

Her voice carried to every corner of the chamber. The maids clearly realized the statement was intended for their ears. Shona directed them, and she was lowering herself before Rhedyn, which would place Rhedyn's position in the household just below Cora's.

Buchanan had clearly decided on the next step after sharing a drink with her...

But Rhedyn discovered herself at a loss on just how to think of Buchanan if she didn't keep him clearly labeled as her captor.

"How...considerate of Laird Mackenzie." Rhedyn nearly choked on the words.

A memory stirred, rising up suddenly from where it had lingered during the night. Her cheek tingled as she recalled in vivid detail the way he'd stroked the side of her face. A little shiver went down her body, shocking her with just how responsive to his touch she appeared to be.

How could a memory stir her emotions so deeply?

"This way, Mistress Lindsey."

Rhedyn discovered herself blinking several times before her mind grasped Shona's words. Heat touched her cheeks as she nodded and followed Shona down three flights of stairs. The morning sun was streaming in through the arrow slits, brightening everything. Once they reached the main floor, the passageway opened up. The sounds of others working and talking floated between the stone walls.

She'd missed such things.

Rhedyn couldn't stop from smiling, and she didn't try. Why be sullen when life would no doubt offer her plenty of times to be downhearted? Savor the moments of joy and look for the blessings she had in her hand instead of the ones beyond her reach. It had always been her way and now, well, such behavior seemed far more important than ever before.

It wasn't as if she hadn't always known her future would involve going to a place where she was a stranger. As a daughter of a laird, the matter of her marriage would be decided upon with an eye on alliances and gain for her clan. If she wanted happiness, she'd have to cultivate it with whatever circumstances reality delivered her into. Marriage might make her the mistress of a household, but true friendship would have to be carefully cultivated if she didn't want an empty life with naught but her position to keep her happy.

Rhedyn shook off her thoughts. She was *not* Buchanan's bride. The pain in her shoulders and arms were proof that she wasn't the mistress of this stronghold. Yet, he'd given her status.

And freed ye from the tower room…

Rhedyn closed her mind to any other thoughts but positive ones. Soon, the entire affair would be only a memory. One she looked to as a reminder her life was good. No, Buchanan hadn't told her he was sending her home, but it really was only a matter of time now. She would be his guest until his captains agreed with letting her go.

The bathhouse was on the main floor behind a kitchen. It was not the huge kitchen Fenella ran but a smaller one which would likely date further back in time to before the great hall had been added to the Mackenzie stronghold.

Now the chamber served as a bathhouse. The hearth had a fire built in it and several large iron hooks had pots suspended over the flames. There were three large tubs set up against one wall. Their insides faced the fire where the wood was dry from the heat. Near the hearth, one tub was waiting. It had been filled with cold water in anticipation of her arrival. One of the maids lifted a long, iron hook and used it to pull one of the pots out of the flames. She wrapped the handle with a thick piece of wool to protect her fingers from burning before carrying it to the tub and dumping it.

There was a hiss as the hot water mixed with the cold. The other pots were added and then the contents were mixed with a long, wooden paddle.

Two of the maids began to open Rhedyn's dressing robe, but she tried to stop them.

"I can see to meself, thank ye."

Shona turned her attention away from a chest she had taken soap from.

"That will nae do, mistress," Shona replied softly as she came close and finished untying the belt which held the dressing robe together.

She locked gazes with Rhedyn. "Gossip has already landed ye here, with no care for right or wrong or fairness." Shona continued in a smooth tone, "Best to no' allow any more vicious tongues to wag on account of any marks yer body might have but does nae."

Rhedyn drew in a stiff breath, but there was no denying the truth of her words. Modesty might be considered a virtue, but among only women in a bathhouse, it could also be wielded as a weapon by those who might want to accuse Rhedyn of having a witch mark or any number of other ailments.

Yet, she faced such things on Lindsey land, too, so it was far from personal.

It was simply the way things were.

"As ye say," Rhedyn agreed.

She released the edges of the dressing grown. The maids knew their duties well, easing the robe down Rhedyn's arms and carrying it away.

Such was another lesson she'd learned young as the daughter of a laird. There would be eyes upon her. And it was wise to keep yer enemy close.

Truly, life was far too vicious.

One of the maids was frozen. She stood with Rhedyn's smock in her fingers, staring at the purple bruises on Rhedyn's forearms. Another hiss from the tub sounded, and Rhedyn was far more interested in making the most of her time to bathe. The bruises would still be there when she finished.

It wasn't as if there was anyone who didn't know how the bruises had gotten there.

The soap had lavender oil in it. Once it was worked through her wet hair, her senses were filled with the delightful scent. A maid scooped up water to pour over Rhedyn's head while another used a soft brush to make sure her toenails were clean. Unfortunately, the water cooled off quickly. Shona snapped her fingers as Rhedyn stood and stepped out of the tub. A length of linen was pulled from a rack where it had been warming near the hearth. The fabric soaked up the water left on her skin.

"Turn around now so yer hair can dry," Shona advised.

A maid placed a stool near the hearth as another held a fresh smock. The garment settled into place as Rhedyn sat down, and Shona began to work the tangles from her hair with a comb.

"Thank ye, Shona."

There was a soft hum from behind her as Shona continued with her work. Before long, Rhedyn's hair was a fluffy cloud. She now wore stockings, garters, and shoes, which made it possible for her to stand without placing her feet on the bare floor.

"Yer dress is ill suited to the highlands beyond an afternoon celebration," Shona said. "I brought a few to try for sizing, but we'll have something made up by next week."

Shona was a master of her position. The woman kept her tone even and sweet, as though she were speaking of nothing but the weather instead of a new dress, which was an expense. A large one, for wool was only produced once a year. The fresh smock Rhedyn wore would have been considered generous, for it was made of the finest hemp and soft. The edges of the garment had been carefully rolled and sewn.

But her words weren't lost on the maids. More than one pair of eyes widened as Shona lifted a petticoat up for Rhedyn to put her arms through. Shona helped settle the garment around her waist, where she then used a tie to secure it in place.

"A good enough fit," Shona remarked as she went back to where a set of stays were laying on a table.

"Good day, Mistress Lindsey."

Rhedyn turned to see Cora. The girl stopped just inside the doorway and lowered herself in a proper greeting. Her eyes sparkled.

"We meet again, Cora," Rhedyn said.

"I am very glad ye have come out of the tower," Cora said. "Me birthday is just two days away, and I will be very happy to have ye here to help guide me."

Cora's zeal for life was infectious. Rhedyn smiled at her. "And how old will ye be this year?"

"Seventeen."

Cora had made it nearly all the way into the room. She looked Rhedyn over—clearly there to inspect her bruises. The maids waited to see what the laird's sister would do.

"Fenella should have a taste of her own actions," Cora muttered darkly.

"Please, be at ease," Rhedyn said. "Yer brother has dealt with the matter."

"Words do nae make amends for deeds," Cora insisted. "Fenella gave ye more than ten blows because it's been far too long since she felt the rod on her own flesh. Ye are being polite, just the way me tutors tell me I will have to behave when I am wed. But Fenella is me kin, and I am not some bride brought here for the sake of the clan. She'll get what she deserves."

The girl didn't intend to stay and listen. She turned and bolted toward the door.

"Cora." It was too late. Cora's skirt was just clearing the door-frame.

Rhedyn went after the girl, leaving the bathhouse behind as she charged into the passageway.

But an arm snaked out and caught Rhedyn around her middle. Buchanan's scent filled her nostrils as he hefted her right off her feet.

"What?" Rhedyn exclaimed. She pushed at him, but she might as well have tried to force her way through a stone wall. Buchanan didn't budge.

He grunted and hauled her back into the chamber.

"Are ye daft, woman?" he demanded as he placed himself in the doorway. "Are ye senseless enough to go running through the passageway in naught but yer shift?"

The look on his face made it plain that he was expecting her to bend to his will, but something stirred inside her. Whatever had awakened between them, refused to allow her to lower her head. It was as if she needed to prove her worth.

"How dare ye accuse me of being foolish," Rhedyn chastised. "Cora is going to have Fenella beaten."

"Cora is none of yer concern, Rhedyn," Buchanan's tone lowered. Something flickered in his eyes which made Rhedyn think he actually agreed with his sister's actions.

"Doing such will only cause more animosity between the Lindseys and Mackenzies," Rhedyn implored.

"Me sister is plenty old enough to take the household in hand if she feels it is needed."

Rhedyn did not wish to be responsible for more pain. She wanted her time with the Mackenzies in the past. A memory.

"I forgive Fenella," Rhedyn informed him. "There is time for ye to send someone after yer sister. Time to intervene…"

Buchanan clamped his hand over her mouth, trapping the rest of her words. He lowered his head so their faces were inches apart. "It's time for ye to know that while I didn't dare order Fenella be given a taste of that rod because I must always try to maintain the standing of those in me household, it doesn't mean I am not fully in support of me sister doing what should be done. Fenella needs a reminder of just how painful a single blow is. That is why she is not allowed to deliver more than ten. I'm grateful Cora is wise enough to see the need of the lesson. Otherwise, I would see to the matter myself."

Rhedyn stiffened, her eyes widening as she caught the glitter of determination in his eyes. His attention lowered to her forearms. Large purple bruises marked where Fenella had applied the rod.

"It is not so important." She turned her back on him, intent on returning to where Shona stood with a pair of stays in her hands.

Buchanan caught a handful of the petticoat and jerked her to a stop. "Be still," he rasped before she felt him pulling the neckline of her smock down to show her back.

"As I said, it is naught to be concerned about."

Buchanan cupped her shoulder and turned her around to face him. Her next argument died on her lips as she caught sight of the rage flickering in his eyes. For certain, she'd seen him enraged before, only this time, it was on her behalf. Such an idea opened a door she hadn't realized she was keeping several feelings locked behind.

"It is a matter for concern," Buchanan spoke up. He looked toward Shona and the other maids before returning his gaze to Rhedyn. "Every one of ye are witness to the bruises on our guest. The household rules will be strictly followed or the offender will answer to me. If a single one of ye says anything but the truth of what ye saw here, ye can have a taste of the rod yerself so ye learn not to make light of such punishments."

"Aye, laird," came the mutters of agreement from the maids.

Rhedyn did not see Buchanan leave, but the maids relaxed, telling her he was gone. Shona continued helping her dress as the pressure in her chest eased.

Breathless?

Really?

As if she didn't have enough difficulties to face.

Yet it was undeniable. She felt something speeding through her veins. A sense of satisfaction that was at best unkind toward Fenella, but there was no point in trying to deny it.

What claimed Rhedyn's attention the most was the look in Buchanan's eyes. The man who had called himself her captor was long gone. Now, staring back at her was someone who was willing to defend her. The maids were attending to her with the most careful motions. They'd heard their laird clearly and weren't interested in stepping over the line Buchanan had just drawn.

Right in front of her.

Her pride might like to argue against the need for it, but she couldn't hide how warm it made her feel at the same time.

Did she really want to be protected by the man who had stolen her?

Beggars can't be choosers…

True. But there was something else that was true as well; she liked seeing the rage in Buchanan's eyes on her behalf.

※》》》《《《

TYREE DIDN'T HAVE to hold Fenella down.

The Head-of-House faced off with Cora for a long moment before she nodded. "Well…ye are the mistress."

Fenella walked over to the wall and took the rod from where it hung. She turned and marched back to the place Cora was still standing. Fenella turned the rod in her hands, sticking the handle out toward Cora.

There was deathly silence all around them. It wasn't the look of doubt on Fenella's face that made Cora reach for the rod, it was the memory of the horrible bruises all over Rhedyn.

She had never wielded it.

But she'd felt it sure enough. Cora broke into a sweat as she grasped the weapon. Fenella's eyes narrowed before she turned and positioned herself over the table. She stretched her arms out with her palms up.

Everyone watched Cora, waiting to see if she'd just been sputtering like a child or intent on exercising her authority.

She might order Tyree to do it but such would be cowardly. Cora set her teeth into her bottom lip and raised the rod.

>>>><<<<

SHONA RAPPED ON Cora's chamber door later in the day.

"Yes?"

Shona pushed the door open with her hip because her hands were full. "I brought ye some bread and mutton."

Cora's belly still heaved. "I am no' very hungry."

Shona placed the tray on a table and straightened up. "Second thoughts then? Ye seemed very determined this morning when ye went toward the kitchens."

"Fenella committed a grave injustice," Cora defended her actions.

Shona stood for a long moment without giving Cora any further argument. Just a steady look which made Cora sigh with frustration. "Me brother should have seen to the matter."

"Ye are no longer a child, Cora. And yer brother is laird now. He must always be mindful of keeping the peace. Do nae look to him to do the things a mistress of the house should."

"I saw to the matter, didn't I?" Cora demanded.

Shona nodded. "All which needs doing now is for ye to stop hiding in this chamber as though ye are feeling guilty."

Cora shrugged. "I wasn't supposed to enjoy it. Wouldn't that make me terrible?"

Shona nodded before she pointed at the chair in front of the tray. "It's to yer credit that yer face was pale the whole time."

Cora sat down. "I held onto me composure better than that."

Shona merely shook out a linen and laid it across Cora's right shoulder.

"Ye must show yer face in the kitchens," Shona advised. "But I warn ye against sampling any of the fair for a few days. Fenella's skills might just be suffering a wee bit if ye grasp me meaning."

Cora did. Sometimes a person had to choose between being happy or right. The Head-of-House just might burn supper in retaliation.

As laird and mistress of the Mackenzies, it might appear Buchanan and Cora held all the power, but the truth was, all they really had was a much longer fall should they lose their positions. She shouldn't argue against the position she'd been born to, for it was God's will.

And yet, Cora felt a longing for something far simpler in life.

⇶⇷

HAMISH MACKENZIE WAS cold and hungry.

He grinned as he guided his horse into the back yard near the entrance to the kitchens of the Mackenzie stronghold. Younger lads began streaming out from the stables to grasp the reins as Hamish and his men dismounted. There was more than one groan from them, for they'd ridden hard and long.

He stretched his back before letting out a whistle. "We're home, lads! Let's enjoy the comforts to be had!"

He took the steps two at a time and burst into the kitchens. There was a squeal as two of the maids caught sight of him. "Who has a kiss for me?" Hamish demanded.

"Here, now." Fenella admonished him with a click of her tongue. "This is a kitchen, no' a brothel, Hamish."

Hamish reached up to tug on the corner of his cap. But he looked past Fenella, toward one of the maids. There was another sound of disapproval from the Head-of-House before the burly Retainer was grinning and leaning over to kiss her cheek.

"Una," Fenella said. "Go and make certain there is hot water in the men's bathhouse for Hamish."

Una's face didn't reflect happiness. But she lowered herself and turned to hurry off to see to the chore she'd been given. Fenella swept the long table with a stern look where the rest of her staff was toiling. She then turned her full attention to Hamish and his men. "I would have a word with ye first."

Hamish gave the woman her due respect. His men took their lead from him, the conversation dying away until only the crackle of the fire in the hearth was left.

"It seems someone," she began, "saw fit to carry some bundles of pelts abovestairs to the storage chamber over me kitchen."

Several of the men who had ridden in with Hamish cleared their throats. But Hamish wasn't going to argue over some pelts or the reason his men had taken them to the tower.

"If me men caused damage to goods belonging to the clan," Hamish said firmly, "I will settle the account." He reached for the tie on his purse hanging at his waist.

Fenella drew in a stiff breath. "As it happens, the damage was done by that Lindsey bitch the laird brought here."

Hamish grunted.

Fenella's lips twitched. "Aye," she continued. "She made free use of the pelts. Sewed them into a blanket for herself without permission."

"I hope ye took their worth out of her hide."

His men rumbled with approval.

"The laird's sister took the rod to Mistress Fenella for beating the Lindsey lass," Tyree spoke up from where he was hovering in one of the stone archways.

Hamish turned on the Butler, intent on starting a fight. He thought twice about it when he took in Tyree's bulk.

Fenella scoffed. "If I did nae make certain everyone knew there would be a price to be paid for pilfering, we'd all starve in the winter. It was worth being reprimanded. Cora is too young to understand. She'll be gone soon."

Hamish's men all muttered in agreement.

Fenella turned and stared at the Butler. Tyree did not strictly answer to her. The Head-of-House understood she needed him, even if, at the moment, she was irritated by his disagreement with her.

Hamish looked at the Tyree. "The laird is soft on that bitch?"

Tyree kept his mouth firmly shut.

"Oh, aye," Fenella answered. "The laird is beguiled by her. Took her away and placed her in the north tower as though she's some manner of guest."

Fenella made a sound under her breath that made it clear what manner of relationship she thought was going on.

Hamish grunted. "Well, I'll see what's what now that I am back. The laird saw reason in me case against the Lindsey. I'll take the matter up with him."

Fenella nodded. She turned her attention back to the meal being prepared, snapping her fingers at her staff. But there was a smug smile on her lips that none of the women mistook as anything but a warning. They'd seen it before, and none of them wanted a *lesson* imposed on them.

The Lindsey lass had better stay far away from the kitchens.

⫸⫷

"DOES THIS CHAMBER suit ye, mistress?" Shona asked.

Rhedyn could see she was serious. Yes, Shona understood the situation, and unless Rhedyn was wrong, Shona was enjoying knowing she held the authority to make her feel welcome.

"Yes, thank you, Shona."

Shona offered her a nod before she turned and left. Freshly bathed and dressed, Rhedyn might have believed she'd simply woken from a nightmare. Yet, she wouldn't let her guard down. Reality was harsh, and if you turned your back on it, well, it was likely you'd suffer all the more for not keeping an eye on the beast intent on devouring you!

The chamber was beautiful with a bed that came with fine, thick curtains to keep out the winter wind. There was a hearth with a stack of wood at the ready and two fine, padded chairs to sit in front of the fire while reading or sewing. A wardrobe stood against one wall, and next to it was a small vanity with a polished mirror. Rhedyn counted three candles about the room, each one ready to cheerfully chase away the night whenever she desired.

But Rhedyn looked toward the door.

There was no sound of the chain...

She moved toward it, testing it to see if it would open. The hinges didn't make a sound as the door opened. Rhedyn realized she'd been holding her breath. She let it out in a whoosh as she moved through the doors and onto the steps.

She could breathe...

Of course, she had no idea where to go. It did seem a shameful waste to remain in the chamber when the choice was hers. She spared a momentary thought for the animosity she'd been greeted with upon her arrival. Still, the chance to get outside was too tempting.

Besides, she was sick to death of idleness. Spring was a time of plenty to do. She rubbed her hands together in anticipation of accomplishing something.

It didn't take her very long to find a task. At the bottom of the north tower, there was a small courtyard. Several women were there. Young girls came and went, delivering ashes from the numerous hearths in the stronghold. The ashes would be put into half barrels that the slats in the bottom had dried and separated on. Water was poured on top of the ashes and left to seep through them. Lye water was the result.

To get the finished soap though, they'd have to boil the lye water with tallow until it all condensed into a thick syrup which might be put into wooden molds for drying.

"Are ye here to help or no'?" one of the women asked.

The woman was doing the hardest part of the process. A large cauldron was set on the ground over a pit which was lined with stones. A fire burned beneath it. The lye water and fat inside it was bubbling away. The woman was stirring it with a large paddle. It was hot, hard, and dangerous work, for the hem of her skirts could easily catch fire.

"I'm here to work," Rhedyn said. She tucked her skirts up and picked up another paddle. The other woman never really looked at her. The bubbling soap took all their attention. They worked in tandem, scraping the surface of the cauldron in steady stokes as they slowly circled one another.

Sweat was trickling down Rhedyn's neck and her arms ached. As more of the water boiled away, the chore became harder. She worked until her arms burned from the effort. Just before it was finished, two of the younger girls tossed in huge piles of rosemary needles. The scent made her smile in spite of the hard labor.

"Get the molds!" the woman in charge ordered. "Keep going," she instructed Rhedyn as she turned and picked up a ladle.

The younger girls had wooden molds in their hands. They lined up for the lead woman to pour the hot soap in. They took the full molds over to a table and returned with new ones.

Round and round they went until the last of the soap was scooped up. Only then did the woman in charge stop and draw her arm across her forehead to mop the sweat away. She raised her face and smiled at Rhedyn.

"Well now, right glad I am to have...had....yer...." Her words trailed off as she got a good look at Rhedyn.

"Pleased to have been of assistance," Rhedyn finished for her as the women suddenly recognized her.

"Mistress Lindsey."

Rhedyn jumped, but Cora was smiling as she came down the last few steps into the courtyard.

"Mistress Cora," the lead woman muttered before she lowered herself quickly and turned to hurry over to where the soap molds were.

Cora winked at Rhedyn before she gestured for her to follow her back to the tower.

"I'm pleased to see ye dressed." Cora went to the passageway doors and peered both ways. "Are we alone?"

"Aye," Rhedyn answered. "As such, I would like to speak with ye about Fenella."

It was Cora's clan and home. Arguing with her wasn't something to do.

"Fenella has received seven strikes for what she did to you. She went over the limit by seven strikes, and the kitchens have always had guidelines for such punishments. Even the Head-of-House must follow the rules. Do nae tell me it is different on Lindsey land? That yer father's Head-of-House may decide on punishments?"

"Only when it comes to who receives them," Rhedyn admitted. "Still, I would rather ye did not reprimand Fenella. The kitchen staff does no' need more reason to hate me."

Cora propped her hands on her hips. "Ye are no' so many years older than me. Did ye no' ever get tired of the list of rules ye were expected to obey?"

"I am not too much older than ye, Cora, but one thing I know is that sometimes it's wiser to let things go," Rhedyn advised. "Yer kin are not going to see ye were following the rules, all they will think about is that I was the cause of the unrest."

Cora let out a huff. "I know it." She looked behind her once again. When she was looking at Rhedyn once more, there was a flicker of determination in her eyes. "I came looking for ye because I realize me kin is no' going to see how unjust yer situation is. So, I will deal with ye meself."

Cora's cheeks were pink, and her eyes sparkled with excitement. She looked down the stairway before she reached down and pulled her skirt aside. "We need to get ye far away from here, before anything worse than a beating befalls ye."

Cora pulled something from where it was stuck in the top of her ankle-high boot. As she straightened, the afternoon light flickered off the edge of a knife. The blade was long and sharp.

Rhedyn recoiled.

"We'll sneak down to the stables together, and then ye can hold this knife at me throat if anyone tries to stop ye…"

Rhedyn felt her blood run cold at the idea of Cora trusting someone she knew so little about. A need to protect the girl rushed through her.

"I will do no such thing, Cora," Rhedyn exclaimed as she took the knife from her hand.

"But why no'?" she demanded. "It's a fine plan. No one will risk me being harmed."

Rhedyn drew in a deep breath, relying on all of her patience to deal with the girl in front of her. "Cora," she began. "Ye must never, never offer yerself and a weapon to just anyone who has come to this stronghold. I might be so frightened, so desperate to escape, that I would take yer offer and place ye in harm's way."

"But ye do need to escape," Cora insisted. "Ye were beaten even though me brother told one and all he'd investigate the matter at the tavern. Me kin will not wait. They are blinded by their anger. I saw the angry way that woman looked at ye." Cora was breathing hard with agitation. "Those bruises on yer arms are proof I need to take action."

"Yer brother did not have me beaten, Cora."

"But he is laird. He brought ye here and can no' protect ye."

"Matters such as these…can often be complicated," Rhedyn said.

"Ye are making excuses for me kin," Cora argued. She reached out and grabbed the knife. "I won't see ye being treated horribly here. I am the mistress of this stronghold, and I will see ye set free before something else happens."

Rather than struggle with the girl, Rhedyn released her grip on the knife.

Cora smiled brightly as she held it up. "Now, come with me to the stables, Rhedyn."

The knife was jerked from her hand a second later as Buchanan emerged from the shadows of the passageway. "Cora." he began tightly. "Get to yer chamber and stay there."

Cora's temper flared. "Ye are horrible!" she exclaimed. "And I will never, ever be sorry for trying to help Mistress Lindsey, for it seems to be our fate to be used in settling men's fights."

Buchanan wasn't pleased with his sister's outburst. "Graham..."

"Aye, Laird," the captain answered from further down the passageway. "I'll escort Mistress Cora to her chamber."

"So ye will resort to treating me like a child when I choose to take action where ye claim ye cannot because ye are laird. Do nae think I will forget it, brother." Cora snorted before she turned and disappeared from sight.

"I am glad ye overheard that," Rhedyn spoke once Cora and Graham's steps faded.

Buchanan glared at her. "Happy to see ye've inspired me sister to rebellion against her own clan?"

Rhedyn lifted her chin, refusing to give an inch of ground.

"It was so reckless of her. Ye must teach her the folly of trusting a stranger."

Cora's flare of passion somehow got started inside Rhedyn. Shutting her mouth would have been wise, instead, she stepped toward Buchanan, intent on making him see her point.

"Ye must..."

"Ye must no' attempt to escape, Rhedyn," he growled as he clamped his hand across her mouth. "Outside the walls, some of me kin might take the opportunity to kill ye."

The sudden contact between them was shocking. The way he just put his hands on her was something she struggled to understand. All of her life there had been proper protocol between herself and men. Buchanan seemed to not know it existed.

The boldness of that idea made her heart pound as though she was running. The contact between their skin was something she was keenly aware of.

And she was not alone in her awareness of him.

She watched his nostrils flare. His eyes narrowed as his hand slipped away from her mouth, gliding across her cheek and beneath her unbound hair to grasp her nape. He clasped her waist, pulling her against his body as he angled his face so he might press his lips against hers.

She gasped, shifting as her body erupted with sensation. She flattened her hands against his chest, pressing against him as she tried to escape.

Buchanan held her close as he kissed her. He held back his passion after she hesitated to respond to his kiss. The sensation was like a living force within her, beating its wings as it made ready to take flight.

Suddenly, kissing him back became as necessary as her next breath. The hands she had pressed against his chest in defense, now drew in the warmth of his body, allowing her to feel the rapid beat of his heart. She wanted to live inside the moment.

Buchanan suddenly withdrew, lifting his mouth from hers. "Sweet, lass," he whispered roughly. He didn't want to stop kissing her.

That idea tormented her because she didn't want to return to thinking about what they were doing. She wanted to immerse herself in the pleasure and forget every other detail surrounding them. But he pulled her to the base of the stairs.

"Get up to yer chamber before I forget I once had a mother who taught me decency." A moment later, he was cupping her shoulders. He sent her forward with a soft push. "Now, Rhedyn."

Her mind suddenly snapped back into the present. She dashed up the stairs and through the chamber door, slipping because she went so carelessly. One knee twisted slightly as she fought to keep her balance. She stood still, feeling her cheeks burn and a tingle on her lips.

She was losing her sanity.

There was no other explanation for the way she'd enjoyed his kiss. What horrified her was the fact that it wasn't her first kiss. No, she'd been pushed into a dark alcove just a season before as Rolfe Munro tried his luck at impressing her.

He'd failed.

His attention hadn't moved her. She'd balled up her hand and rubbed her knuckles roughly against his breastbone as her father's captain had taught her in order to defend herself. Rolfe hadn't yelped as the captain had promised, but he'd broken off the kiss and fixed her with a frustrated look.

Why should one man's kiss be so vastly different from another's? Rolfe Munro was every bit as tall and handsome as Buchanan.

And Rolfe hadn't kidnapped her.

He'd sat at the high table and offered for her hand, seeking a marriage which made sense for the benefits it would bring both their clans. His kiss had left her feeling in full control of her senses.

Buchanan's had muddled her mind so fast, she was forced to admit it to herself.

Suddenly, Cora's plan wasn't so unreasonable after all.

⇒⇒⇒✦⇐⇐⇐

HE NEEDED TO control himself. But Rhedyn's taste lingered on his lips. It made him aware of an appetite he hadn't realized he had for her. He stared at the entrance to her chamber.

It was just a door…

"Ye'll be wanting to come away now, Laird."

Buchanan jerked back. Graham was in the stairwell, toying with the end of his gray beard.

"I sent ye with Cora."

"Aye." Graham responded with a nod. "But the lass can find the way to her chamber, for she is no' a child. Ye on the other hand...well...the look in yer eyes tells me ye need a wee bit of encouragement to get yerself to where ye need to be going."

Buchanan glared at his captain.

"Well now, lad," Graham continued. "I suppose we could just discuss the matter of what ye might do with that little lass inside that chamber. Of course, if ye go inside, there will be no going back."

Buchanan was suddenly moving away from the door. He growled on his way down the stairwell.

But his captain caught him at the base of the stairs. Graham looked both ways to ensure they were alone before he leaned in closer. "Do nae let yer pride be wounded, Laird. I've a wee bit more experience in life than ye. I'm content to follow ye, but since yer father is no' here, it also falls to me to speak the truth on the matter we have in front of us."

Graham's tone cut through Buchanan's attempt to hide his feelings. A laird needed to maintain his appearance of being in control, but right there in the passageway with the afternoon shadows beginning to grow long and dark, well, it seemed more arrogant than anything else to refuse to discuss the subject.

"I did the wrong thing for the right reasons," Buchanan confessed. "Taking that lass from her father. I never thought I'd have to resort to doing something like it."

"Aye, Hamish pressed ye sure enough," Graham agreed. "Ye avoided bloodshed."

"But at the cost of depriving the lass of her freedom."

"Every daughter of a laird will find herself facing an arrangement made on what it brings her clan," Graham remarked. "Yer need to see justice prevail is to yer credit. However, there is business to be done, and ye had to settle the score with the Lindsey or face the disgruntlement of yer men."

"Are ye telling me the lass was bound for an arranged marriage, so I shouldn't worry too much about stealing her?" Buchanan asked to clarify. "Knowing such will absolve me of guilt. There is precious little evidence to convict Colum Lindsey of betraying us. Iain was a hothead, and ye know it as well as I do."

"Aye, it's a fact that I was glad to no' be at Iain's back," Graham said. "But ye're no' a lad. Ye understand that being laird often means ye must make decisions based on what is best for the clan. Someone loses in those situations, lasses most often. But a woman can accept such a situation better than a man. As for the Lindsey lass…"

Graham looked up the stairwell and twisted the ends of his beard.

"I do nae need suggestions on what to do with her," Buchanan said. It wasn't the wisest thing he might have done. Graham had experience on his side, which meant the man's words were given respect by other members of the clan.

Graham slapped him on the back. "Aye, ye know what to do with her. But the devil is in the details."

Buchanan started down the passageway, and Graham followed.

"As Colum Lindsey's daughter and the other one only half grown," his captain began, "breeding a son on her would be advantageous. As a mistress, that would suit the men who believe her father is guilty of betraying Iain. Leave the girl without the respect of being yer wife as retribution to her father."

"Are ye telling me to have no compassion for a child of mine who would be bastard born?" Buchanan demanded. "Be done, man."

"And allow ye to think ye have the matter in hand?" Graham asked. "Ye do nae, lad. Ye've had a taste of her now. Why do ye think I came after ye? I see the fire in yer eyes. And as for the little lass, well, she'll bend to yer demands seeking protection. The lassies always do, ye know. That's why ye should no' worry too much about why she landed here. A lass is meant to adjust. I tell ye to come away, so ye can make yer decision concerning her with a clear head."

Buchanan's head was clearing.

The trouble was, the desire to turn around and pull Rhedyn back into his arms wasn't dimming in the least. That desire burned like a great fire in the middle of winter.

He had unlimited access to Rhedyn if he so chose.

The knowledge needled him as he forced himself to continue walking away from her. What kind of beast had he turned into? When had his manners gone astray? It was unlike him, especially the lust burning in his blood for one lass over another.

❊

CASTLES ALWAYS HAD dark alcoves.

Cora felt the cold stone of the wall against her back as Graham and Buchanan passed by.

Women were meant to adjust?

She bit her lower lip to contain the scoff that rose from her chest.

She would never bend.

Graham, Buchanan, Hamish, well, they could all forget their plans to send her to the Grants as a sacrificial lamb. She stood in the passageway facing the fact that what had once been her home was now crumbling around her. All of the love she'd always taken for granted was naught more than a façade.

Meant to adjust?

What a way to say her happiness wasn't as important as the business of the clan. For just a moment, she felt a sting of guilt, for part of her recognized the value of sacrifice for the greater good. She was the laird's daughter. Her position came with many privileges, but there was also responsibility to help secure peace through her marriage.

So, should she just accept everything as Graham seemed to think she should?

Rebellion bubbled up inside her. It was intertwined with resentment against those who already deemed her future as something she didn't need to choose.

Rhedyn faced a similar, unjust fate…

And Cora had failed to help her.

She'd better get a grasp on her emotions before she lost the chance to make a difference. No one would take her seriously until she showed them something worthy of respecting.

Helping Rhedyn escape was a fine place to start, and it would be good practice, for there was no way she was going to be presented to the Grants against her will.

⟫⟫⟫⟪⟪⟪

"WHAT DO YE mean by allowing that Lindsey bitch to stay in the north tower?"

Buchanan's irritation doubled as Hamish issued his demand the moment Buchanan made it into the hall.

"Welcome back, cousin," Buchanan muttered.

Hamish didn't change his challenging stance, but at least a few of the men intent on backing him up appeared to have a bit of shame over just how rude the man was behaving.

"Some welcome." Hamish spit on the floor. "Shall I look forward to seeing her sitting at the head table tonight? Dining as though she's some honored guest? While Iain is rotting in his grave? Along with every Mackenzie who rode with him?"

Maids had appeared at every opening of the hall to get a good look at what the argument was about. Buchanan walked toward his cousin but stopped several paces from him.

"I would no' have chosen to have a public confrontation over this matter, Hamish, but I will no' shirk from the fight ye are clearly intent on picking with me. Since ye are yelling at me, ye can tell me here and now what evidence ye have against Colum Lindsey."

Hamish took a moment before responding. "He was at the Sow's Troth."

"Was he the only one in the tavern?"

"He seemed to be running the place sure enough from the way I heard it," Hamish said. "Threw Iain out."

"For what reason?" Buchanan asked.

"Does it matter?"

"It does," Buchanan answered firmly. "The Sow's Troth caters to different clans. Iain was known for his temper. If he was asked to leave because he was picking a fight, Colum was acting within his rights to keep his night from being ruined."

Hamish's eyes narrowed. Buchanan reached forward and cupped the man on the shoulder.

"I would have someone answer for the crime but only the guilty one." Buchanan gazed at the men standing behind his cousin. "It's a solid fact that Iain was no' known for being very interested in winning the favor of the women he kept company with. Even I know what other services the Sow's Troth offers. I also understand the rules of the place. Iain would have found it difficult to comply."

Buchanan watched as several of the men shifted on their feet. Doubt was making its way through their minds.

"And when there is solid proof?" Hamish demanded.

Buchanan gripped his belt. "What would ye have me promise, Hamish? Am I some bloody savage to declare to one and all that I will spill that girl's blood?"

"Aye!"

Buchanan growled. "Enough! Do nae raise yer voice to me again. There will be no murder done here so long as I am laird."

Hamish didn't like his words.

Buchanan sent his man a look which made it plain he had no taste for the way he was demanding blood. The need to shelter Rhedyn grew stronger.

"Mind me, Hamish." Buchanan lowered his voice so their words remained between them. "There will be no vengeance inside this stronghold while I am laird of the Mackenzie."

⟫⟫⟩⟨⟨⟨

HAMISH WATCHED BUCHANAN leave. His temper turned blistering hot. Innis knew what it looked like on a man. Rage was something a woman was wise to understand the warning signs of. She hung back, but her mind was racing with ideas. All she needed to do was carefully plan and utilize the resources she had.

Una passed by on the way to the bathhouse. There was a look of reluctant acceptance on her face.

"I'll see to Hamish," Innis told her.

Una's eyes brightened, and Innis came closer and smiled. "I see ye have no liking for the duty."

"It's no' the scrubbing of his back I refuse to do...." Una's voice squeaked with embarrassment as her cheeks turned red. "It's just... Young Cory treats me well, and Fenella promised to arrange a match between us. But now, she orders me to the bathhouse."

"Go on. Stay out of sight for a bit," Innis told the girl.

Una nodded and hugged Innis before hurrying away.

Innis went toward the bathhouse, opened the door, and stepped inside.

"I was expecting the blonde," Hamish said.

He was already disrobing, his member sticking out. Men were forever proud of their appendages. Innis had no understanding as to why.

"Cory has plans to wed her," she remarked softly as she pulled one of the kettles from where it was heating in the fire. "He's yer man." She met Hamish's gaze.

He grunted. Innis looked back down as she poured the boiling water into the tub.

"Come here, woman," he ordered in spite of her subtle warning.

122

Innis looked at him again. "I came to do ye a different sort of service."

His eyes narrowed.

"Ye'll no' last long in command of yer men if they feel ye do nae have any respect for who they consider their women."

Hamish would never tell her he agreed. No, he had far too much pride for that. Still, a man who could be led by his pride had uses.

"I meant for ye to unlace me boots, woman."

Hamish sat down on a stool and waited for her to approach. She began to work the laces free from his shoes. They were caked with mud and stiff from long hours in the cold.

"What manner of service do ye offer?" he asked once his boots were off.

Innis studied his face briefly before she turned and went back to the hearth to pull another pot of water off the fire. Lust and ambition were both flickering in his eyes. As she poured the water into the tub, she looked through the cloud of steam which rose up between them.

"The laird can nae deal directly with the Lindsey bitch. I do nae believe it means he favors being soft on her." Innis used a paddle to stir the water. "Appearances among the other lairds are important."

Hamish came over and settled into the tub. Innis used a bowl to dip up some water and pour it over his shoulders. He flexed and rotated his arms.

"Are ye suggesting we take care of the matter for the laird?" he asked.

"For Iain."

Hamish grunted in approval of her answer. He leaned forward so she could scrub his back. For a long time, there was only the sound of splashing water in the room. But once she finished with his back, he boldly grasped her hand and tried to place it over his member.

Innis withdrew her hand. "If that is all ye are about, I will send Orla in."

Hamish shifted in the tub. "Think yerself too good for me?"

Innis meet his stare. "I'm clever, and I will have the place I want for meself. No' simply a moment of yer lust. I will be the laird's mistress. To do that, I need the Lindsey girl out of the way before the laird's pity turns to something stronger."

Hamish didn't finish rising from the tub. He sat back down and held her gaze. One side of his mouth twitched when she didn't look away.

"He would do something like that." He finally stood, then walked over and picked up a length of linen to dry himself with. He reached for a shirt once he was finished and put it on. "The thought of that bitch as lady of this stronghold sickens me."

"So, we must make certain it does no' happen." Innis looked up from where she'd been pleating his kilt on the floor. "We can be of use to one another. I can get near her. Ye cannot."

She was being bold, for a man such as Hamish didn't see women as anything but a vessel for release of their lust. But she was clever and saw the effect her words had on him as he contemplated her.

Hamish came closer. He stopped and looked her in the eyes. "Ye have a spine woman. That's a fine thing for the laird to have in any offspring ye give him. Get the Lindsey bitch out to the stables tonight, and I will make sure she never returns to tempt the laird away from ye."

Innis nodded. She paused at the door, looking both ways before leaving the bathhouse. The deal was struck. She smiled on her way back to the kitchens. Even Fenella's glare wasn't enough to dispel the pleasure speeding through her body. Soon, the Head-of-House would mind how she spoke to Innis. That wasn't to say Fenella wouldn't have her uses. Innis minded her eyes, keeping them downcast, because the path to her success wasn't something to take lightly.

CHAPTER FOUR

"M ISTRESS."

Rhedyn looked up as a maid appeared in the doorway after a light rap on the door.

"Yes?" Rhedyn asked. Perhaps she spoke too quickly, but the truth was, she'd walked endless circles inside the chamber. Could she go where she pleased? Would it be a risk, or was she simply hiding like a coward?

Both were valid questions that had kept her contained to her room as the afternoon stretched on.

"The laird mentioned ye might enjoy a ride. There are plenty of horses if ye care to take a bit of air," the maid offered.

An invitation.

But why?

Did Buchanan plan to make a public display of treating her well?

Was he planning to court her?

Rhedyn bit her lip as her thoughts flew like a flock of startled birds.

Did she want to be courted?

Buchanan's kiss *had* pleased her. The idea of returning to Lindsey land and waiting for Rolfe to return left her cold.

Stop being ridiculous. Buchanan is simply making it clear ye have his protection.

And such was for Cora's sake more than Rhedyn's. Buchanan was intent on seeing his sister's fears soothed.

Well, it was an invitation.

"I am coming," Rhedyn told the maid. She was halfway to the door when she thought to turn and pick up her arisaid. The length of Lindsey cloth was neatly folded and placed on a table.

She stopped short, wondering if it might be better not to announce her clan affiliation. Her temper flickered in response. Buchanan should never have brought her to a place where she was placed in a position of choosing to hide her father's colors.

"Mistress?" the maid inquired.

"Yes, I am coming."

In the end, Rhedyn left her arisaid on the table. Temper aside, she didn't need to go looking for a fight. The Mackenzies had lost the laird's brother, after all. Until the matter was settled, keeping quiet wouldn't hurt.

Besides, what mattered was making sure peace remained between Cora and her brother.

Ye're excited about seeing him again....

Rhedyn didn't bother to chastise herself over her thoughts. Later, she might, but for the moment, she would enjoy her time away from her chamber.

Her heart hummed as she nearly danced down the steps. The maid walked quickly, but Rhedyn was happy to follow. Once outside, she drew in a deep breath.

Fresh air. It nearly made her dizzy.

The maid kept going through a yard. Rhedyn heard the chickens which roosted near the kitchens. Most of the birds were still in the grass, hunting worms and insects. The chill of evening hadn't sent them inside their nesting boxes.

That meant there was time for a long ride.

The maid continued down a slope to where the stables were. Built of stone, the scent of animals reached her nose. It wasn't unpleasant, which meant the stables were well attended to. Off to one side, she spied two wagons. They were empty now, but the inside of the beds bore the marks of having been used to haul away manure.

"This way," the maid said. She stopped outside a doorway. Her apron and linen cap spoke of kitchen duty.

"Thank ye for showing me the way." Rhedyn walked inside.

It was dark. For a moment, she couldn't see anything. But the place was filled with the snorting of horses and the stamping of their feet.

A hard hand clamped over her mouth as she was drug into the shadowed corners of the stalls. She tried to scream, but all that escaped the hold on her mouth were muffled sounds.

"Iain was my friend," Hamish grunted next to her ear. "I will have vengeance for his blood."

Rhedyn remembered Hamish's voice well.

It was a sound she didn't think she would ever forget, even if she lived a hundred years. He was pulling her deeper into a stall. His hold impossible to break.

A perfect place to kill her.

She suddenly fought with strength she didn't realize she had. There was no method to her struggle, just a blind, panicked need to escape. She tasted blood as she sunk her teeth into the fingers sealing her mouth.

"Ye bitch!" Hamish exclaimed as he pulled away from her.

"Ye will no' kill me so easily!" Her words sounded pathetic. Hamish was huge and blocking the only escape.

At least it looked that way. Tipping her head back, Rhedyn saw the beams of the ceiling and a faint trickle of sunlight where it came through a spot in the thatching piled on the roof. The cold winter had worn the roof down. She climbed onto a beam that formed the stall, and reached for the wood above her.

"Ye won't escape," he promised menacingly.

But she'd gained a good grip on the beams and pushed off the rail to send herself up into the thick layer of thatch. Hamish caught her legs, pulling her down. She refused to go without a fight. The thatch was dry and full of dirt as her head popped through it.

"Help!" she screamed.

If anyone was in the yard to hear her, she didn't get a glimpse of them. Hamish yanked her back down violently.

She fell in a heap on the floor of the stall. A horse pawed and snorted nearby as Hamish reached down for her.

"No!" she snarled at him, then rolled onto her back and kicked at him.

For a moment, it felt like his weight was too great. But she flattened her hands against the floor and shoved with her legs. What felt immovable, suddenly gave way. Hamish went stumbling back, giving her the chance to get onto her feet.

"Ye will no' leave my body in a dark corner of this stable!" Rhedyn yelled at him.

"I will no' face Iain in the afterlife without being able to tell him I exacted the revenge due him!"

His hands were up, his fingers looking like talons as he started toward her again.

"Ye might just meet Iain sooner than ye think, cousin!"

Hamish was suddenly skidding back. The entrance to the stall was clear. Rhedyn bolted through it, but had to stop because Buchanan stood in her path. He reached out and closed his fingers around her wrist. With one swift jerk, she was stumbling toward him. He shifted out of her way so she could get behind him.

"Ye are a sorry excuse of a laird," Hamish accused Buchanan. "Weakness might be suffered in a damned English noble, but no' here in the Highlands!"

"And yer plan is what precisely?" Buchanan demanded. "To kill a lass in a dark stable and take pleasure in knowing ye did such a thing?"

"Colum must pay for what he did!" Hamish snarled.

Hamish launched himself at Buchanan. Rhedyn should have run, but she was frozen in place as the two men collided. Buchanan twisted and sent a hard fist into Hamish's midsection. There was a grunt as the blow landed, followed by Buchanan recoiling from a similar hit. They fell toward the railing on the other side of the walkway. Horses let out startled sounds, but neither man stopped. They fully intended to kill one another.

"Stop!" Rhedyn insisted.

Hamish had stumbled back and blood trickled from the corner of one of his eyes. "Listen to the way the bitch begs!" he sneered. "Weakling Lindsey!"

"It is no' a weakness to not want to see murder done!" Rhedyn insisted. She grabbed a pitch fork from where it was leaning against the wall, pointing the sharp ends at Hamish.

"Get out the door, woman," Buchanan ordered. He turned his head and shot her a hard look. "Now."

His words were laced with unshakeable authority. She should have obeyed.

But she was rooted in place as firmly as a hundred-year-old tree.

Hamish took advantage of Buchanan's inattention by attacking first. Buchanan twisted and turned, locking his arm around the other man's neck. Both were covered in sweat as they strained to best the other. There wasn't a hint of mercy in either one.

"Ye heard the laird, lass." Graham was suddenly there. He grabbed two handfuls of her skirt and yanked her out of the way.

She tried to see what was happening to Buchanan, but a stream of Retainers flooded in. Someone yanked her further from the stables. Graham looked back from the doorway at whoever held her arm.

"Get her inside, and do nae leave her for a moment," the captain issued his order before he disappeared inside the building.

Rhedyn tried to get to Buchanan again.

"Mistress!"

The young man holding onto her arm wasn't happy about his duty. His tone was edged with impatience and irritation, but he wouldn't release her until he was standing in front of her. He stretched his arms out wide to block her path when she started to go around him.

"Do no' make this difficult for me."

When she still looked around him, he let out a whistle. The sound brought two more Retainers to his aid. They formed a wall that was impossible to breach.

"But…"

"The captain said ye are to go inside," the first man told her. "So, ye may walk or make me carry ye."

"But ye are going," another man added.

They weren't going to allow her much time to contemplate the matter. It seemed the words were barely out of their mouths when the Retainers began to move toward her.

Rhedyn jumped back. "All right!" The idea of them touching her was too horrible to endure. She was suddenly chilled to the bone and trembling.

But she still didn't want to go inside. No, she wanted to get back to Buchanan's side.

To do what, precisely?

Rhedyn sighed and headed toward the hall. Not because she was being made to by her escort, but because her own thoughts held her captive as she tried to understand just why she was drawn to Buchanan.

Clearly, her mind was breaking.

>>>×<<<

HAMISH SPAT ON the floor at Buchanan's feet. "Ye are a bastard, and no mistake! How can ye protect that Lindsey bitch?"

"Bastard?" Buchanan asked as he slowly circled him. "I've lost me temper with ye over the matter. We're Mackenzies, no savages."

"I've lost faith in ye!" Hamish exclaimed. "Ye have made the Mackenzies the laughing stock of the Highlands! And I am no' alone in me thinking!"

"Is that a fact?" Buchanan straightened. He took his attention off Hamish and aimed it at the men crowding behind him.

"Who among ye agrees with murdering a lass in the stable?" Buchanan demanded. He turned and sent a glare toward the men clustered behind him. "Speak up, for I am no' afraid to tell all of ye that such an idea turns me stomach."

"As it should, Laird."

It was Graham who spoke. "Murder is no' the Mackenzie way."

"She is Colum Lindsey's daughter!" Hamish argued. "She is here in retribution."

"Aye, she is Colum's daughter," Buchanan agreed. "And I find meself no' so happy to admit I took a her from her father, no matter the reasoning. How many of ye have daughters?" He looked around again. "Would ye have them treated in such a way?"

There was muttering among the men. Buchanan gritted his teeth as he strove for patience, allowing them to think the matter through.

"Taking the lass was a punishment toward her father," Graham spoke. "This business in the stable..." He shook his head. "It's altogether different, and I'll say it plainly, it is no' to me liking."

"An old man speaks up for ye," Hamish mocked Graham. "Will it be the chambermaids next?"

"It will be me," a new voice came from the back of the group.

"Yer actions are wrong," Fenella raised her voice so it was heard throughout the stable.

Hamish glared at her. "Yer son was cut down along with Iain."

Fenella's eyes glistened with unshed tears, but there was strong disapproval on her face. She had her apron gripped in her hands so tightly, her knuckles were white. "Aye, me son is gone." She gazed at Hamish. "And I'm ashamed to say I behaved poorly toward the girl....but this...." The Head-of-House looked toward the stall where Hamish had taken Rhedyn. "Seeing that girl's head poke up from the thatch...a woman should no' ever look so frightened."

The men at Hamish's back began to shift away from him. Only a few stood steadfast in their positions.

"Seems we need to find a solution to the lass's problem." It was Graham who spoke again.

The stable was packed with people now, not a single foot of space unoccupied. There were mutters of agreement.

"Her father's guilt is no' proven conclusively," Buchanan stated. "He was no' the only man in the Sow's Troth that night. I took the lass so that tempers could cool. Before we started a feud with the wrong clan."

It was a risky thing to say out loud. Buchanan understood that while his father's men were following him, it didn't mean they didn't have private opinions that differed from his own. But when it came to Rhedyn, he seemed to have no reservations about making his own position crystal clear.

"I will no' stand for having the girl harmed." He pointed at Hamish. "Ye said clearly ye meant to kill the lass. There are witnesses. Ye are stripped of yer rank and banished from the castle. Murder will not be done on Mackenzie land while I am laird."

There was muttering among the men.

Buchanan let his harsh stare sweep over them. "Go with him if ye think the same, for the next man who tries to commit murder on this land will be hanged."

⇶✕⇷

BUCHANAN STOOD ON the steps of the largest tower in the Mackenzie stronghold. The yard was unusually quiet. Only the sounds of saddles being secured and horses stamping at the ground could be heard.

Fortunately, Hamish only had a few followers.

Fenella stood just behind Buchanan. She wasn't just there to lend her weight to the matter, she had two of her maids standing behind her, their arms laden with lengths of wool in a greenish-brown color.

"Ye'll leave the Mackenzie colors before ye go, Hamish," Buchanan declared.

It was the harshest sentence he'd ever had to deliver. Even in the last couple of years as age had taken more and more of a toll on his father, there had never been an incident worthy of banishment.

Hamish came close and opened his belt. The Mackenzie kilt he wore puddled in the dirt at his feet. "I will no' wear them again until ye are no longer laird."

Hamish and his men didn't stop to pleat up the lengths of material waiting for them. Instead, they slung them over the saddles and mounted. Then they were gone. The wind blew through the yard, hitting their backs as they rode out of the main gate.

"'Tis for the best," Fenella muttered.

Buchanan heard the lament in her tone, but she drew in a deep breath before making eye contact with him.

The eldest captain of the clan had taken up a position on the other side of Buchanan. Several other men with gray hair, stood near him, too. They nodded in support of Graham.

Buchanan turned to face them. He'd been raised to shoulder the weight of the clan on his own, but today, he felt like it was heavier than ever.

Rhedyn's fate hung in the balance.

"The lass is a hostage," Buchanan stated.

"Even if Colum is proven guilty," Graham said, "it's been made clear ye will no' stand to see the girl harmed."

"Correct." Buchanan wasn't really listening. His focus was on

Hamish as he rode down the road and out of sight.

One matter finished. Which left something he considered very important left to do.

He turned and left his captains on the landing. If they turned to look at him, he didn't notice. He marched into the great hall; his men had Rhedyn there. They'd lined up between her and the doorway—barring her from leaving. She stood with a frustrated look on her face. But what caught his attention more was the way she was still attempting to think of a way around them.

"Ye're dismissed," Buchanan growled as he broke through the line his men had made. He caught Rhedyn by the upper arm and turned her around.

"What are ye doing?" she demanded under her breath.

>>><<<

BUCHANAN DIDN'T ANSWER her.

Instead, he pulled her along beside him. She had to nearly run to keep pace with his longer stride. The great hall passed by in a blur before they were in the passageway and past the opening to the kitchens. They didn't go unnoticed. There were two gasps as maids spied them.

Rhedyn reached for his fingers, trying to pry them off her arm, but he spun her though a doorway first.

"Just what are ye about, Buchanan Mackenzie?"

He shoved the door shut first, sealing them inside what was clearly his study.

"What am I about?" he asked softly.

"Yes..." What else could she say?

"First, ye'll tell me why ye went to the stables. How could ye be so foolish? Did I not warn ye about the temper of me kin? Must I lock ye inside this chamber?"

"A maid came to me and said ye were waiting for me." Rhedyn tried to break free of his grasp, but he held tight.

"And ye believed her?" Buchanan demanded. "Why would I be inviting ye somewhere?"

The reproach on his expression infuriated her. As did the grip on her wrist because he seemed so intent on disciplining her.

"Because ye kissed me!" An outburst Rhedyn didn't regret.

Surprise registered on his face as his grip slackened. She twisted free. "It's improper for me to be in a closed room with ye."

→≫≫≪≪←

IMPROPER?

Buchanan stood staring at the door of his study for several moments after Rhedyn had disappeared through it.

Improper?

Aye, their relationship was that all right.

With no one able to see him, he indulged in a grin. Oh, he grinned in front of his clan from time to time, but it was a controlled expression. Just like every emotion was. This smile was personal. He enjoyed it because he would have bet his last piece of silver on the fact that he could feel the curving of his lips all the way to his marrow.

She affects ye deep, laddie.

Another emotion threatened his enjoyment. It was a sense of vulnerability. With anything else, he might have shaken it off, denying it because a laird just couldn't afford to have a weakness. Yet, there was no denying Rhedyn awakened something that made him willing to stand up to his clan for her.

The incident in the stables somehow making it grow deeper roots. What had begun as a means to avoiding bloodshed was now a desire to protect Rhedyn.

And she'd walked right into danger.

He grunted at that hard reality. His gut knotted at the knowledge of just how easy Hamish had found it to lure Rhedyn away from the safety of her chamber.

'Because ye kissed me!'...

Her admission made his lips twitch. He had kissed her. And he wasn't sorry. Nor was he going to apologize for closing the door to his study with her inside. Such would cause gossip, but that idea gave him another thought. One which offered him a solution to the trouble he'd been brooding over.

⇒⇒⇒⟪⟪⟪

"MORNING, MISTRESS."

Shona arrived with a tone filled with happiness. She was followed by four maids. One of them set a tray on the table as two went to begin making up the bed Rhedyn had barely slept in. The bedding was a mess from her tossing and turning throughout the night. Shona's eyes narrowed as she took the scene in.

"How kind of ye," Rhedyn said to distract Shona.

It was kind, even if Buchanan's words rose from her memory.

"Did I not warn ye about the temper of me kin? Must I lock ye inside this chamber?"

The chamber was simply a finer prison.

"I have brought ye a doublet," Shona replied as she pointed to the last maid who was waiting with a garment in her hands.

It was an over doublet, which would fit on top of the bodice her dress had. It was a fine garment and a luxury to own, for the highlands often experienced weather which changed quickly.

"The laird has requested ye join him for a ride this morning."

Rhedyn's eyes narrowed. A flash of rebellion went through her. She bit her lip though, questioning her own need to deny doing something she knew full well she was more than hungry for.

Yer temper is flaring...

Life was so very unfair sometimes...

"It is a fine day for a ride," Shona said carefully.

Rhedyn finished off her breakfast, still contemplating the doublet.

Shona stared straight at her. "It's well thought out of the laird to ensure there are no further misunderstandings as to yer position here, mistress."

The nightmares which had made her wake over and over again during the dark hours gave her every hope Shona's words were true.

"Mistress?"

Rhedyn jerked as Shona came closer, peering intently at her face. "I'm fine," Rhedyn declared.

"The lack of color in yer face says otherwise."

Rhedyn smiled. "If I'm pale, an outing is precisely what I need."

Shona raised an eyebrow, but Rhedyn stood, and the maids came forward to help her dress. The doublet did sit very nicely over the bodice of the dress. It had a high collar which would protect her from the wind.

There was a rap on the outer door.

"Bring it in," Shona spoke to whoever was there.

The door opened, revealing two Retainers. They were carrying something large and bulky between them.

"Mistress," they muttered on their way inside the chamber.

"Right here, please," Shona directed them.

They placed their burden down carefully and then reached for their knitted caps, tugging on the corner of them before they turned and left.

"This belonged to the laird's mother." Shona pulled the length of fabric off whatever the Retainers had delivered.

Rhedyn gasped as a full-length mirror was revealed. It offered her a perfect reflection of herself. "This is far too valuable for me."

"Ye are the laird's personal guest," Shona assured her. "Ye shall have the best."

Rhedyn caught sight of the maids behind her sharing a look between them. Shona knew precisely what she was doing.

So, all which remained was for Rhedyn to play her part. "Yer laird is quite thoughtful."

The dress fit her well. Rhedyn looked at the way her hair was braided and dressed with ribbons. The doublet was a lovely, burnt-orange color. It had been sewn with an eye on beauty as well as function. There were tabs at the shoulders, piped and lined. The front of it closed with small silver buttons, each one worked with a rose on its face.

"This is too fine," Rhedyn remarked in awe. "I dare not take it outside where it might be soiled."

"Does leaving it locked in a wardrobe make any sense?" Shona asked as she tugged on some of the shoulder treatments gently to make sure they were perfectly placed. "The laird bid me see ye attired as yer station demands."

Standing behind her, Rhedyn caught a glimpse of Shona's expression. There was a firm look of determination on her face.

There was no use arguing, at least not with Shona.

But what did Buchanan intend?

Ye will no' know the answer until ye face him...

"Thank you," Rhedyn said to the maids and Shona.

The maids all lowered themselves as Shona handed Rhedyn a set of gloves. One of the girls hurried to open the door for her as Shona escorted her down the stairs.

Buchanan was waiting for her on the same steps she'd come up when she'd first arrived at the stronghold. There were nearly as many people there was well. Oh, they were trying to appear as though they weren't there to gawk, but they simply weren't doing a very good job of appearing busy.

Buchanan turned, revealing a freshly shaved face. His shirt sleeves were rolled down and the cuffs buttoned. He also had a doublet on. The sleeves were open along the inner arm, but the cuffs were also secured at his wrists.

He was a fine-looking man.

He's yer captor...

That thought didn't gain any traction as Buchanan swept her from head to toe and slowly smiled. "Thank ye, Shona."

Shona lowered herself and then melted away. A number of those watching took the hint and hurried to disappear. There were still a number of Retainers peeking over the edge of the upper walls though. Rhedyn felt heat teasing her cheeks as Buchanan extended his hand to her.

"Will ye join me, lass?" he asked.

It was an invitation. One which caused her to feel just a bit breathless. She stretched out her hand, placing it into his as he waited on her response.

What are ye doing?...

Honestly, Rhedyn had no idea, but it simply felt so good, there was no reason to insist she employ self-discipline. Should she give him a cold shoulder? Who would it hurt in the end?

Only herself.

⟫⟫⟪⟪

SHE'D PLACED HER hand into his.

Buchanan had never noticed before just how much of a compliment such a thing was from a lass. The polite gesture had always seemed like a chore, one he'd been forced to master as a young lad at the direction of his mother.

Now, he felt the trust Rhedyn was granting him.

Felt it down to the soles of his feet.

The intensity of his awareness was shocking, but it also opened up a door he had never realized was inside himself. Behind it, there was a whole new sort of feelings. Ones with far more intensity than he'd ever associated with women.

No, not women.

Rhedyn.

She was unique. He helped her up and onto the back of his stallion before joining her. She let out a little breathless sound as he settled behind her. Riding with her was another thing she'd label improper, but he wasn't repentant.

Not one little bit.

⟫⟫⟫⟪⟪⟪

"IT'S JUST A wee bit further."

Buchanan's voice touched something inside her.

All right, perhaps it was having him pressed against her back which made her feel like she was trembling. Honestly, there seemed no way to control her reaction to him.

He guided the horse away from the Mackenzie stronghold. A neat little column of Retainers followed them, ensuring her cheeks never cooled. Even with the chill of heading into the wind, she could still feel the blush.

No laird rode out alone. At least not one who wanted to live long.

"Just up here, lass." Buchanan sounded eager.

Whatever was over the top of the next rise, he urged the stallion toward it. She lifted her chin, but he suddenly covered her eyes.

"I want yer first look to be perfect, Rhedyn."

She felt the horse gain the top of the ridge. It stood for a moment before Buchanan guided the animal downward. He let out a whistle. His men answered him, and then they were descending further. All the while, he kept her eyes covered.

Anticipation was bubbling up inside her. She finally felt him stop the horse.

"Now, keep yer eyes closed," he instructed. "No peeking."

"All right."

He slid off the stallion as she squeezed her eyes shut. Her mind was racing as she contemplated what he might have in store for her.

Would it be her father?

That thought should have pleased her, but it had the opposite effect. She was suddenly nervous at the idea of opening her eyes and seeing her own clan; it felt like something to be dreaded.

Buchanan guided her gently by the shoulders. "Open yer eyes."

The sun was shining. Rhedyn blinked a few times before she got a look at whatever he'd brought her to see. A little sound of wonder passed her lips as her eyes focused.

"I hoped ye'd find it breathtaking."

Stretching out all around them was heather. The purple and white blooms were so plentiful, it looked like someone could walk across it. Below the ridge was a small meadow. Across the highlands there were hundreds of them, but only in early spring did the heather bloom.

"I know ye likely have a spot on yer father's land where ye go to see the heather," Buchanan remarked. "I did no' want ye to miss it this season on account of me."

"That is…kind."

She'd stepped away from him, moving among the flowers as she drew in a deep breath. When she opened them, she discovered him watching her. Behind him, his men were on the high ground, all of them looking somewhere except at them.

Her belly knotted with nervousness. She looked around at the heather and then back at Buchanan.

"Do ye mean to make me yer mistress?"

If her boldness surprised him, his expression didn't show it. In-stead, he reached forward, gently touching the side of her face. "I mean to ensure ye do nae ever have such dark circles beneath yer eyes again."

The connection between their flesh made her breath freeze in her chest. Time felt like it slowed down.

"I let Hamish off too lightly," Buchanan finished with a tone full of disgust.

"So, this outing is to make sure there is gossip about us."

"It was also intended to make ye smile, lass."

He crossed his arms over his chest. His expression didn't really give her any hint as to his mood, but there was something flickering in his eyes which hinted at vulnerability.

Did he truly care if she enjoyed the moment?

Rhedyn slowly smiled. He tilted his head to one side as he flashed his teeth at her in a smile. She discovered herself at a loss for words. All she was certain of was the way the grin on her lips felt perfect. She turned and looked at the field again.

≫≫≪≪

THE MOMENT WAS perfect.

Buchanan had never really contemplated if a single place or time was better than others before. For certain, a good night spent in song and drinking was preferable to working hard under the midday sun.

But watching Rhedyn among the heather was different from the moments he'd enjoyed with his friends. There was something about the way she stood so still, which made him not want to move and ruin the intimate moment. She reached out and touched a blossom, moving slowly away from him. It prompted him to follow her. She looked back at him, her eyelashes fluttering as she resumed her slow walk.

He was compelled to follow.

No, enticed.

Something drew him to her, and ignoring the impulse was inconceivable. Later, he'd likely console his pride by thinking it played into his plan.

For the moment, though, all Buchanan was thinking was just how much enjoyment he was experiencing. Somehow, he'd never noticed life held such an opportunity before.

>>>><<<<

A CRACK OF thunder startled Rhedyn.

She jumped, looking up at the sky. Dark clouds had rolled in while she was distracted.

By Buchanan…

Hush, she chided. After the last few weeks of being a captive, there was no way she was going to deny herself for enjoying the morning.

"Come, lass!" Buchanan reached for her.

She put her hand into his, and he tugged her up the incline. His stallion was dancing as the wind whipped up.

"Easy now," Buchanan whispered to the animal.

There was such warmth in his voice, and the way he smoothed his hand along the creature's neck sent heat through her veins. She struggled to conceal her thoughts as Buchanan calmed the horse and helped her up onto its wide back.

She was clearly losing her sanity if she found the way he calmed a beast enticing. Just a few weeks before, she'd been a proper daughter. Now, as Buchanan mounted behind her, she felt a tingle in her breasts as her nipples drew into tight little nubs which had nothing to do with the storm.

In fact, the wildness of the weather only made her long for some privacy where she might indulge in her impulses.

But the Mackenzie Retainers closed around them, escorting them quickly back to the Mackenzie stronghold. She couldn't stop the feeling of dread as she once again rode into the yard.

This time, Shona was waiting in the passageway. Rhedyn turned around, though, looking for Buchanan. But the formal laird was what she found behind her. The man who had taken her to see a meadow of heather was stern-faced now.

"Come away," Shona advised her softly. "There is business for the laird."

Rhedyn looked into the passageway. A new group of men stood there. They wore the colors of the McLeod's and there wasn't a hint of a smile on any of their faces. Laird McLeod stood with several of his captains at his back. Whatever their reason to be in the Mackenzie stronghold, it was a grave matter.

⟫⟫⟫⟪⟪⟪

"I'D HOPED IT was nae true," Cedric McLeod began. "Vychan told me ye had Rhedyn Lindsey, but I still had hope that ye'd have sent her on home by now."

Buchanan stood in front of the hearth in his study. Someone had laid a fire in it, even if he personally didn't find the weather cold.

"Colum Lindsey is no' a difficult man," Cedric continued.

"Which is why I had no stomach for running him through," Buchanan cut to the heart of the matter. "Why are the McLeods making this their business?"

"Colum wed me sister," Cedric announced.

Buchannan felt something shift inside him. "Yer sister? As far as I know, ye had but one sister who bore Colum Lindsey a child. A child she birthed on McLeod land because the couple split. McLeod and Lindsey have no' been on friendly terms due to the matter of Colum and yer sister never wedding."

"Aye," Cedric said. "But Colum rode down to Edinburgh and got the Archbishop to approve of the union. Me nephew, Vychan, is now the heir of Clan Lindsey."

Buchanan might have normally enjoyed a good chuckle over hearing of a wedding where the bride was dead, but if the Church had sealed the matter, it was nothing for him to take lightly. The authority of the Church was not to be argued with.

"Give the lass to me," Cedric boldly said.

Buchanan shook his head. "She stays with me."

He should have thought the idea over. As far as strategy went, it would have been a good move to keep the McLeod laird happy. His own clan would have seen the merit in not having both Lindseys and McLeods angry with them.

But the words were out of his mouth long before he thought of any reasons other than what he wanted. And Rhedyn leaving was something he discovered himself dead set against.

"Ye've no proof Colum is guilty," Cedric pressed the matter.

"What I have is a clan ready to demand retribution for over a dozen dead Makenzie Retainers," Buchanan retorted. "Ye saw with yer own eyes. The lass is treated well."

"Aye," Graham took the opportunity to voice his support. "The lass is treated very nicely by our laird."

"As I saw," Cedric agreed. "But the lass is me niece now. If ye do nae release her, I have to join with the Lindsey against ye." He opened his arms up wide. "We've been allies for generations. It is no' to me liking, but blood is blood. I can no' leave her here as a hostage."

McLeod's men stood on one side of his study, Buchanan's on the other.

"So, it might be best to see the girl settled here." Graham lifted his chin so his voice would carry. "She was taken to avoid bloodshed."

"Ye need to talk to her father about that," Cedric insisted.

"We should take advantage of her presence here," one of the men behind Graham stated. "Even if her father is guilty, she is his legitimate child. And if not guilty, we shouldn't let the prize go, either."

Buchanan watched the way Cedric looked toward his own captains. It was clear some of them had no liking for the new family obligation they had inherited.

"Twelve Retainers is no' a light matter," Graham said. "The McLeod will have to respect our actions."

The McLeod captains had taken to toying with their beards. They leaned in, whispering between themselves. It was Cedric who finally lifted his hands to quiet them. He turned and took a deep breath.

"As her uncle, I am open to discussing a union," Cedric declared firmly.

There was silence for a long moment before the men began to discuss it. Buchanan watched the way the information settled into them. Many began to nod in agreement before a growing course of 'ayes' was heard.

Something flashed through him. A sensation sharper and more brilliant than anything he'd ever experienced.

But Graham cleared his throat, recalling Buchanan to the fact that everyone was waiting for him to answer.

"As it appears to be settled," Buchanan said. "I will wed her."

The McLeod captains grinned, obviously pleased. Preened was actually a better word for the way their faces lit with pleasure for having made him bend to their will.

Buchanan locked gazes with Cedric.

"Now that the business is settled, off to supper with ye all," Cedric announced. "I plan to have a drink with me new family."

The captains filed out of the study, leaving Buchanan and Cedric. For a long moment, there was only the crackle of the fire filling the silence.

"It's a good solution, lad, and ye know it." Cedric began to help himself to the whiskey kept off to the far side of the hearth. He poured two generous measures before offering one to Buchanan.

"It's a fine way for the McLeods to gain ties with the Mackenzie without ever having done a thing to raise the bride," Buchanan remarked.

Cedric chuckled over the rim of his glass. "Ye're young. However, the way I hear it, ye are no fool." He paused to take another sip. "Me sister refused to wed Colum Lindsey. Aye, the fault was hers, and I know it well."

"But now ye have a way to see yer nephew in line for the Lindsey lairdship."

"Ye begrudge me that?" Cedric asked. "It's no' his fault me sister was so stubborn. She followed her passion and should no' have been so surprised to have to face the consequences. Besides, Vychan is no' assured of gaining the lairdship."

"Colum has always considered the lad his son," Buchanan stated.

"Once the old man is gone, there will be men in the clan who consider Vychan an outsider. Ye faced a similar fight against Iain," Cedric pointed out. "Him being gone is no' going to make ye lose sleep."

"I did no' wish him ill," Buchanan defended himself.

"Ye did no' have to," Cedric said. "He had the same temper me sister had. Once either of them decided upon a path, they'd no' step off it." Cedric pointed around the room. "In this study, ye and I are lairds. We can say things to one another which may no' be kind, but they are true nonetheless."

Buchanan nodded and sipped at his whiskey.

Cedric grunted. "Colum has ensured Vychan has a chance at the lairdship. It's the lad's due. Being me nephew did no' shield him from the harsh view of being bastard born."

Cedric picked up the bottle of liquor and crossed the space between them to refill Buchanan's glass.

"Drink up, lad, ye have a bride to woo and me to thank for agreeing to leave her here with ye."

"Is that so?" Buchanan asked.

Cedric had refilled his own glass and was setting the bottle back down. He turned and raised an eyebrow. "It certainly is. Do ye think I do nae understand the Munro would thank me well for taking Rhedyn home for Rolfe to come and collect? And do nae waste yer breath telling me ye'd no relinquish the lass to me. Ye would when faced with four clans united against ye. So...get on with showing yer appreciation."

Buchanan lifted his glass. "Ye're drinking me best whiskey."

Cedric tossed down the remains in his glass and reached for the bottle once more. "Ye can be sure I am going to drink a fair amount of it." Cedric crossed the room and laid a hand on Buchanan's shoulder.

"Off with ye now, lad. I'll need to be witness to yer wedding tomorrow morning," Cedric said. "Unless ye prefer I talk to her."

"I took her, so I will speak to her."

Buchanan should have been struggling to maintain a grip on his temper with the way Cedric was so intent on doing everything the way he'd decided things should go.

But Buchanan discovered himself grinning instead. There was a pulse of anticipation growing stronger with every second. Something gave way inside him, like a barrier had been smashed. With the collapse, he was flooded with sensations so strong, they were dangerously close to being needs.

Would that be so terrible?

To need Rhedyn? Buchanan stopped in the passageway. Cedric walked beside him.

Lust was something Buchanan understood. The nature of his own flesh was something he'd battled more than once, but this was something different. Having his marriage arranged had always been a matter he'd expected to face. But nowhere in the planning of it all had he expected to feel, well, to feel such a surge of excitement.

Cedric slapped him in the center of his back. "Off ye go, lad. I'll be at yer high table waiting on the good news."

The idea of facing Rhedyn drew him toward her, just as surely as the scent of dinner did when he'd been out riding for too long. She would satisfy him and make him feel whole.

Hunger?

Was that the right word? He hesitated outside the door of the north tower chamber. Craving Rhedyn would put him at her mercy. But he still wasn't interested in turning around and leaving.

Rolfe Munro would never have her…

He knocked on the door. Barely reining in his desire enough to afford her that courtesy.

>>><<<

WHOEVER WAS KNOCKING didn't wait for her to invite them in. Buchanan pushed the door open as though it was his right to do so.

"Yes?" Rhedyn asked.

A tingle touched her nape as she gained a glimpse of Buchanan's face. For certain, whatever business the McLeods had with him, it had been serious.

"Did Laird McLeod bring evidence against my father?" Rhedyn asked. Her damned heart was thumping at a frantic pace.

He made sure the door was shut behind him. For some reason, she was far more aware of just how much bigger he was than herself. The chamber seemed to enhance it, making her feel like she was trapped inside with a bear.

"He brought news of yer father sure enough," he began. "It seems yer father has married."

Rhedyn's eyes widened in surprise. "To…who?"

"Ye have a brother, Vychan," Buchannan continued. "He's the legitimate heir now."

A silence stretched between them as she processed what he'd told her.

"Yes," Rhedyn remarked, still caught up in thinking. "I do know who Vychan is. I suppose it's a good thing."

Even if it was shocking. She wasn't going to ask for the details.

Such facts were likely to make her head ache. She was certain the arrangements had entailed a large amount of money, but she really didn't have the heart to question the matter.

"My father had many regrets concerning Vychan," Rhedyn remarked. "It's good to hear the matter has been resolved."

She drew in a deep breath, feeling as though she'd accomplished some important task.

"I heard Rolfe Munro was courting ye," Buchanan said abruptly. "Do ye have affection for him?"

The question caught her off guard.

"No, I did nae care for his..." She realized words were just spilling out of her mouth before she thought anything through.

The corners of Buchanan's mouth twitched as a gleam of enjoyment entered his eyes. "Ye did nae care for what?" he asked as he stepped toward her.

She felt like her breath was frozen in her chest, and her lips went dry.

"His kiss?" Buchanan guessed correctly.

Rhedyn stepped back. He was too imposing in that moment, her mind filled completely with the idea of him. Her senses were heightened, making it hard to think as he closed the distance between them.

"Rolfe tried his luck with ye, lass?" Buchanan asked softly.

"Ye make it sound sordid," she said. "A kiss in the passageway is acceptable when he'd made his suit known to me father. Ye kissed me, too."

Buchanan chuckled, but it wasn't a good-natured sound. No, it was a dark rumbling like the purr of a wolf as it cornered its prey.

"I did at that. And ye kissed me back."

There was solid confidence in his tone. Something flashed in his eyes as she moved back again.

"This is the strangest conversation," she said. "If me father is wed now, and Vychan is legitimate, then Laird McLeod is me uncle."

Of course it made sense. Even if her father's bride was dead.

"He's here to take me home, else he'll have to help me father raid ye." Rhedyn pieced it all together. Her stomach suddenly felt like someone had planted their fist into her midsection.

"He's here to witness our wedding," Buchanan informed her softly.

"What?" Her astonishment was clear.

"The McLeods and the Mackenzies have been allies for generations," Buchanan continued. "Yer uncle…" He paused for a moment. "Does nae care to end up fighting against me clan. Since ye are here, and yer reputation stained by this matter, the best solution is for us to marry."

"Do nae be ridiculous!"

It was absurd. She turned and walked across the room but stopped when she found herself just three paces from the bed. Rhedyn whirled around to discover Buchanan had kept pace with her.

"Laird McLeod can simply escort me home."

Buchanan crossed his arms over his chest. The posture made him look even larger and more imposing than ever.

And she liked the sight…

Rhedyn scolded herself for losing focus. Clearly, it was in fact sage advice for young women to stay well away from men, for being too close to Buchanan was affecting her sanity.

"Ye prefer Rolfe?"

There was a glint in his eyes now. Rhedyn peered at him intently.

"Ye can nae be jealous." The words were across her lips before she thought about them.

"Why no'?" he asked. "Because I kidnapped ye?"

Rhedyn nodded.

He chuckled.

"I assure ye, Rhedyn, I am most serious about wedding ye."

He looked it, too. Rhedyn blinked, but his expression remained steadfast. Her heart was hammering away, sending her blood rushing through her veins so fast, she felt lightheaded.

But the bed was too close. Rhedyn fell onto it but bounced right back off it in alarm. She tried to duck beneath his arms, only to have him clamp his arms around her body.

"Release me!"

Buchanan only lifted her off her feet. She kicked in the air, but he held her firmly against his body, lowering her only once she'd stopped straining against his hold.

She was trembling.

It made no sense, but the contact between them was so intense, she felt the tremor running along her limbs. Each inhalation of breath drew his scent into her head.

How could a man smell so good?

"I would have ye release me." The sound of her voice was wrong. It was husky and breathless.

His chest rumbled again with that purring sound.

He suddenly moved his hands, sliding them along her arms. "Truly, Rhedyn?" he asked against her ear. "Do ye claim to no' enjoy being so close to me?"

"I..." Her voice refused to cooperate as she attempted to deny it.

Why had she never learned how to lie?

"I shouldn't." There. It was a denial at least. "Release me."

His arms opened. She ended up standing in place because she hadn't really expected him to comply. It took her a long moment to believe she was free and to get her feet to move. Once she made it across the chamber, she turned and looked back to find Buchanan contemplating her.

He raised an eyebrow. "Surprised, lass?"

She nodded.

His lips twitched into a grin. "Good. I have no desire to have a wife who cringes when she sees me."

"I have not agreed to wed ye," Rhedyn informed him. Her temper finally flickered to life, affording her some relief from the trembling in her body. "Do nae be thinking that ye and Laird McLeod can simply discuss the matter and consider it done."

Except that they could. She was forced to recognize that she was in his stronghold and therefore very much under his control.

His expression tightened. She knew well what he looked like when he was serious, and there was no mistaking the way he appeared right then.

"I think I might just be very thankful for the chain of events which brought ye to me notice, Rhedyn, for now I can make certain Rolfe Munro doesn't have the chance to claim ye."

He suddenly jumped forward, reaching out to grasp her forearms. "Ye tremble when I touch ye, lass."

She did. Understanding why he affected her so deeply eluded her. He suddenly scooped her up.

Once again, she was cradled against him, her breaths drawing in the scent of his body. This time, she found it oddly comforting as he turned and crossed the space back to the bed. He sat her down on the edge of the mattress and then sat next to her.

"Buchanan." She propped her hands behind her. "Ye must rethink the matter."

He pressed his thumb against her lips. "I have made my decision." Determination flashed in his eyes, and his face became a mask of unrelenting firmness.

"No one," he began gruffly, "no one will ever lay hands on ye again without knowing ye belong to me, Rhedyn. The next man who frightens ye will understand he will no' just be banished, but I will choke the life from his body for the crime of putting fear into yer eyes."

"Ye can ensure me protection by sending me home with Laird McLeod."

He stroked her face, sending a shiver down her spine. Only it wasn't the cold sensation that the memory of Hamish's attack had produced. No, this was a jolt of warmth that burned through that chill, making her quiver.

"Ye will be me wife," he muttered firmly. "Because I want to put me hands on ye, lass. It would be far better for me to send ye home, for there are plenty in me clan who will not be pleased to see me making ye the lady of this stronghold."

"So...send me...home." It was the logical thing to say, yet the words stuck in her throat.

Whatever she might have said was caught beneath his kiss. He cupped the back of her neck and pressed his mouth against her. Rhedyn shifted nervously, but the truth was, she was far more interested in getting closer to him. His strength drew her to him, the way his mouth moved against hers unleashed a rush of sensation that thrilled her all the way to her toes. When he lifted his head, she was breathless, a tingling mass of indecision. Her mind, simply unable to deal with anything.

"Shall I send ye home, Rhedyn?" he asked as he stroked her neck gently. "Do ye prefer a cold marriage to what is between us?"

He held her in place so that their eyes met. "I confess, I would consider myself ten kinds of a fool if I were to allow ye to ride away with yer uncle for whatever is between us, I know it is rare. And that I've never felt it before."

She should have told him no.

Should have voiced some sort of denial.

Should have managed a retort.

Instead, all of her 'should have's' remained unspoken as Buchanan stood and left. Her thoughts returned in a rush, leaving her perched on the bed as she tried to decide what it was she needed to argue with him about.

No wonder she had been warned to stay away from men.

They addled the brain for certain!

⇛⇚

RHEDYN WASN'T GOING to hide.

An hour after her confrontation with Buchanan, she brushed her hair from her face. Somehow, she'd fallen asleep, but now, she was wide awake. And the closed door of the chamber was irritating her.

Actually, it taunted her.

Laird McLeod might just have a different view of her wedding Buchanan. How could she have fallen asleep when there was an opportunity to escape?

Rhedyn paused in front of the mirror. Her reflection showed her so many things. One of which was that she was no longer a girl.

Rolfe Munro would be back to press the matter of a union between them. He'd told her as much.

So, does that mean you're going to marry Buchanan?

Rhedyn refused to answer her own question. Instead, she headed toward the door and opened it. The stairway was dark, but light flickered at the bottom where candles had been lit in the passageway. She realized she'd held her breath as she left the chamber. By the time she was standing in the passageway, the tension had broken. She drew in a deep breath.

"Ye've perfect timing, mistress."

Rhedyn jumped. The man who had spoken seemed to expect her startled response. He remained where he was, reaching up to tug on the corner of his knitted cap.

"Muir, ma'am," he introduced himself. "I'd be happy to show ye the way to the hall for supper."

The passageway was nothing but a place to get from the tower to the other parts of the castle. Here, there were not even storerooms, for she was beneath one of the walls which formed the inner yard. The

155

north tower afforded a secondary defense position in the event of attack.

"I know me way, thank ye." She started down the passageway.

Muir keep pace with her.

She turned and peered at him. He reached up and tugged on the corner of his cap once again. "The laird tasked me with seeing to ye, mistress."

Rhedyn felt her chest tighten once again. "I am perfectly well upon me own."

The words were barely past her lips when the events of the day rose from her memory. Muir's expression changed, too, making it clear he was thinking the same thing. Her words were foolish, but there was no getting them back.

"Did ye say it was supper time?"

"Aye, this way, mistress," he replied jovially.

But he didn't lead the way. Instead, the Retainer remained behind her as he extended his hand.

Conversation drifted out of the hall as they drew closer. It was full of Mackenzie Retainers. Long tables ran the length of it, and the scent of roasting meat hung on the evening air. There were over two hundred Retainers. It was a staggering amount, for her own father would be hard pressed to assemble a hundred. The Mackenzies had always been a clan with strong numbers.

Her father would have considered a match with Buchanan as something grand.

Should ye take the opportunity?

"Ye will be me wife," he muttered firmly. *"Because I want to put me hands on ye, lass."*

Rhedyn felt her cheeks heating. Putting his hands on her was something she understood very well. Seeing Buchanan sitting at the end of the hall where a platform held the high table, she discovered her mouth going dry.

Did she dare?

words fitting for the moment. 'Damn' wasn't nearly strong enough for the way she felt.

She needed to escape.

⟫⟫⟫⟪⟪⟪

IT WASN'T THE first time Cora had left her chamber after dark. She stuffed her hair into a bonnet and slipped down the steps.

"Go back to yer chamber, Cora."

She stiffened. Shona emerged from the shadows at the base of the stairs.

"Did me brother set ye here to watch me? Ye are no' a fool." Cora faced off with her. "I know well that ye are me half-sister in spite of everyone tip toeing around the truth as though the words would scorch me ears. But must ye do everything he demands of ye?"

Shona didn't recoil from the bite in Cora's tone. Instead, she moved closer, keeping a steady connection between their gazes. "I would have introduced ye to being an adult long before now, Cora. Still, it is not up to me to make the rules of the house."

Cora tossed her head. "Oh, aye, I understand well enough that men run this world."

"Ye've naught to be so concerned about. Yer brother does not treat Rhedyn poorly. And if she returns home, marriage is something she will face even there."

Cora wasn't in the mood to back down. "Rhedyn being forced to wed is a matter I think worthy of being concerned over."

Shona merely lifted an eyebrow. "Are ye planning to ride out into the unknown of the night? Just the pair of ye against anyone who might be raiding or drunk?"

"She shouldn't be forced to wed. I don't want to wed Cormac Grant, either," Cora insisted.

"Ye do nae even know the man."

"Are ye going to tell me to make the best of my arranged marriage?"

Shona tilted her head to one side. "I'll advise ye to no' throw something away without taking a look to see what it is first. Only a child cries for fruit in the dead of winter while refusing a bowl of porridge to fill its belly."

Cora understood well enough.

"Raging has its place, Cora," Shona continued. "What ye need to learn is when to fight and when to realize ye might lose what ye already have. For the moment, yer wedding date has not been set."

"Agreed," Cora said quickly. "We should be talking about ways to help Rhedyn escape."

"Did ye no' hear me advice about taking a look at what ye have before discarding it?" Shona asked. "There is a spark between yer brother and Rhedyn Lindsey."

"But he stole her."

"Does it differ so vastly from a contracted bride?" Shona asked. "I do nae believe so. Either way, Rhedyn would no' have been asked her opinion on the matter of who her groom was. Yer brother was willing to make it clear in the hall tonight that he will no' tolerate Rhedyn being disrespected. If she leaves here, her father will wed her to someone who might decide to feud against us over the offense of her being stolen. This is about more than just one woman."

Just as Cora wasn't going to be consulted on the matter of her marriage to Cormac Grant.

He might not be so terrible…

She forced herself to repeat that bit of logic. Shona made a good point about taking a look at the man before forming an opinion.

But Rhedyn was a different matter.

"Ye owe everything to me brother," Cora boldly spoke her mind. "So, ye are here to make certain I do nae help Rhedyn escape."

"Yes, I am also a sibling of the laird," Shona agreed. "Decisions must be made for the good of the clan. Ye are being childish by not seeing the dangers of running away. If ye are found dead tomorrow, there will be plenty of blood spilled over it."

Shona planted herself in front of Cora, making it clear she wasn't going to back down. For the moment, it was only the pair of them, but if there was a scuffle, Cora was sure some of the Retainers asleep in the hall would hear them.

She didn't care for the feeling of helplessness that enveloped her.

And there was no way to escape it.

⟩⟩⟩⟨⟨⟨

SHONA WATCHED CORA turn around and begin climbing the stairs to her chamber. The bottom of her skirts were just disappearing when Buchanan joined her. Shona inclined her head.

"I will no' forget yer help tonight," he said.

"I advise ye to think more about the fact yer sister will no' forget that she lost this battle tonight."

Buchanan locked gazes with Shona. "I did no' make the match between her and the Grants. Ending it will be a tricky matter. Do nae make the mistake of thinking I favor the alliance over Cora's happiness. But as ye pointed out to her, raging against a man she has never met is no' a solution." He left her alone.

Shona was left pondering his words. She set her back against the stone wall, something she'd done many, many times in the past, for a bastard daughter's life was easier when she didn't stick out too often.

Fight for what she wants?

Shona smiled.

Well, what was good for Cora was good for her brother.

Shona felt her mind settling on a decision. Once made, she turned and walked through the dark passageways until she came to the stillroom. Inside were the herbs. Some were used as spices and others for medicines. She withdrew a small key and fit it into the lock.

⟫⟫⟩⟨⟨⟨

SOMEONE KNOCKED ON the chamber door later that night. Rhedyn looked up as Buchanan opened it and came inside. He contemplated her for a long moment, as though he was still debating with himself just what it was he wanted to do.

"Come here, lass, and kiss me."

He went so far as to beckon to her with his finger. But the look on his face made it clear he expected her to refuse him.

Which was likely why she started toward him. Surprise flashed through his eyes, fanning her need to shock him.

What precisely was she doing? Rhedyn had no idea beyond the fact that she liked feeling brazen far more than the panic which had so recently been threatening to consume her. Whatever the reason, she moved so quickly, Buchanan stumbled back against the door.

"Christ," he muttered under his breath.

Rhedyn stopped two paces from him. A smile softened his expression as he recognized the humor in the moment. He reached up and tugged on the corner of his knitted cap.

"I'm impressed, lass."

"If ye came up here expecting to find me weeping," she said, "ye can take yerself back the way ye came."

She turned away from him.

He caught her wrist. "I came to offer to take ye away if ye do nae want to marry me."

"What?"

"Ye heard me, Rhedyn. I will take ye out of this stronghold and return ye to yer father."

The expression on his face told her he was serious, and she was close enough to him to tell that he wasn't soaked in whiskey. "Why

164

would ye offer me such a thing?"

"Because if I do nae offer ye escape, the matter of how ye became me wife will always be between us."

It would be.

His offer left her standing there, staring at him without a clear idea of just how to proceed. "I do nae know what to do."

Should she leave?

Dare she stay?

She'd thought coming to terms with her circumstances was difficult, but it was nothing compared to how overwhelmed she felt now that he was offering her freedom.

"If ye are undecided, kiss me."

She tugged to free herself from his grasp, but he didn't let her go. "Why would I do something like that?"

"Because Rolfe Munro will be waiting for ye if I return ye to yer father. Dare ye go back and chance being wed to him while thinking about me?"

Her eyes widened. "Ye arrogant—"

She finally managed to pull away from him.

"Ye said Rolfe Munro stole a kiss from ye."

"Aye," she said. "But I should no' have told ye."

Buchanan moved toward her, and Rhedyn shifted to one side. It wasn't really retreating, just adjusting.

"Ye said his kiss did nae move ye."

Her body tingled with need. Her belly tightened as she watched the way his lips thinned as he looked her over. He raised his hand and curled his finger once more in her direction.

"Come and see what ye think of *my* kiss."

Rhedyn shook her head. It drew a husky chuckle from Buchanan.

"And why no'?" he asked devilishly. "Do ye believe that because I am a man, I do no' care to have a woman who fancies me? Let us see if we have the makings of a good match."

"Do you care what a woman thinks of ye?" She really shouldn't have asked the question. It was devoid of modesty, but she just couldn't help herself. He was right. Rolfe would come back. And although he offered her a fine match in many ways, she didn't blush for him.

"We were both born to our positions, Rhedyn," he said. "I know the woman I wed must be one who brings an alliance. I would have passion as well."

"Ye can have a mistress of yer choice."

He shook his head. "No' if I wish to keep me word. The wedding vows require faithfulness of both husband and wife."

"They do," she said slowly. "Although I'm surprised to see ye noting it."

"It is nae the first time ye have noticed that I have no liking to play a villain."

It was an admission. And there was no missing the seriousness in his tone. The sound struck something inside her. Something deep down where there was no arguing about any reasons. There was simply right and wrong.

"Ye are no' a villain," she whispered. Her words were like a fragile bubble floating through the air between them. While it held, everything she saw through it was magical.

"I am not," Buchanan confirmed as he stepped closer. "And if I send ye home, Rolfe Munro will be back to try his hand at securing ye. I came up here tonight to see if ye want to make a choice between us...for yerself."

It was a challenge.

One which heated her blood even more. Buchanan was the most surprising of creatures, for she'd never heard of a man who was willing to be faithful. His men surely wouldn't fault him. But she would be expected to mind her tongue and suffer his husbandly needs without complaint.

With a quick tug to her arm, she fell against him.

"Buchanan."

He clamped her against his body. "Shh. I have promised I will no act the villain. But I will no' allow ye to go without a true test, lass. We will see if this union might be a good one."

He was behind her now, his body hard and oddly pleasant to be held against.

Why had she never noticed how delightful it was to be embraced? His breath teased the top of her head, sending ripples of awareness across her skin. Beneath her clothing, gooseflesh rose up. She shifted, and he held her securely. Every little breath drew his scent into her head.

The result was intoxicating.

Her thoughts were scattering as the need for intimacy became undeniable. His chest rumbled with appreciation to the way her body reacted to his.

"Would ye ignore that, lass?" he asked. A moment later, he was turning her so he could lock gazes with her.

Her breath caught as she witnessed the look of longing in his eyes.

"Kiss me, Rhedyn."

His tone was firm. He cupped the back of her head and pressed his mouth over hers to seal the demand. It was a kiss full of promise and intention.

But it didn't hurt.

She suddenly couldn't get close enough to him. She reached for him, stroking him as she mimicked the motions of his mouth. Their clothing frustrated her, separating her from what she craved. She slipped her hand into the open collar of his shirt, delighting at the sound which came from him.

A groan of pleasure.

He repaid her in kind. Stroking her nape below the collar of her dressing robe. She arched, muttering with enjoyment before he suddenly cupped her shoulders and set her away from him.

"What?" she questioned, feeling as though he'd been ripped from her arms.

"If we're going," he said, "now is the time to leave."

She bit her lip. Everything she'd been raised to believe conflicted with what she felt.

"Ye must make a choice Rhedyn," he persisted. "I'll not have this matter between us."

He'd take her home.

She witnessed the flash of determination in his eyes.

Marry him?

Christ, she'd never been so tempted to do something in her life!

And she suddenly held the choice in her own hands. A gift from a man who she'd be wise not to toss aside. Was it so simple?

Actually, Rhedyn decided that it was.

"Good night, Buchanan," she said before she turned and headed back toward the bed. She looked back at him over her shoulder. "I will see ye in the morning."

CHAPTER FIVE

R HEDYN DIDN'T FALL asleep until late.

Which meant she was jerked awake by someone pounding on the door of the chamber. Enclosed in the bed with its heavy curtains, the daylight had failed to wake her.

"Morning to ye, mistress," Shona declared with joy. There was the patter of steps on the wood floor as others entered the chamber along with her.

Someone took hold of the bed curtains and pulled them back. Rhedyn blinked, her eyes shocked by the bright light of midmorning.

"Since it's yer wedding day, I thought it best to allow ye to sleep late," Shona said.

The maids exchanged smirks. One of them sent Rhedyn a wink along with a look that made it plain the girl thought Rhedyn was a lucky girl to be getting the right to share a bed with Buchanan.

Rhedyn felt her belly knot. But there was also a flicker of heat at the top of her sex. It was by far the most carnal feeling she'd ever experienced.

"Up with ye, mistress!" Shona didn't grant Rhedyn any time to ponder her thoughts.

Today, the tub was brought up the stairs to the chamber for her bath. Rhedyn attempted to protest, but there was little point, because there was a line of boys hauling water right behind the two men who sat the tub down.

Shona watched it all with a practiced eye. The maids knew their places as well. Rhedyn found herself stripped and washed in no time at all. And then, she was pulled from the tub so her hair might begin drying.

There was a skidding sound as the tub was pushed to the far side of the room. Shona nodded approvingly before she looked toward the maids.

"Wait at the bottom of the stairs," Shona instructed them firmly.

The women looked at one another before Shona snapped her fingers, and they all dropped Rhedyn a curtsy before hurrying from the room.

"I brewed this for ye this morning," Shona explained. "It will keep yer belly flat for as long as ye drink it every day without fail. The matter will remain between us."

Such concoctions were whispered about, but they could so easily be connected with charges of witchery.

"I would not see ye trapped in a union with me brother, if ye truly cannot be content," Shona continued.

"Yer brother?" Rhedyn gasped.

"Aye." Shona lifted the cup higher. "Me mother learned to make this brew after discovering how difficult it would be to have her children branded with the stain of her choice to love a married man. Even if that man's wife was happy to see her husband in anyone's bed but her own."

It was a common enough arrangement.

But being in control of when she conceived, well, there was an idea Rhedyn hadn't ever thought of before. She reached for the cup, even before she realized her intention to do so.

"'Tis bitter," Shona warned.

"So is a marriage without affection." Rhedyn hesitated. "Barren is a harsh word. Buchanan could send me back to my father in disgrace."

Shona let out a little huff. "Since he stole ye, yer father could call him a liar and pay off the midwife to testify ye are still a maiden before yer next wedding."

"Ye would allow yer brother to be spoken of in such a way?" Rhedyn asked.

"Me brother stole ye," Shona replied. "He has already ensured that the Lindseys have naught good to say about him."

Shona pointed at the cup. "Escaping this castle will not grant ye freedom from getting married. That brew, though, will make it so ye can leave if ye find the arrangement with me brother unbearable."

Many brides didn't get such a blessing. There was a glitter of hope in Shona's eyes. The sight made Rhedyn grin, for hope was infectious. So was freedom, for she suddenly had the ability to follow her impulses without regret.

She would just need the courage to make her own decision.

Rhedyn lifted the cup to her lips and drank it. The bitterness was sweet on her tongue.

Buchanan would be disappointed when she didn't conceive.

The thought was unexpected and undermining to everything she thought she was so very certain of.

Such as going home.

When had she started to embrace the idea of making the Mackenzie castle her home?

Buchanan wasn't a villain...

It was more than a thought now. Rhedyn realized it was growing deep down inside her heart. Forming a growing sense of trust. A contracted groom would have been bound to treat her kindly but not be faithful. Hence, Buchanan offered her something personal.

Do ye want it, though?

Rhedyn looked around the room. A gown was laid out on the foot of the made bed. There was a wreath of new spring greens twisted with ribbons for her head. The only thing missing was her father's approval.

'Ye kissed me back...'

She had, and the memory of it made her cheeks heat. Her father wouldn't be blind to the alliance the union with Buchanan would bring. She moved toward the dress, reaching out to touch the fabric.

"The dress was made for Cora to meet her betrothed in this season," Shona supplied the details. "She has no' even tried it on."

Shona's tone made it clear she felt Cora was being difficult over the matter of her contracted marriage.

"Cora has set her mind against her match," Rhedyn said.

"She has, indeed," Shona agreed. "What I wonder is, which way are ye thinking to set yer own mind?"

Rhedyn lifted her gaze off the dress and looked at Shona. "I'm thinking ye are by far the best companion to have at me side, for ye speak plainly."

"No' worried I am twisting the facts in an effort to beguile ye?" Shona lifted a pair of stockings up from where they'd been left on the side of the bed.

Rhedyn sat down on a stool so she could put them on. "My consent isn't necessary. Buchanan could simply have me delivered to the church doors."

She reached for one of the stockings and worked her thumbs down the inside of one, until she reached the toe.

"Ye're right," Shona agreed. "He does no' need yer compliance, yet he asks for it."

Rhedyn put her foot into the stocking and pulled it up her leg. She secured it just below her knee with a leather garter before moving onto the second one.

If Shona was curious as to what Rhedyn was thinking, she didn't ask.

What are ye thinking?

To form it into words seemed impossible. The only solid thought Rhedyn held onto as she got dressed was the memory of Buchanan holding her the night before. It had left her thinking of him in the wee hours of the night when there was nothing to shield herself from the blunt honesty of just who she was.

She had kissed him back.

And she'd enjoyed his touch.

Both were considered sins and reasons to avoid one another. But what had her lifting her arms so Shona might put the first skirt over her head was the fact that Rolfe Munro's kiss had left her cold.

Her father approved of Rolfe Munro.

But his kiss left her feeling nothing.

"Ye seem to have thought it through," Shona observed.

Rhedyn looked at her. "It's a matter of courage really. I've been raised to think of the alliance my wedding would bring to me clan. Well, this union will accomplish a fine one."

"Ye might hide behind that reasoning," Shona agreed.

"I could," Rhedyn responded. "The truth is, being locked above the kitchen gave me a taste of true loneliness. Perhaps before I might have believed I could wed at my father's direction and never given into the need to find the warmth me union lacked."

"Ye do have courage," Shona said.

"Because I've admitted to me lack of obedience?"

"Because ye have been honest," Shona said. "The pair of us have been neatly born into our places. As a legitimate daughter, ye should have admonished me for bringing ye that brew."

"And ye should have lectured me on not longing for carnal desires."

Shona nodded.

"So, I am getting married." Rhedyn smiled. "For at least if I am a wanton, I will have the blessing of the Church."

"Such will make yer life much simpler." Shona picked up the stays laying on the foot of the bed and held them up for Rhedyn to put her hands through.

Courage.

She discovered she liked the feeling of knowing she was making her own choice.

She liked it quite a bit.

Buchanan would just have to live with the fact that he'd encouraged her to make her own choice, for Rhedyn was certain it would not be her last one.

⟫⟫⟫⟪⟪⟪

SHE MIGHT REFUSE him.

Buchanan was up at first light, doubts plaguing him.

Men do nae follow a laird who is nae bold.

His father had given him many lessons about the need for confidence. No one followed a man who didn't keep his chin held high. But he couldn't deny the fact that he wanted Rhedyn to choose him.

He pulled a cloth off a polished mirror. He couldn't recall the last time he used it. Today, he carefully cut away his facial hair. Shaving was a vanity he didn't often indulge in. There were far too many tasks needing his attention during the day to worry about something which grew naturally on his face.

But he wanted Rhedyn to like him.

There was a feeling deep in his chest that made him edgy. Whatever it was, he couldn't recall feeling it before. He leaned over and peered closer in the mirror, turning his head to make sure he'd gotten every last whisker.

Would she be pleased?

He was finished before anyone came to get him. It afforded him time to contemplate just how likely it was that Rhedyn would refuse to wed him of her own free will.

His belly knotted in response to that idea.

He didn't want to force her. Plenty of his own men would likely wonder what his problem was for even thinking such a thing.

Aye, that much was true. However, marriage was a business first when it came to the laird.

Rhedyn had been raised knowing men would come for her dowry and connection with her father. She was only a key to unlock those goods. Something to be used.

Would she appear at their wedding because she saw it as a duty? Or because Rolfe Munro's kiss hadn't moved her?

Buchanan wanted it to be because she saw him as more than her captor.

Well lad, ye'll likely have to temper yer desire to bed her...

Buchanan grinned at his reflection in the mirror, turning side to side so he could see his face. Was he frightening?

Well, to a lass, perhaps.

Rhedyn's head only came to his shoulder. He could close his fingers on one hand around her wrist. That sensation inside his chest intensified as he thought about the way he could hold her against his body and tuck her head beneath his chin. The reason he liked it mystified him.

Lust?

For certain, many of his men would use that word. And he'd be a liar if he didn't admit his cock was hardening in reaction to his thoughts. But the feeling was more than simple lust. He wasn't a lad who didn't understand the difference. Whatever the sensations brewing inside him, it made him worry that Rhedyn wouldn't walk to the Church doors with him. He wanted to see a shy smile on her face and feel her fingers clasping his as they crossed the yard.

Foolish?

Perhaps.

But even acknowledging it didn't seem to be enough to stop the yearning growing within him. Would he have her anyway? There was no one to stop him and yet, a bitter taste filled his mouth as he realized that without a doubt, he wouldn't force her to wed him.

But if she does appear, lad?

Buchanan was turning for the door as he felt his anticipation growing. Standing still was impossible because he had to know if she was going to accept him. His years of experience seemed to matter little as he stood there. It made him grin, for he'd stood by his friends' sides as they waited for their brides and witnessed the way they'd tried to conceal their own doubts.

That was the thing he truly craved. He wanted to be a groom. One whose bride chose him. Not for his position but for who he was.

She didn't let ye take her home...

The look Rhedyn gave him the night before rose from his memory. He closed his eyes so he could give himself over to it completely.

"Good Night Buchanan." She spoke clearly before she turned and headed toward the bed. She stopped and looked back at him. "I will see ye in the morning."

Buchanan felt his confidence flare.

She'd promised.

And if he wanted her to trust him, he'd have to return the favor. So, he drew a deep breath and went to greet his bride.

She'd be there.

Because she'd chosen to stay.

Because she'd chosen him.

⟫⟩⟨⟨

THE MACKENZIES HAD turned out in large numbers to see the wedding of their laird.

The yard was packed full, and a quick look up showed Rhedyn that there wasn't a spare spot along the walls, either. Everywhere she looked, there were gazes upon her, waiting to see just what she'd do.

But Rhedyn wasn't very interested in what others thought. She hesitated in the doorway of the north tower. The wreath of greens on her head smelled wet. Shona had brushed out her hair so that it hung in a curtain behind her. There was a ripple of approval from those waiting to get a peek at her when she appeared. It was a wedding day any girl would have dreamed of.

But her father wasn't there.

She felt his loss deeply, but only for a moment before Buchanan stepped into view. It was her turn to let out a little sound of delight, for he'd cleaned up rather well.

He was a handsome brute. There was simply no denying it. With his chin smooth and his hair combed and washed, he was everything any bride could have wished for.

And he was looking to see if she was there.

Oh, it was only a brief moment. But she caught a glimpse of him searching for her. As he spied her, his expression relaxed, his lips curving into a grin which lit his eyes.

"Mistress?" he asked with his hand extended.

"Laird Mackenzie," Rhedyn answered in kind with a small curtsy.

He closed his fingers around hers. She felt the connection deep inside. Something flickered in his eyes that made her think he felt the same. But there wasn't really time to ponder her thoughts, for the assembled people all began to part, making a path toward the church.

There would be a larger church in the village, but no fortification was complete without a place dedicated to God. The priest was waiting for them in the doorway, his hands tucked into the wide arms of his simple robe.

They stopped at the doorway, kneeling before the priest invited them into what was considered the House of God. In centuries past, most couples would receive the blessing of marriage at the doors, for only the completely devoted might enter the sanctuary. However, newer times brought different customs.

Rhedyn heard footsteps behind them as the senior-ranking men of Clan Mackenzie crowded into the tiny space to witness the vows.

She lost track of everything as the priest turned and sent her a piercing look designed to impress upon her the holy nature of the ceremony he was preparing to perform.

Buchanan's fingers tightened on hers, making her realize the look was for both of them. A strange sense of companionship blossomed inside her. It burned all the uncertainty away, leaving her feeling like she wasn't alone for the first time since she'd left her father's side. It wasn't the look the priest gave them which gave her such a feeling. No, it rose up from the experience she'd had with Buchanan. She snuck another look at him, smiling.

No, he wasn't a villain.

And she was going to marry him.

⫸⫸⫷⫷

"TIME TO TAKE the bride abovestairs."

Three cups of French wine still weren't enough to dull the impact of those words. Rhedyn started to reach for her goblet as Fenella announced to everyone that it was time for the last part of the wedding celebration.

The bedding.

There was a ripple of amusement from the Retainers who were all packed onto the lower tables just waiting for the Head-of-House to appear and escort the bride away.

Rhedyn stopped short of her goblet as she realized Buchanan was watching her. She flattened her hand on the table top and used it to push herself up.

Courage...

She'd chosen her path, and there was no point in hesitating.

"Mistress," Fenella said.

She still wasn't certain what to think of the Head-of-House. But there was a small smile on Fenella's face, so there was no reason to sour the moment by holding grudges.

Rhedyn followed her up four flights of stairs. These were wider than the ones in the north tower. The chamber at the top was grander as well.

The laird's chamber.

Inside, there were two large arm chairs near the hearth. On one end of the chamber, there was the biggest bed Rhedyn had ever seen. If she lay in the center of it and stretched her arms out wide, she doubted her fingertips would reach the edges.

"Now, there is no need to look so concerned," Fenella said. She looked Rhedyn up and down. "Ye are no' too young to not have been told a thing or two about what to expect on yer wedding night."

Rhedyn held her hands up. "I am well informed. Thank ye, Fenella."

A look of relief crossed the servant's face. Rhedyn was sure she appeared just about the same, but it was short lived, for two maids who had followed them began undressing her. They knew their duties and had the dress peeled away in mere moments. Rhedyn stood still, time tormenting her with just how long they might last as she forced herself to remain in place and not dash to the bed to cover herself. There was a cluster of older women near the door, and they had a duty to attend her.

Witnesses.

Rhedyn might have taken comfort in their presence if her father had given his blessing to the union. These were Mackenzie women, and she doubted any of them would defend her if Buchanan decided to annul their union on the basis of there being something unhealthy about her body.

Still, forgoing the custom would have bred rumors. The women peered at her, two of them making a full circle around her before they nodded.

"Into bed with ye," Fenella said at last.

It seemed Fenella wasn't planning to hold grudges, either. The bedding smelled of rosemary and lavender. Just as it should. The two candles burning near the headboard were made of bee wax, the soft scent of honey mixing with the herbs. The maids leaned in to tuck the thick bedding up to her chin.

They didn't finish too soon. The men were coming up the stairs. Their voices were raised in song as they escorted the groom to the chamber.

"Open the door for them," Fenella ordered one of the maids.

The entire party of half-drunken men fell into the room in a jumble of kilts and bare knees. They had Buchanan surrounded as they sang out the last verse of the song.

"Ye've had yer fun now, lads." Buchanan tried to work his way free.

"But ye haven't had yers!" Alpin exclaimed.

Buchanan didn't fare any better than she did when it came to his clothing. His men stripped it away, leaving him fighting to keep his shirt. She looked up at the canopy above the bed as they pushed him onto his back to take his boots as well.

"Out!" he roared at them. "The lot of ye!"

"I do nae know if me old knees can carry me," Graham announced as he wheezed. "I might need to sit down and rest a bit..."

The maids giggled before Fenella snapped her fingers and sent them scurrying out the door.

"Follow them," Buchanan ordered his men.

Graham limped toward the door, each step slower than the last one, as the rest of the men made a mockery of assisting the elder. He finally made it to the doorway and leaned against it as he drew in a deep breath. But he winked at Buchanan and then disappeared a moment later.

"Just wait until the lot of ye wed," Buchanan grumbled.

"So, ye've never escorted one of yer captains to their brides?"

Rhedyn's question seemed to surprise him. He stiffened before he turned to look at her.

"I'm sorry, lass." He stumbled across the floor and grabbed the length of his kilt, holding it up to cover his lower body. "I did no' mean to startle ye."

"Yer shirt linen is not that thin," Rhedyn remarked. Her clothing was laid over one of the chairs. She looked at her smock and dismissed the longing for it.

Buchanan moved toward her clothing, plucking the undergarment from where it sat neatly folded. He carried it to the bed. "I do nae wish to have ye feeling uneasy, Rhedyn."

He laid the smock on the bed and turned his back.

What she felt was surprise. She forced her frozen fingers to release the coverlet and reach for her undergarment. The bed ropes groaned as she moved and struggled to dress. Her bare feet made a slapping sound as she crawled out of the bed. She stood for a moment as the idea of walking around in nothing but her undergarment made her think about getting back into bed.

Fenella had timed things perfectly. The sun had set, leaving the chamber lit by a few candles. The semi-darkness offered her a haven to hide in. Buchanan had shifted back toward the wall, near a window. The shutters were firmly shut against the evening chill. In spite of the thick wood covering, the bed had thick curtains. For now, they were pushed back and secured.

"Are ye cold?" Buchanan asked.

"No," Rhedyn said quickly.

"I was going to offer to light the hearth."

Rhedyn looked toward the neat stack of wood and kindling just waiting for a flint stone to be used to fire it.

"Oh…of course ye were," Rhedyn responded. "I didn't want ye to waste the wood. Not when the weather is so fine and warm."

In truth, her feet were cold and her nipples were hard beneath the fabric of her smock. But her cheeks were hot and burned hotter when she realized she was looking down her body, and Buchanan wouldn't miss the reason why.

Would he fondle her breasts?

She'd heard whispers about what lovers did. Lovers, well, they spent far more time going about their marital duty because they were indulging in the pleasures of the flesh.

Do ye want him to handle yer breasts?

Thank God for the dim light. It allowed her to hide her red cheeks.

"What are ye thinking, Rhedyn?"

Of course he asked. She was standing there in naught but her smock and biting her lower lip like a simpleton.

"I was just noticing the effort Fenella put forth in preparing this chamber." She couldn't help but glance down at the bruises still fading from her arms.

"She has seen the error of her ways," Buchanan replied. "Yet, I still cannot abide her actions. If ye wish to replace her, I will not argue against it."

Rhedyn was stunned.

"Ye think I would deny ye the authority of the mistress of this house?" Buchanan inquired as he watched her face.

"I really hadn't thought about it at all," Rhedyn answered. "Things have happened rather suddenly."

"Ye've been educated in running a large house, have ye not?"

"Of course."

"So, the timing of it all matters not." He shrugged. "Fenella has run the house since me mother died. But she's overburdened."

"Aye," Rhedyn agreed. "This is such a large stronghold, the kitchens alone are a huge task. The books should be kept by someone else."

"By me wife," Buchanan said firmly as he sent her a solid look.

For a moment, they stared at each other, and Rhedyn felt like she was suspended between heartbeats. Just waiting for the next one to commence while she held her breath.

Waiting.

But for what, she wasn't entirely sure. At least, she wasn't quite clear on just how it all should begin. Did he kiss her first, or might she initiate since they were now wed? Should she lay on her back in obedience or touch him as the maids had whispered about in the kitchens? It was really very confusing, for none of the instruction she'd been given officially matched what she'd heard being spoken about.

"Ye were correct about how thin linen is, lass." Buchanan suddenly switched topics. He cocked his head and grinned. "At least it's true until ye stand in front of a flame."

Rhedyn jumped away from the light cast by the candle. She was suddenly tongue-tied.

What had made her think she should wed a man such as Buchanan?

She realized the wine must have had more of a hold on her than she'd realized, for she had been so contently conversing with him while forgetting just where she was.

It was her wedding night.

And he had the right to do whatever he pleased with her. She'd given him that right when she spoke her vows.

"Why did ye marry me, lass?"

He hadn't moved, and was still leaning against the wall. She realized he'd selected a spot half in the shadows, to mask his larger frame.

He didn't have to help her feel at ease.

Rhedyn swallowed the lump in her throat. "Because ye were right."

He raised an eyebrow. "On what account, Rhedyn?"

A small ripple of pleasure traveled across her skin as he spoke her name. It was so very intimate in his bedchamber. She drew in a deep breath and shrugged. "About Rolfe Munro's kiss not moving me." She watched his face as her words reached his ears.

"Are ye admitting ye kissed me back?" he asked with a raised eyebrow.

She had.

And the knowledge burned away her current nervousness. She'd made her choice. The sense of awkwardness making her worry about the fabric of her smock suddenly felt ridiculous.

"I'm twenty-three this summer."

Buchanan nodded. "It's reasonable for Rolfe Munro to be at yer father's table. Ye are no' a girl."

But she felt like she was acting like one. "Me father has no one except me and Bree. He was in no hurry to see us off to our own households."

Yet it would have happened soon.

And now it had.

Rhedyn stared at Buchanan.

Her groom…

For the better part of the last ten years, the topic of marriage had always been on the tip of people's tongues. Advice, warnings, and predictions. All of it aimed toward the moment she'd stand right where she was.

"Ye are being kind," she said softly. "Waiting on me."

Buchanan straightened up. "Well, I've never actually shared a bed with a woman, either."

"Ye are no virgin," Rhedyn declared. "No with the way ye kiss."

His bare feet made a soft sound against the floor as he closed the distance between them. "No. But me bed…I never brought a lass here because it would be the place I shared with my wife."

He stopped a pace from her. In the semidarkness of the chamber, he was almost mythical, cast in silver and darkness. It was a whimsical thought, but she decided she enjoyed it greatly.

She flattened her hands on his chest. Her fingertips felt the heat of his skin through the fabric of his shirt. Rising up onto her toes, she aimed for his mouth. He met her more than halfway, the façade of patience shattering the moment she touched him.

He kissed her slowly at first. Allowing her to move against him as he closed his arms around her. The embrace sent a shiver down her back as she sought a firmer connection with his mouth.

Buchanan didn't deny her. His hand cradled the back of her head as he tilted his own to the side so their mouths might fit together. The kiss changed, becoming demanding, but she discovered that she wanted to demand things of him, too.

She pressed up against him, marveling at the way her body appeared to be softer so that it might mesh with his completely.

Buchanan trailed his lips down the side of her jaw, and she gasped for breath. Her heart was hammering away, making her lightheaded. And she didn't care a bit. All that seemed to matter was touching him. There was so much of his body she wanted to slide her hands over. He was solid, delighting her in a way she'd never realized she might find enjoyment in.

And he seemed to find her body just as worthy of touching. He slid his hands down her sides until he closed his hands on each of her hips. She jerked, a jolt of sensation going through her lower body. It was sharp and intense, leaving behind a throbbing at the top of her sex.

"Do ye want me to stop, lass?"

His question made her open her eyes.

"I will respect yer wishes."

She gazed sincerely at him, realizing he could be trusted in every way.

But there was something else, too. And that glint of heat was what she truly craved. It seemed to mirror something inside her. A need she'd never realized she yearned to feed.

"I married ye," she said. It was as if she'd suddenly burst into flames, but instead of pain, there was a delicious pleasure to be experienced.

His lips twitched. This grin wasn't the sort she'd ever seen before. This was a promise, one he completed by tugging at the fabric of her smock. He pulled it up and over her head. The coolness of the room felt pleasant on her bare skin.

"Aye, ye married me…*wife.*"

Buchanan scooped her off her feet. The bedding was still pushed to one side from when she'd climbed out of it. He laid her down and ripped his shirt off in nearly the same moment. The bed rocked as he joined her on its soft surface.

And then he was lowering himself down. Their skin felt so amazing as it connected. A sound of pure enjoyment escaped her lips. Normally, she would have tried to contain such a thing, but now, there was no controlling anything. There seemed to only be the yearning burning inside her and Buchanan; the thing she needed to satisfy her need.

He cupped one breast, sending her arching. But not away from him, into him, and she wanted to offer herself up to his touch.

"Ye are not timid, Rhedyn," he muttered as his mouth hovered over her nipple.

She locked gazes with him. "I am not."

He brushed his thumb across her nipple. She gasped, stunned by the intensity of the contact.

"Never change, lass," he muttered his last words as he bent down and licked her.

The little nub tightened more as she withered with enjoyment. Pleasure was flowing down her body to the top of her sex. Encased between the folds of it was a pulsing point that begged for attention.

Buchanan appeared to know it. He smoothed his hand down her body, across her ribs, and onto her belly. She'd never realized she might enjoy a touch so much. She closed her eyes as she surrendered completely to the moment.

But Buchanan intended to go lower.

"What are ye doing?" she asked, opening her eyes.

The question just sailed out of her astonishment. His fingers were resting on the curls that crowned her sex.

"I'm planning to tease ye, wife."

His eyes glittered with glee, alarming her almost as much as the sight of him so close to her sex kindled a wave of anticipation.

"Why?"

It was the sort of question she should never have voiced. It was personal and indecent, and she looked away as she realized the deed was already done.

Buchanan chuckled. "Look at me, Rhedyn."

His fingers moved, sending little prickles of delight through her. Part of her wanted to refuse, so she might maintain her sense of dignity.

But she realized she didn't want to have anything negative between them. In fact, the mere thought of placing a barrier between them made her snap her head back so their gazes met. What she seemed to crave at that moment was complete intimacy.

He sent her a pleased look. "I'm going to tease ye so yer insides are hot and ready for me."

His words made her bite her lower lip. And he kissed her hard. It was a hungry kiss, one that showed her just how controlled he'd been before. Now, he let her feel his hunger, and she reached for his head, pushing her fingers through his hair in an attempt to hold onto him.

"I don't think I can stand to be any hotter, Buchanan."

"Ye can, I swear it."

He didn't explain more, but nuzzled against her throat for a moment, teasing the delicate skin of her neck with kisses. Nothing mattered beyond experiencing the moment. She was floating, surrounded by sensations so enjoyable, there was no reason to think.

There was only reacting.

Buchanan pulled one taut nipple into his mouth. His fingers moved on her mons, toying with the hairs. The sensitive spot at the top of her sex that had been throbbing was now insistent with need.

He knew it. He sent his fingertip through the folds guarding the entrance to her body and found that spot. She cried out, arching up toward his hands without realizing why she was doing so. It was impossible to resist.

Her reward was pleasure.

Every stroke took her closer and closer to something she didn't understand. She was wet, making his fingers slide easily across her little nub. The pleasure traveled to her core, making her desperate for some form of release.

When it burst, she twisted with pleasure. It was blinding and threatened to carry her away. It was pulsing through her, ebbing, but still enough to keep her panting softly.

"That's it, lass, that's the reason I want to build the heat in ye," he whispered next to her ear. Then he smoothed her hair back from her face and placed a kiss against her temple before kissing her lips once more.

The yearning had subsided, but not completely. Deep inside, she was still hungry. Somehow, she understood he was what she needed to be fully satisfied. The knowledge was there in her mind, somewhere from a moment when an older woman had explained being a woman to her.

Now, though, thinking was something she wasn't even remotely interested in. She clung to her lover, needing to touch him, stroke him, and share the moment with him.

And she liked it that way.

Somehow, they had both become hot.

"I'm very wet now, Buchanan."

He lifted his head, the candlelight reflecting in his eyes. There was a look in them that made her shiver. It was primal and dangerous, and it thrilled her.

"Aye, ye are, lass..." He straightened his arms, pushing his upper body up and away from hers.

He settled back on his knees, his expression settling into one of male satisfaction.

"I like the sight of it," he whispered as he pressed her thighs wide. "The sight of ye aroused and eager for me."

He trailed his finger through the folds of her slit.

"Um…" She was suddenly feeling vulnerable.

He pressed her thighs wider.

"I want to see my woman," he said huskily. "I just swore that I will have none but ye…and I would have all of ye Rhedyn."

He caressed her opening, circling it before thrusting his finger inside her. She let out a little sound of delight as her eyelids began to feel heavy again.

"Are ye frightened, Rhedyn?" he asked softly. "We do nae have to go any further tonight."

"But…it's our wedding night," she said. Her mind wasn't on her words, but on the thick length of flesh standing up between his thighs.

"Aye, it is."

His jaw was tight with need. She could see frustration glittering in his eyes, but there was also something else. A determination to keep his word to her.

She slowly smiled, trust making her bold. "Ye have touched me…there."

He thrust his finger into her again. "Aye…"

"So, let me touch ye the same way."

His lips curled back from his teeth. It was a primal form of male enjoyment, one she found intoxicating to witness.

Had she truly affected him so deeply?

Apparently, she had. The knowledge gave her courage. She rolled up, reaching for his cock. He sucked in his breath as her fingertips brushed it. The skin was smooth as silk, but it was coated with a length of flesh that was hard. She drew her fingers from the tip, down to the base.

"Christ…" he muttered.

So, she had the power to reduce him to the same mindless state she'd been in.

She reached all the way forward so she could close her fingers around his staff. But he pulled her hand away a moment later.

"Forgive me, lass, but I do nae have the discipline to endure yer sweet touch."

"Will ye feel...good...as I did?"

One side of his mouth twitched. He pressed her back onto the surface of the bed. His breath teased her lips. "It will feel very good, lass. I can nae think of anything I want more than to have ye under me."

His cock was pressed against her opening. She shivered, caught between the desire to understand his words and the need to just sink back down into the swirling mist of sensation and yearning.

"But tonight, I need me cock to no' fail me before we finish the business at hand, for I would no' have it on yer mind."

Understanding didn't elude her. Consummating a marriage was serious business, for more than one bride had been branded barren when the truth was, her groom had never visited her bed.

It was business and yet, she felt anything but the cold detachment of getting a chore done.

No, ye're eager, like peering into a locked chest ye're finally old enough to know the contents of...

"Let us be married," she said.

He held her gaze for a moment.

A long moment stretched out. He was waiting on her, allowing her to make the final choice. The knowledge settled the last of her nerves, leaving her ready to embrace the woman she was ready to become.

"Come, husband, I would be yer wife in every way."

Pleasure lit his features in response. He smoothed his hands along the inside of her thighs. In the semidarkness, they were both shadow creatures, and it suited the moment. There was something very primal about it. He reached down and clasped his cock, rubbing the head of it through the center of her slit.

She gasped as it connected with the little bundle of nerves at the top of her slit. She covered her mouth with her hand to prevent any more sounds from escaping.

"I enjoy the sounds ye make," he said, gazing at her.

She might have replied, but he was distracting her by moving his cock up and down. Pleasure was rippling through her as need gnawed inside her. But she wasn't the only one caught in the grip of need. His face betrayed how much it cost him to hold back. His jaw was tight, his lips thin as he took a few more moments to stroke her.

She knew the moment he lost the battle.

She was more than wet enough to accommodate him, yet she felt the resistance as he pressed into her.

"Christ…" he growled.

He started to pull back, and she clamped her thighs around his hips. "More."

It was a demand. But she didn't regret it. No, she reached up and gripped his forearms.

"Do it," she encouraged him.

He caught the side of face, his fingers twisting in her hair. "Tell me ye are me wife."

"I married ye."

He pressed a hard kiss against her mouth as he moved his length back into her. This time, there was pain. Her body protested as he entered her. She lifted her hips, and he grunted as he sent his length deep into her. The pain was hot, searing her in those first few moments.

Yet, it didn't last. Buchanan began to move, unleashing a new yearning. She wanted to keep pace with him now. She raised her hips up to take every thrust, delighting in the sensation of having his flesh deep inside her. Somehow, she understood the method of seeking out satisfaction. She moved with him, striving toward some mutual goal.

It was an all-encompassing need, one she found held her captive.

When it all burst, the pleasure was so bright, she cried out with the sheer intensity of experiencing it. She twisted in its grip, her body shredding.

But she wasn't alone. Buchanan let out a growl, burying himself deep as he arched back, every muscle in his body tight. She was left gasping for breath as he rolled away from her. The sound of their deep breathing filled the chamber.

Sometime later, Buchanan rolled back toward her. He gathered her close. There was something very intimate about the way he pulled her into the curve of his body. A sense of contentment came with the contact. It was so serene, she drifted off to sleep, unwilling to ruin the moment by thinking.

Tomorrow would come soon enough, and she would have to face the reality of her choice.

≫≫≪≪

INNIS NORMALLY ENJOYED the good moments in life as they came.

It was a practical attitude for a girl in her position. But tonight, she sat at the long table in the kitchen without remembering that being allowed to get off her feet was a rare comfort. There were platters of sweet breads and cheese on the tables still. There was even part of the tart, which had been baked especially for the bridal couple, left over. Everything was made with spices and fruits to celebrate the wedding of the laird.

Innis should have been eating as much of it as she could, for tomorrow, there would only be common fare. Fenella was a strict mistress, but she did manage to make certain her girls had a taste of the dishes they worked hard to produce.

"The laird had to wed."

Innis jumped. Fenella emerged from the shadows, a knowing look in her eyes.

"Of course, mistress."

Fenella let out a snort. "And yet, ye sit here looking so forlorn. Girl, the laird was never going to belong to ye alone."

The Head-of-House reached over and sliced off a generous portion of the tart. She lifted it to her nose and inhaled its scent before she took a bite.

"Ye can nae be too pleased about it either," Innis remarked softly. She looked about, but the two boys who slept in the kitchen were both snoring. "That Lindsey might put ye out of yer position tomorrow."

Fenella took another bite of the tart before she replied. "Aye, she could at that. Which is why I am going to enjoy partaking of this feast while I might." Fenella finished off her slice of tart and looked over what else the table offered. "She is still in the laird's chamber, so the matter is done now. Worrying about me fate will no change it."

It was done. Innis's heart ached.

Fenella sliced off more of the sweet treat and dropped it onto a plate, which she slid in front of Innis.

"Enjoy it while ye may, girl. What will happen tomorrow will be upon us soon enough with the rising of the sun." Fenella winked at her. "Who knows? There might yet be a place for ye in the laird's affection. As soon as his wife breeds, well, she'll be back in the north tower."

Innis felt her mood brighten. Oh, yes. She hadn't thought about the matter like that. Buchanan was doing his duty. It didn't mean he liked his new wife.

No, it didn't mean that at all.

❯❯❯❮❮❮

THERE WAS A hard rap on the laird's chamber door at first light.

Rhedyn opened her eyes and felt a stab of pain go through her skull. The three goblets of wine she'd consumed the night before was taking its toll for certain. She groaned.

"Aye, that's the word for this morning," Buchanan grumbled.

Rhedyn jumped. The bed ropes groaned as she moved, and Buchanan chuckled at her surprise.

"Good morning to ye, wife," he said with a grin.

Whoever was on the other side of the door laid their fist on the wood panels again with more force.

"Enter!" Buchanan barked.

"Wait," Rhedyn protested.

The door was pushed in, and Graham was there, smiling wide enough to show off all of his missing teeth.

"A fine morning to ye both," he called out congenially. "Time to be out of bed."

"Ye'll wait." Shona appeared behind the captain. She turned and sent him a hard look before she was hurrying around to where a dressing robe was draped over the back of a chair. She shook it out with a snap.

"Up with ye, mistress." Shona held the robe open as there was the unmistakable sound of more steps on the floor outside the chamber door.

Even knowing there were others making ready to enter the chamber, it was still hard to force herself to slip out from beneath the bedding. Graham was looking at the ceiling, affording her the chance to make it to the robe. She quickly shoved her arms into it.

But everyone knew she was naked. And one glance at the bed showed the dark stain on the sheets. Buchanan had taken the opportunity to get up and put his shirt on. Graham didn't wait very long. Shona was just tying the sash on the robe when the captain came across the floor. The rest of Buchanan's captains were right on his heels. They tore the bedding all the way off and shook out the sheet.

"Here now." It was Fenella who raised her voice above their enjoyment. "Hang it already, and get out so the mistress can dress."

Buchanan added a grunt to her order. The men appeared to be astonished to discover everyone wasn't as gleeful as they were with the stained sheet.

"Now!" Buchanan instructed them.

They shuffled toward the window. Fenella opened the shutters, allowing the bright morning light in. A few moments later, the sheet was hanging out of the open window to the delight of those waiting in the courtyard. A cheer rose up.

Rhedyn was certain she was going to die right where she stood. There was an ache between her thighs, and everyone, absolutely everyone in the castle knew what she'd been about the night before.

Fenella started pushing them all toward the door. "Ye have had yer fun! Stop wasting the daylight!"

And she was intent on pushing Buchanan out of the chamber as well.

"It's my chamber," Buchanan protested.

Shona had already gathered up his clothing. She handed them off to the laird. "I believe yer bride has had her fill of men for the moment. Go on with ye."

Fenella shut the door in his startled face.

"There," the Head-of-House said as she nodded with satisfaction.

"It is his chamber," Rhedyn said in surprise. But a moment later, she was giggling. "The look on his face!"

Shona wore a smile as she began to lay out new garments for Rhedyn to put on. Fenella gathered up all of the wedding dress parts before she turned and faced Rhedyn. The tension in the chamber was suddenly high. A quick glance around made Rhedyn realize there were no other maids.

"I'm ready," Fenella spoke firmly. She stood in front of Rhedyn, her chin steady and her expression set. "Best to have this done now."

"Aye," Shona agreed. She'd taken up a position to one side, clearly there to serve as witness.

Rhedyn suddenly understood very well what the two women were expecting.

Appearances. Always maintain appearances.

Her mother had pressed that lesson deep into Rhedyn.

"I wronged ye," Fenella stated, her expression one of confidence. "Ye are the mistress now, and I'll make no excuses."

Rhedyn felt something inside her shift. Whatever she did at that moment, it would have a severe impact on more than just the people in the room. Once done, it could never be undone. She had to make a choice on how she would appear to the rest of the staff.

"I am newly arrived here," Rhedyn began. "Of course, ye know this well. I mention it because there is no true way for me to judge yer character since I have only just met you, Fenella. Perhaps ye might tell me how long ye have served here?"

Fenella's expression eased. The love she had for the Mackenzies was evident. "Me mother was a cook here. In those days, before the great hall was finished, there were three main kitchens. Me mother ran the north tower one."

Rhedyn didn't just hear the words. She noticed the stains on Fenella's apron. So early in the day and yet, the fabric already sported several marks. Fenella wasn't one to let her staff rise early and produce the morning fare while she enjoyed being at her leisure.

"The wedding celebration ye presented was very fine."

Fenella hadn't been expecting a compliment. She raised an eyebrow. "I'm pleased to hear it met with yer approval."

"Ye are a competent Head-of-House," Rhedyn continued. "I would be foolish to remove ye from the position."

Her words surprised Fenella and Shona. The two women shared a look as Rhedyn realized she'd also stunned herself. But she liked the feeling she gained for knowing she'd resisted the urge to strike out at someone, simply because circumstances had changed.

"As to the matter of discipline," Rhedyn addressed the subject directly.

Fenella's face tightened.

"It is the laird's rule that ye give no more than ten blows without his approval, correct?" Rhedyn fought the urge to retch as she remembered the sound of the rod sailing through the air.

"It is," Fenella confirmed.

"Best we all adhere to that standard henceforth."

There was silence. Fenella contemplated Rhedyn for a long moment. "Yer mother saw to yer education well."

"As did yer own," Rhedyn responded in kind. "A household this large will require all of our efforts to see it running smoothly."

"Well said," Shona spoke at last.

"I'll be getting back to the kitchens now, mistress." The Head-of-House inclined her head before she turned and left.

Rhedyn sat down to pull the stockings onto her feet. Her heart was racing, but the sense of accomplishment flowing through her made her smile.

"Ye should be pleased with yerself," Shona said once they were alone. "No' too many would have been kind to her while still wearing the bruises she gave ye."

Rhedyn looked at her forearms. The bruises were faded now. In fact, it was a marvel to realize just how far in the past her first few days with Buchanan felt. Time was truly a wondrous elixir. The memory of the meadow rose from her thoughts, overshadowing the time she'd spent in the storeroom above the kitchens. It did in fact appear that the future might be bright if she merely looked at the positive things around her instead of the negative.

Her mother would have called it prudent.

"She was grieving," Rhedyn remarked as she secured her garters. "She spoke up against Hamish for me. I think it better to remember that."

Could life truly be what she made of it? Rhedyn wasn't sure, but the morning light was suddenly warm and full of opportunities. She was eager to see what the day held.

Trusting yer captor?

The thought didn't give her pause. No, she ignored it as she continued dressing. And she refused to entertain any further doubts. The sheet was flapping outside the window–she'd made her choice.

Her husband.

So, she'd make the best of her marriage.

⟫⟫⟫⟪⟪⟪

HAMISH LET OUT a roar. He crumpled the paper in his hand and threw it away. "He wed that Lindsey bitch!"

"I am grateful I was no' there to witness it." Rory sat on the floor.

It was a rough cottage they'd taken refuge in. One side of the roof allowed the rain in, but the rest of it was sound enough. The remains of the last occupant had been just a pile of bones when they'd arrived, so there wouldn't be anyone protesting them living there.

None of the inns in the village had been willing to take them once word reached them of their Mackenzie colors being stripped away. But that didn't mean they didn't have friends. By midday, there were plenty of Mackenzies clustered inside the cottage. Their brooding filled Hamish with hope.

"They flew the sheet this morning," one man recounted. "Rumor is, the laird is going to go begging Laird Lindsey to settle accounts."

There was another round of grumbling.

"We need a strategy." Hamish held up his hand. "A plan."

The men looked to him. Hamish knew it was his chance to unseat Buchanan at last. Where bloodline had failed him, wit just might make the difference. In the Highlands, men followed the victor.

Hamish looked at the men. "I'm going to use that Lindsey bitch to put an end to Buchanan."

Smiles curved the lips of those watching. Hamish felt the challenge warming his blood. The chill in the air added fuel to his determination. Aye, Buchanan had made a fatal error in taking the woman to his bed. An error Hamish would be happy to use to his advantage.

＞≫≪≪

"ENOUGH OF YER sour mood, Innis." It was Orla who scolded her. The woman was second in charge of the kitchens. "Ye can go see to the chicken nests, and do nae come back inside until ye have stopped pouting."

The sun was a scarlet ribbon on the horizon when Innis stepped outside. She enjoyed the fresh air but was smarting over the scolding. It would always be her lot to suffer such reprimands unless she secured herself a man with a high position.

The chickens were settling down for the night. They had stone nesting blocks built up along one side of the inner wall. There was a low doorway and a narrow aisle to walk before another stone wall stood to protect the birds from the weather. A slanted roof was overhead. Inside, it was dark but warm and dry. The birds didn't like her searching their nests for eggs. They pecked at her, but she persevered because there would be more suffering in the morning if she failed to find any eggs. She carried the few she found back to the door to find that a Retainer had followed her.

"I've no time to dally," she told him firmly.

He didn't move out of her path. She stopped a few paces from him and propped her hand on her hip. "Ye heard me. Do nae get to scuffling with me. If these eggs are broken, Orla will be very cross with ye for causing waste."

The eggs were nestled in her apron, which she'd pulled up and tucked into her waistband to form a pouch.

The Retainer lifted his finger to his lips. "I'm here to deliver a letter. I am Egan."

He looked over his shoulder before he reached inside his doublet and pulled a small, folded parchment out. But he held it just out of her reach. "Hamish believes ye loyal to him. If ye are not, say it now. For if ye read this and betray him, I'll snap yer neck."

Loyal or not, she still reached for the letter. Information was the key to her future. The Retainer ducked beneath the entrance of the nesting area and disappeared.

With no light to read by, Innis tucked the note into her bodice and returned to the kitchens. Davina eyed her. She kept her chin lowered as she placed the eggs in a bowl on the long table used for turning bread. Then she went to scrub her hands. Davina lost interest in her, affording her the opportunity to sneak away.

She went down a passageway and looked both ways before pulling the letter out. It seemed as though it crinkled far too loudly when she opened it.

'Do whatever ye can to cause discontent between the laird and his bride. Loyalty will be rewarded.'

She read it twice before holding it near a flame. The paper caught fire quickly. Innis made sure the entire note was consumed and reduced to ashes before she began to contemplate her options.

Her hope flourished with the idea of having another chance. She might go straight away to Buchanan and tell him of Hamish's plan. But Buchanan might only thank her and offer naught else. He had never returned her advances.

Hamish, though… Well, he was a man who enjoyed women often. He would never be faithful to her, but so long as she gave him a son, it wouldn't matter.

Innis smiled, a new plan forming in her mind.

Chapter Six

"'T IS A FRIGHTFUL mess, and I'm ashamed to have ye see it," Fenella declared as she showed Rhedyn to where the estate account books were kept.

"Ye should not have been burdened with them," Rhedyn said as she followed her.

Fenella stepped inside the room. There were two long tables, one piled high with notes and letters. It looked unorganized until she looked closer and realized that sealed letters were sorted from the pages of accounts.

"Shona would bring young Cora here often to teach her the duties of the mistress of the house," Fenella said carefully. "Young Cora has other tutors as well."

"As it should be," Rhedyn said.

Fenella nodded approvingly. "I will be in the kitchens if ye need me, mistress."

And Rhedyn would be here for the better part of the next year by the look of the books and letters waiting to be answered. A large book was sitting on one of the tables. An ink well was nearby, along with a silver-tipped quill. This was the duty of Lady Mackenzie. Poor attention to the accounts might translate into shortages of essential food stuffs during the winter when the roads were piled high with snow and there was no possible way to get more. Shona was needed for other duties.

And the letters… Well, there was another important matter.

A lady's education included learning at least three languages. French, Latin, English, and in the Highlands, Gaelic. Rhedyn sat down, avoiding thinking about Cora for the moment. First, she needed to work through some of the piles of goods traded for rent.

"I suppose I should be slightly ashamed to have ye taking this over." Cora appeared in the doorway. "At least in its current state." She stared at Rhedyn, contemplating her.

"It was no' terrible," Rhedyn said. "Me wedding night."

Cora drew in a startled breath. But a moment later, she was looking over her shoulder, checking both directions before she came all the way into the chamber and firmly shut the door.

"And yer brother offered to take me home the night before."

Cora skidded to a halt. She blinked a couple of times before her lips curved up into a smile.

"So, stop arguing with him," Rhedyn instructed Cora.

"Taking ye was worthy of argument," Cora insisted. "He truly offered to take ye home?"

"Snuck into me chamber in the dark of night to do it."

"And left ye a maiden?"

"Yer brother is no' a villain."

Cora considered her for a long moment. "Nae, he is not. But do ye truly have faith in this union being a good one?"

"I know me duty. Just as ye understand yers. But it's important to remember that yer brother has a duty as well. Yer kin wanted me father's blood the day he took me. He managed to avoid giving it to them."

"He did," Cora remarked softly.

"And he has wed me now. I plan to give my marriage a good effort."

"Ye truly do nae wish to escape?"

"The time to do so was before yesterday," Rhedyn said. She felt a touch of guilt, for she was not being fully truthful. The brew Shona had delivered to her would make it possible to leave still.

But there was something surprising about it. Rhedyn discovered herself feeling free for the first time in her life. The future was hers to explore and decide upon.

Was she making a mockery of her wedding vows?

Perhaps.

But it seemed far more of a sin to bring a child into a marriage where there was hatred.

So, Buchanan is yer lover...

She supposed that was true enough. She wasn't going to think about the fact that she was a captive just ten days ago.

No, far better to center her attention on the way Buchanan had treated her last night.

Far, far, better.

➤➤➤◄◄◄

"THIS WAY, MISTRESS."

Rhedyn recognized the maid. "Innis?"

The girl lowered herself. "I'll escort ye to the north tower. Yer chamber is ready."

Rhedyn felt her belly knot. The happiness she had carried around all day disappeared.

Innis was already leading the way. Not a hint of concern for taking Rhedyn away from her new husband.

The north tower.

She drew in a stiff breath. Pain was slicing through her, threatening to crush her composure. She hurried to catch up with the maid before the despair swallowed her up.

"Ye missed supper, so I brought ye some," Innis spoke kindly before she lowered herself and left the chamber.

There were candles lit, but Rhedyn felt like it was icy cold in the room. The chill came from inside her.

It wasn't an uncommon arrangement.

No, in fact, to have shared the laird's chamber would have been a deviation from the normal living conditions she'd been raised to expect.

Suddenly drinking the morning brew seemed very shortsighted, for without a child, she might have just condemned herself to a lifetime of loneliness.

Ye made yer choice…

She had, but freedom suddenly didn't seem so very promising.

She drew in another deep breath and forced herself to walk toward the table where her supper waited. Innis had laid the table with fine ware. A covered dish held a warm stew that was thick and likely tasty. Beneath a clean cloth, there was fresh bread. There was even some cheese to complete the meal.

A fine supper. She could find no fault with it.

The stinging in her eyes frustrated her. Was she accepting the situation so easily? Was she going to cry while the memory of her wedding night was so very fresh in her mind?

Truthfully, she should have been counting her blessings for having such a fine memory of her wedding night. Rhedyn wasn't an innocent. In spite of how her father had given orders that she be guarded against hearing the harsher side of life, there had still been times when she'd been in the kitchens and the maids had thought themselves alone and spoke freely.

More than one bride had been thrown out of her new husband's bed less than an hour after she'd been escorted into it. She should be grateful Buchanan had arrived sober instead of so deep in his cups that he'd have cheerfully deflowered her while his captains watched.

Rhedyn knew all of it. Those ugly details of the life of a mistress of a stronghold such as the Mackenzie one. Wed with purpose in mind, not affection.

Yet, there had been warmth in their bed the night before. She had not imagined it.

Logic was failing to hold back her misery. The chamber was lonely and silent compared to the way her husband had so tenderly introduced her to passion.

All she felt was the emptiness around her.

"Why are ye here, Rhedyn?"

Perhaps because she'd been so deep in thought about him, Buchanan had appeared.

He closed the door. It hit hard, jolting her. She drew in a startled breath.

"Ye're real," she muttered.

He crossed his arms over his chest and tilted his head to one side. "Have ye been drinking?"

Rhedyn shook her head. "I was thinking."

He nodded. "Ah...thinking...good. Since that's the case, ye can tell me what ye are doing here? Did ye forget where me chamber was?"

It took a moment for her mind to grasp the meaning of his words. His expression tightened as the silence stretched out between them. But he looked past her at the supper waiting on the table.

"Perhaps I should have made things clear between us last night," he informed her in a low tone. "I expect ye to share me chamber."

"Ye do?" She bit her lower lip.

"I do." There was a firm edge of authority in his voice. "So, ye will not be instructing the staff to set yer supper here again."

She didn't know what to say. She was afraid that if she spoke, she'd shatter the image of him standing there.

"Do ye really want to live apart?" Buchanan demanded in frustration. "Ye prefer it here? Was last night so terrible?"

"No." She jumped. "I just...did not think ye'd want me...in yer chamber every night."

His expression eased. He drew in a breath before moving toward her. "I suppose it's fair enough of ye to think I would no' want ye near." He nodded. "That's my fault. I have no' courted ye."

"Courted?" Rhedyn asked in astonishment. "I certainly did not expect such."

"Rolfe Munro courted ye."

She looked at Buchanan, wondering if what she heard in his voice was actual jealousy. "What does it matter if he did?"

"I see, lass."

"Ye see...what precisely?" Something flashed in his eyes. It was a warning, but the reaction she had to it wasn't one of foreboding.

No, a little tingle of anticipation went down her spine.

"I see ye would like to be impressed, lass." He closed the distance between them.

His intense stare made her back away. "And just how do ye plan to do that?"

He paused before taking another step toward her. "I've a few ideas."

He reached out and caressed her lips. The contact was jarring, making her gasp as his lips curled up into a smug grin.

"Ideas that make me happy to be in the north tower, far away from the rest of me kin."

"What do ye mean?" Her voice came out breathless.

Buchanan slid his hand up and across one side of her face, sending little ripples of sensation across her skin. He kept going until he'd threaded his hands into her hair. Stepping closer, he began to pull the pins from her tresses.

She shuddered as her hair was released. There was something very intimate about it.

"I never held any affection for linen caps on lasses until now," he said as he combed his fingers through her tresses. He leaned down so that his breath hit the delicate surface of her lips. "I want ye to hide this from every other man. Keeping it for me, and the moments when I can take it down for ye."

He captured the gasp that escaped her with his mouth as he pressed a kiss against her lips. It was a hard kiss, one that stirred that need which had driven her half mad the night before. She knew it now, understood the intensity of the impulse. The knowledge seemed to have the effect of making her impatient for her yearning to be soothed. She reached for his clothing, pulling at his doublet and pushing it down his arms.

The garment hit the floor as he twisted to pull his arms free and renew his hold on her. They were moving around one another, their mouths still fused as they tried to satisfy their cravings. Clothing was something neither of them were willing to tolerate. Stripping it away was essential.

"I can nae wait," he rasped against her lips.

"Do not!" she encouraged him. Having almost been denied his touch, she was frantic to indulge now that it was hers to take.

She gasped as he cupped her hips while moving up behind her.

He chuckled. "There is one of those sounds I want to keep all to meself, lass." He bent her over the footboard, rubbing her back and all the way down to her bottom. "I want to make ye scream."

She'd flattened her hands on the surface of the bed. He drew his hands over her hips and across her belly to her mons. He threaded through the curls before pressing a fingertip between the folds that guarded her clitoris while his body was flush with her back.

"There is yer little pearl," he whispered next to her ear. "Ye enjoyed having it toyed with last night."

Tonight was no different, but her cheeks burned as she heard him say such a thing out loud. "Ye should no'…"

He pressed down, sending a surge of intense pleasure through her belly.

"Touch ye here?" he finished for her.

She was shaking and grateful for the bed to press her hands against because her knees felt weak. He was rubbing harder across her pearl, intensifying the need burning inside her.

"Ye shouldn't speak of such things," she said.

"How else will I know what ye like, wife?"

She was nearing that point again, the one which would end with a burst of pleasure. She could feel everything tightening inside her, her hips thrusting forward to add more pressure. He pressed his lips against the column of her neck as she began to peak, nipping her delicate skin.

She cried out as everything burst. Buchanan gripped her hips, holding her as she drew in deep breaths.

"It is shameless," she rasped as she straightened up.

"Ye are me wife." His hands rested on her shoulders for a moment. "I am the only man ye might indulge in such brazenness with."

"But…"

He cupped her breasts.

"Is it wrong?" he asked earnestly. "Wrong to enjoy touching ye, lass? I have pledged to be faithful to ye for the rest of me life. And ye would label it shameless?"

He scooped her up and carried her to the bed.

He looked at her, waiting for her to finish. When she bit her lip, he flattened his hands on either side of her, crawling up the mattress.

"Well, lass?"

She lifted her hands, touching his face. Somehow, she'd never thought very much beyond the rights her husband had over her body, but now, she was enticed by being able to initiate the contact she craved.

"Rhedyn?"

She pressed her fingertip over his lips. "Shh. I am thinking about what I would like to do to you."

He growled, and it filled her with desire. She pushed him until he rolled onto his back so she might be the one on top. Then she boldly straddled him. She'd never contemplated exciting him on purpose.

He must have read her thoughts. "Put yer hands on me, Rhedyn. I belong to ye every bit as much as ye do to me."

The idea was magical, like falling into the world of the fae. Where joy and pleasure were the only pursuits and concocting dreams was the purpose of life.

She played with the coarse hair on his chest as she kissed her way to his jaw. As she leaned up to kiss his mouth, her breast made contact with his skin. Being naked together felt so natural, so essential.

He sighed and suddenly rolled her onto her back, his kiss growing demanding as he settled between her thighs. As he pressed his length inside her, she hugged him tight with her thighs. She didn't care about anything else. She'd discovered true joy. She'd found her lover.

⟫⟫⟩⟨⟨⟪⟪

RHEDYN'S BREATH WAS slow and even. She'd fallen asleep with the candlelight illuminating her breasts. He contemplated her for a long time, not wanting to wake her. There was a sense of peace settling over him as he listened to her breathing.

But he wanted her closer.

His few partners had been meetings in dark alcoves and a hay stack or two, but he'd never brought them back to his chamber.

The gossip would have linked them together forever if he had. But he'd woken more than once and longed to have someone else there in the cold hours of the night.

And he would never allow her to sleep apart from him.

His temper stirred. Hearing that she'd gone to the north tower had enraged him. Half his captains had seen him charging off to confront her. He didn't care.

He eased the bedding over her as the night grew colder. She nestled against his side, their legs tangling as he caught the scent of her hair. It stirred something inside him, quelling a thirst he hadn't realized he suffered from. Everything he thought he knew about marriage didn't seem to fit the situation he found himself in. He wasn't trying to just do his duty.

In truth, getting back to his bride was distracting him from every other duty he had.

His mind had returned again and again to the unforgettable night they'd spent together. Buchanan tightened his arms around her. She shifted, making him smile as she snuggled closer.

Would she do the same while awake?

It was a good question. One he needed to get an answer to. Rhedyn had made the best of her circumstances, but if he wanted more from her, well, he'd have to cultivate it.

A surge of determination went through him. It burned through the last of the frustration lingering in his mind at having found Rhedyn in the north tower. He would woo her and make her long to be beside him.

⇶⬿

"I WILL SEE ye tonight, wife."

Rhedyn muttered something in answer. She looked toward the window and confirmed it was barely daybreak, but she was still half asleep.

Buchanan chuckled and tucked the bedding up to her chin. "Ye can go back to sleep, lass. But ye'll remember me words."

There was a firm note of authority in his tone. It stroked something inside her as the warmth in the bedding lured her back to sleep. A sense of security she hadn't felt before in the Mackenzie strong-hold. Did it make sense? She had no idea, because it was a feeling, not something she had thought out.

Buchanan seemed to have that effect on her. He made her aware of things she'd never knew she had inside her before meeting him.

Later, she'd think about why she suddenly felt at ease.

Or maybe she wouldn't, for she liked the of not finding a reason to change her mind. Wasn't that the way of lovers?

It was indeed.

>>>«<<<

THE LAIRD HAD gone to the north tower for his bride.

The kitchen was always a place where everyone's personal details were discussed. Innis didn't have to do anything but listen.

Today, she bit her lip to keep from making a comment.

"What do ye expect?" Orla asked with a wicked smile. "He's got the blessing of the kirk to bed her. Our laird has no mistress, why would he ignore the woman he's allowed to sleep with?"

The other maids giggled.

"All the better to see if she's barren," Davina joined in the conversation while Fenella was out in the hall seeing to the setting of the high table. "Since she is his enemy's daughter, he can plow her fields and see if his seed takes. If it doesn't, he can send her back to her father."

Of course!

There was another round of laughter. One Innis joined in with before she was looking back at her work.

Barren. If the new Mistress failed to conceive, the marriage could be annulled.

Well, there were ways of ensuring the new mistress failed in her primary duty. Ways Innis knew well. She suddenly recalled the letter. Hamish appreciated her. It wasn't about choosing a side yet. She could make certain the mistress didn't conceive without really choosing Hamish over Buchanan.

A perfect solution.

She held tight to that knowledge. It made up for the restless nights she'd spent tossing and turning as the idea of knowing Buchanan was wed burned in her mind.

He had to be hers.

She had nothing else.

Perhaps she had no right to be so jealous, but logic was poor company in the dark hours of the night while she lay in a room with six other maids and consoled herself with just how lucky she was to have a roof over her head.

But with the new idea firmly in her mind, she found renewed hope brightening her outlook for the future.

She looked both ways before venturing into the stillroom later that day. There was a sharp scent in the air from all the dried herbs. A large table was in the center of the room, its surface worn and marked from decades of use. Along the far wall, there were over a hundred small drawers. Each one held different medicinal substances.

"Ye think ye looked around well enough," Fenella said from behind her.

Innis spun around.

Fenella propped her hands on her hips. "Ye do nae belong in here, girl, and ye know it well."

"I came in for both of us."

Fenella raised her eyebrows and stepped inside. "Is that so? Explain yer thinking, girl."

"We do nae have to suffer with the Lindsey girl as mistress forever."

Fenella shook her head. "The wedding sheets have been flown."

"The laird can have her," Innis insisted. "But if we fix the matter...so she does nae conceive... she can be sent back to her father."

Understanding brightened Fenella's face.

Innis smiled and continued. "All we need to do is make certain she is dosed every morning." Innis turned and pulled one of the drawers open, motioning for Fenella to come closer.

"And if her belly doesn't round, the laird will have to annul the marriage?" Fenella finished for Innis.

"Aye." Innis beamed at Fenella.

The Head-of-House only shook her head. "He'll never wed ye."

She waved her hands in front of her. "I don't dare to reach so high. But I might be his mistress."

"There would still be a wife, so what does it matter who that wife is?" Fenella asked. "This one is even tempered enough."

"It matters because Iain died at the hands of her father." Innis suddenly sniffled. "Iain was a fine man. Yer son died with him because of the Lindsey."

"They were both young," Fenella spoke quietly. "Young enough to be led too easily by their ambitions."

The stillroom echoed the soft sounds of grief for a moment. Fenella recovered first, raising one corner of her apron up to dab at her eyes before she let the fabric flutter back down. "Go on with ye, Innis," she ordered. "If anyone sees ye here, they will know something foul is being plotted. I will see to the mistress."

Innis grinned, feeling more confident than she had since hearing the news of the impending wedding. She hurried forward, clasping her arms around Fenella in a firm embrace. Fenella patted her on the back a single time before she was pushing her toward the door. Innis went quickly, checking before she emerged to make sure no one was watching.

Let the laird put the saddle on the Lindsey girl, a ride would be all he'd get.

⋙✦⋘

"THE HEAD-OF-HOUSE WOULD see ye, Laird."

Buchanan looked up as Muir announced Fenella. He felt the muscles along his back tighten. There was only one reason he could think of for her to be seeking him out, and it wasn't a good one. Muir raised his eyebrows and shot him a look which confirmed his man was thinking the same thing. Fenella had beaten Rhedyn, so it wasn't far-fetched to think that his wife would want to dismiss her.

"Show her in," Buchanan said.

She came in and lowered herself.

"Rise, Fenella," Buchanan said. "How may I help ye?"

Honestly, Buchanan had no idea what he was going to do if the two women couldn't get along. He could hardly blame his bride for not wanting to work with the woman who had abused her, but Fenella had served the Mackenzies her entire life. Clearly, his hope the two women would resolve their issues was in vain.

"I've come to talk to ye about the new mistress."

Muir rolled his eyes from where he stood behind the Head-of-House.

"Wait." Buchanan held up his hand before Fenella began. "I believe me wife should be here."

"Yer wife has already dismissed my concerns, Laird. It's why I am here."

Buchanan felt a pain stabbing through his skull. He'd never been one to reach for whiskey before the sun went down, but he suddenly understood why his father had kept a bottle behind his desk. Being laird was taxing in the extreme.

"All the more reason for her to be here where the matter can be firmly decided upon."

Fenella closed her mouth and nodded. Muir reached up and pulled on the corner of his cap. "Come wait outside, mistress, while we get the lady."

"She is tending to the books," Fenella informed them. "I just spoke with her."

Whiskey...

Buchanan took a moment to stand once Fenella was outside his office. He cracked his neck as he paced across the length of the room and back. He'd rather face an enemy bare handed than deal with some of the matters which he had to face across the laird's desk. Diplomacy was something a man couldn't measure in simple right or wrong. Success lay in the murky details.

Muir rapped on the door before he pushed it open. Rhedyn came forward. She offered her husband a polished reverence before she cast a questioning look toward him.

"Now," Buchanan began as he sat back down. "Fenella has some matter to discuss."

Rhedyn's eyebrows lowered. "And I have made it clear what I think on the matter."

"Rhedyn," Buchanan said. "Let us discuss the matter."

"There is naught to discuss," she said firmly. "This is my home now."

Muir looked up at the ceiling and sighed behind the two women.

"Is there truly no way to reconcile? Fenella has served here for decades. I know she treated ye poorly, but surely the pair of ye are no' so inexperienced in life that I must impress upon ye the merits of forgiveness?"

Rhedyn's expression changed, so did Fenella's.

"My laird," his Head-of-House said. "The lady has graciously forgiven me."

"I did not dismiss her!" Rhedyn spoke at the same time.

Muir was looking between them, and Buchanan discovered himself leaning forward to do the same.

"Then what is the matter ye wish to discuss?" he asked Fenella.

"It is naught," Rhedyn declared.

"I disagree," Fenella persisted.

The two women faced off as Buchanan looked toward Muir, attempting to discover just why he didn't have an inkling as to what was happening.

"I have heard rumblings which disturb me," Fenella said.

Buchanan felt a tingle in his nape. "What has happened?"

Fenella looked at him. "There are some among our kin who wish yer marriage to end badly."

"One maid sneaking into the stillroom is no cause to worry," Rhedyn insisted.

Buchanan shoved his chair back and stood abruptly. "Who tried to poison me wife?"

"The girl's intent was to make sure yer bride does nae conceive," Fenella explained. "And yes, such a thing is possible. If the right number of herbs are taken each morning. But it is a delicate balance, Laird. Otherwise, it is indeed poison."

"The name?" Buchanan demanded.

"Young Innis," Fenella answered. "But I worry there is more to the matter, hence I advise ye to wait and watch the girl. She has it in her mind to be yer mistress and gain a position for herself."

"Aye, she's approached me." Buchanan nodded. "I've made it clear I will not be taking her as such."

"She's young and looking for escape from harsh circumstances," Fenella added. "I fear she might be taking orders from Hamish."

Buchanan tightened his fingers into a fist. "What proof do ye have?"

"Rumblings," Fenella answered. "And half-seen meetings in the dark. Naught which might be used against anyone."

"Which is why I told her it is nothing to be concerned about," Rhedyn interrupted. Even if she did understand that anyone sneaking into the still room as very suspicious. All of the stronghold's herbs and precious medicines were stored there. The only reason to sneak into it were to steal or poison. One of the keys on Fenella's belt was for a lock on that door. It would be secured every night. Any maid under her direction would know the penalty for going in without permission.

"I know this stronghold, Mistress," Fenella declared. "Ye have treated me far better than I deserve, and I am no' blind to it. I also know the Mackenzies. Ye have no' been here. Iain was popular and had a way of making those listening to him believe he could smooth out the path in front of them. Many of us know life is never so simple. But I worry that some might be listening to Hamish and be willing to do ye harm. I cannot repay yer kindness in forgiving me by keeping silent when the matter is something I know in me heart there is reason to worry about."

Fenella looked at Buchanan. "I have no more evidence to offer than a single maid who snuck into the still room. But I know the passageways of this stronghold. There are rumors. As for Innis, well, the girl seemed intent on making certain the mistress was sent back to her father. Now, it's possible the girl acted on her own, but I allowed her to believe I would see to the doing of it."

"I'm grateful to ye, Fenella," Buchanan said. "It is no' an easy thing to suspect our own kin of a crime."

Fenella nodded and turned to leave. Rhedyn began to follow.

"Rhedyn, stay."

Muir opened the door for the Head-of-House and followed her out. Rhedyn turned on him.

⋙⋘

"I AM NO' helpless," Rhedyn said. "And Shona is very watchful of my meals."

Buchanan stood in front of the table, his arms crossed over his chest, appearing unyielding.

"I dealt with Hamish in the barn rather well," she continued.

"By nearly getting murdered?"

There was a glint in his eyes which warned her he was struggling to control his temper.

"I just got my freedom back," she said.

Buchanan's expression softened as he heard the concern in her voice. He came forward, reaching out to cup her elbows.

"I would no' have ye feeling imprisoned here, lass."

"Precisely why I told Fenella not to talk to ye," Rhedyn said. "It is only one maid."

Buchanan's hands slipped up to her forearms and held her firmly. "Hamish didn't give ye any warning before he tried to kill ye. That is a man's way."

She shivered.

"I felt that, lass." He pulled her closer.

She wiggled in his arms.

"Be still, Rhedyn," he implored. "Do ye really no' care for me embrace?"

"It's no' that."

He tucked her head beneath his chin and stroked her back. "I feel as though ye strip away everything from me as well, lass. The only way I've found peace with it is knowing I do the same to ye."

She relaxed then. It was the truth; she was at ease in his arms.

She shouldn't be.

That was the single thought needling her. They knew so little about one another and yet, it seemed her life was somehow complete now that she was with him.

"Muir will be keeping an eye on ye."

Rhedyn flattened her hands on his chest and shoved away from him. Buchanan released her, but the expression on his face was unchanged when she faced off with him.

"At least for a time," Buchanan continued. "We'll give me kin a chance to get to know ye. Ye've got a good deed to add credit to yer name now that ye have kept Fenella."

"I didn't keep her to make meself look good."

Buchanan tilted his head to one side. "Why did ye keep her? It's the truth I was grateful the decision didn't fall on me own shoulders, for I have no liking for the way she abused ye. But I could not dismiss me own failing, which led to the matter happening. Punishing her would have been shirking the blame for me own shortcomings."

The admission surprised her.

"Ye should no look so astonished, lass," he said. "Is it so difficult to see me as someone who will treat ye kindly?"

"I'm surprised ye are explaining yerself to me. Ye are me husband. I am bound to obey."

Why did she speak so freely with him? Even with her father, she'd have been careful how she worded her comment in his solar. This was the place where her husband was the laird of the Mackenzie clan. She took a quick look behind her to make certain Muir was still on the other side of the closed door.

"I suppose I have given ye little reason to trust me."

"I would disagree," she said. She bit her lip, once again appalled by her own words. The action didn't go unnoticed by Buchanan. He chuckled.

"I enjoy knowing I inspire impulses from ye."

She scoffed at him. "No man enjoys a wife who doesn't mind her tongue."

He moved closer to her. "In private, I encourage ye to speak yer mind. We each have our place in this marriage, lass."

He lifted her chin, leaning down to press a kiss against her mouth. Heat stirred inside her as she smiled and started to walk away from him.

His lips slowly curled up as he gazed at her face and reached out to catch a handful of her skirt. He pulled her back against him.

"I'm going to kiss ye until ye are breathless, lass."

He made good on his threat. All she managed to do was realize just how much she enjoyed having her hands on him. Her fingertips were pressed to the hard muscle covering his chest, making her regret the layers of clothing between them. She pressed her fingertips through the opening in his shirt, near his collar bones.

"Do nae be shy," he whispered against her throat. "Bare me."

He was too much temptation to ignore. She found the end of the tie that kept his shirt closed at the neck and pulled on it.

"Now touch me," he encouraged.

His hands were threaded into her hair, dislodging the pins she'd used to put it up. She knew what he would do... He would kiss the side of her neck, sending ripples of excitement down her spine before lifting his head and looking at her hair. One hair pin would be plucked and then he'd press his mouth to her skin once more. The knot of her hair was growing heavy, starting to drop.

She drew her hands down to the buttons on his doublet, her fingers fumbling with them because she was trembling. But she managed, finally pushing the sides wide.

"Aye, that's the way, lass."

He buried his face in her hair as he drew in a deep breath.

Her head was pressed against his chest, filling her senses with the scent of his skin. Without a doubt, it was intoxicating, and she wanted more.

More intensity.

More brazenness.

Submission was suddenly not enough for her. The yearning inside her craved something far more aggressive. She wanted to take him. Push him to the same extremes he'd done to her.

"Christ Almighty!" Buchanan lifted his head as she closed her hands around his length.

She looked up, wanting to see his face as she boldly grasped his cock. "I did like it when ye touched me on me sex. Do ye like it?"

His length was hard.

"Aye," he growled in response.

The husky tone encouraged her. It was strangely erotic, introducing her to an entirely new sensation. One she'd heard rumors about when her father's kitchen staff hadn't thought she was around.

Women spoke in hushed, excited whispers of the ways they kept their lovers returning to them time and again.

She pulled her hand up his length and smiled as his breath caught.

"Shall I milk ye, then?" she asked softly.

"Who taught ye such a thing?" His voice quavered.

Never had she imagined to reduce him or any man to such a state. Her confidence swelled as she repeated her motions.

"From the maids...when they thought I was gone to bed," she answered as she made it to the tip of his member. There was a drop of fluid on it.

"Somehow, I do nae think ye learned...what ye....did to me....by just...listening..."

Buchanan clasped his fingers around her nape. His hold was firm, just shy of painful. She froze, wondering if she'd gone too far.

"Stroke me," he implored.

His words were almost more of a sound than words. But she understood the language. It was part instinct, part yearning. She was moving her hand back down to the base of his member as she watched his eyes glitter. The sight set off an intense need to push him toward the edge of his limits as he'd done with her.

She moved her hand faster.

His breath became hard and heavy, but he maintained eye contact with her, sharing the moment. At the top of her sex, her pearl was heating, becoming a live coal that felt as though it were red hot. Then he grunted and covered her hand with his own.

He was at the edge...

"I'm going to have ye now," he said. "Here."

He tugged her to him, lifting her off her feet as he turned her around and sat her on the edge of his desk. She had no care for where the ink well was, for there was nothing in her thoughts except him. The need was raging like a fire on a dry, thatch roof. The flames eagerly consuming everything.

"Take me," she encouraged him. "I will have ye, too."

He pushed her skirts up and pressed her thighs wide. "Aye, ye will Rhedyn." He cupped her chin as he fit the head of his cock against her wet folds. "Do nae ever plan to leave me."

There was a warning in his tone, one he enunciated with a firm thrust. His cock slid inside her, making her gasp in pleasure. Somehow, she'd never realized how much sensation her body was capable of feeling. Now she knew. It was being revealed to her in every powerful stroke. Each thrust made her gasp as the pleasure built. Deep inside her, it felt like a knot was tightening. She lifted her hips, moving toward his thrusts in a quest for fulfilment.

They both craved their reward, straining toward one another, working at a furious pace until satisfaction burst within them. He caught her cry of rapture with his mouth as he thrust deeply and delivered his seed. It filled her body, searing her insides as a deeper tremor went through her.

She'd have collapsed onto the desk if he didn't hold her up. He stroked her back, running his hands down her spine. Sweat coated her skin, and her legs quivered as though she'd been running.

He held her for what seemed an eternity. With her head pressed to his chest, all she heard was his heartbeat.

She didn't need anything else.

〉〉〉《《《

MUIR WAS WAITING outside the door of the chamber where the books were kept when Rhedyn went to seek out supper.

"Evening, mistress." He reached up and tugged on the corner of his cap. "Supper?" he asked hopefully.

Muir was a burly Retainer. His arms were thick with muscle from training with a sword. He'd never looked at her unkindly before but now, there was a slight curve to his lips.

Well, ye are no longer a prisoner.

Yet, she still had a guard. Muir trailed her to the hall. He followed her to the high table and even pulled out the chair for her. The moment she was seated, he hurried to one of the lower tables and sat down with a grin.

Rhedyn looked toward her husband.

"The matter has been discussed and decided upon wife," Buchanan said before she'd opened her mouth. A challenge was glittering in his eyes as he met her gaze. "Yet, I will be happy to retire if ye would like to discuss it again."

A blush heated her cheeks.

But that wasn't the only place warmth teased her flesh. The look of determination in his eyes begged for a retort.

"In truth," she muttered in a near whisper, "I might have confessed just how little I care to sit here, rather than retire, with ye…."

Buchanan leaned toward her to catch her words. She watched his expression change as he considered what she had said.

"But Muir would be deprived of his supper," Rhedyn continued. "I wouldn't want such a sin resting on my conscience."

Buchanan's eyes narrowed. He suddenly pushed his chair back. The heavy piece of furniture made a harsh sound as it skidded.

"Muir!"

Buchanan's voice bounced down the great hall, silencing nearly everyone.

"Me wife craves my attention. Good night."

Muir had a piece of bread in his mouth. He lifted his head and sent Buchanan a huge smile. Buchanan reached down and grasped the back of her chair, pulling it back with her still sitting in it.

God, the man was strong!

Her heart raced as he pulled her out one of the side entrances of the great hall. Behind them, amusement erupted, making her cheeks sting with embarrassment.

By the time they reached his chamber, it felt like her blood was speeding through her veins. She was so warm, her clothing bothered her.

"Do nae begrudge me teasing ye, lass."

Buchanan had turned her loose into his chamber. He took up a position in front of the door. The look on his face gave her a moment of pause, for there was a need there, one which wasn't centered on passion.

No, he was waiting to see what she made of his behavior. He was watching her. Intent on her. She felt her eyelashes fluttering, a strange sense of shyness enveloping her. But her lips were twitching up into a little smile as she shifted back across the length of the chamber.

His chamber.

She recalled it and yet, the scent of the room suddenly struck her as being his. She reached up and drew the linen cap she'd worn off her head.

"Aye," he muttered approvingly, stepping toward her.

Rhedyn dropped the cap on a table and held up a single finger. Buchanan froze, waiting on her command. It filled her with confidence and made her breathless. She began to draw the pins from her hair as he watched. His expression tightened as she freed the entire mass and used her fingers to comb it all.

"More," he said.

His tone was edged with authority, but it suited his nature. She turned her back on him, peeking over her shoulder.

His lips rose into a grin at her response. The circumstances of her arrival meant there were only a few garments available for her to wear. They were more common than the dresses she'd had at home and laced up the front.

Tonight, she enjoyed the simplicity of her wardrobe, pulling the lace free on her bodice. Her breasts relaxed as she let the bodice slip down her arms. Her skirts were dropped quickly, too.

But Buchanan scooped her up before she'd stepped out of the puddle they made around her ankles. She gasped, never having heard him approach.

"I want to carry ye to me bed. And place ye there….and make ye enjoy being in it so much, ye will never be content to sleep anywhere else."

She was eager to test his words. The bed was a strange, unexpected haven. A place where she met a companion she'd never expected to find in life. Together, they were suddenly a force that felt invincible when pitted against the endless challenges of life.

Was that whimsy?

She didn't know.

And what was more, she didn't care. All that mattered was reaching for the man intent on proving himself to her. The result was stunning. It was glorious, filling her with a sense of contentment which lasted far past when passion had ebbed.

Long into the dark hours of the night, he held her close. Intimacy gained a new meaning for her as she felt the way he curved around her, unwilling to let her go.

⟫⟫⟪⟪

HAMISH CRUMPLED A letter as his men watched him. He threw it into the fire before looking back at them. The demanding looks on their face restored his confidence. He was their leader. Something he'd always craved.

"That Lindsey bitch has enchanted the laird," Hamish declared.

There was growling in response.

"She'll taint the bloodline of the Mackenzie if we allow the matter to go unchecked," he continued.

There were nods of agreement.

"What is yer plan?" Arlo asked. "I've no liking for the girl."

Hamish nodded. "We'll use her to lure Buchanan out of the stronghold where I can challenge him."

The words had been inside him, unspoken for a long time. Hamish felt like he'd crossed a bridge at last, one he'd been told he could never tread upon for so long.

He realized he'd craved it more than anything else.

"I would have followed Iain, with loyalty," he raised his voice so the other men might hear. "Now that he is slain, I must step up and ensure the Lindsey do nae go unpunished. Buchanan has betrayed his own brother. He isn't fit to be laird of the Mackenzies!"

CHAPTER SEVEN

TIME WASN'T WAITING for anyone.

Least of all, Rhedyn.

The days began to fly as the summer heat arrived. There was ample work for everyone, but the books stubbornly persisted in occupying her every moment.

Still, it was her duty.

When her monthly courses arrived, she suddenly found herself being the source of gossip once again. Bearing children for her husband had, of course, been something she'd been taught was of the upmost importance.

Somehow, she'd hadn't really realized how dire her circumstances might be if she failed in accomplishing the duty quickly.

She'd been lulled into a sense of security. It was shattered as news of her monthly flow made its way throughout the stronghold. By noon, she was being cast looks of disapproval. Venturing into the hall for the midday meal felt very much like the first time she'd appeared there as a captive.

So, she hurried back to her books, happy to have something which didn't glare at her.

"Do nae allow them to trouble ye," Shona appeared in the doorway of the chamber.

Rhedyn looked up from the pages she was attempting to decipher. A list of goods sold at the local market was scratched out on the parchment, but it had clearly rained that day and water marks made it nearly impossible to read.

Shona placed a plate on the side of the table. "Ye ate nearly naught."

"I didn't think that there would be such a reaction to not conceiving the very first month I am here." Rhedyn reached for the plate, but once she'd moved the cloth covering the food, she realized her belly was tied in knots.

"Being the mistress, the staff feels they have the right to know every last detail of yer personal business," Shona said. "Surely things are not so different on Lindsey land?"

Rhedyn let out a sigh. "The truth is, as a daughter, I was shielded from much of the ugliness."

"Ah...." Shona said. "Kept ignorant so ye will no' make trouble when it comes time to wed the man yer father picked out for ye."

It was the fate of most daughters, and the tone of Shona's voice made it plain the girl considered it something that simply was unavoidable.

Reality was full of sharp edges.

There was a gleam in Shona's eyes. It was both a warning and a look of approval. Rhedyn drew in a deep breath.

She'd face the challenges.

Somehow, she'd dredge up the strength.

Oh? And what about Buchanan? What if he is as disappointed as his kin?

She wanted to shake off the thought. It was gloomy, indeed, and on the heels of such a wonderful two weeks with Buchanan near her, the thought made her eyes sting with unshed tears.

Tears?

Rhedyn was horrified by the idea of crying for no reason.

Yet, she had a reason. Disappointing the staff, well, that was something she could make peace with. But she realized that her heart ached to think of Buchanan being disappointed in her not conceiving.

Would he put her out?

She hated the thought. Looking back down at her work, she tried to force the idea from her mind by concentrating on her task.

Yet it persisted, needling her.

"Why are ye worried?"

Cora was standing in the doorway now. Muir was watching from outside. Cora's eyes glittered as she stepped inside and shut the door.

"I would think it better to know ye are not stuck in this marriage just yet," Cora said.

"I suppose" Rhedyn answered. She took a deep breath and changed the subject. "Since I am getting the accounts into order, it is a perfect time for you to work on yer skills as well."

Cora looked at the stacks of paper waiting to be input into the account ledger. "I have no liking for such tasks."

Rhedyn stood. "Neither do I. However, it is the skill of the mistress of the house. A position ye will have at some point. Hence, ye should make certain ye are up to the task."

Cora crossed her arms over her chest. "What if I refuse to wed?"

Rhedyn took a deep breath and released it. "Ye have not even met the man."

"He has never even written me a letter," Cora said.

"Perhaps he has." Rhedyn pointed to a pile of letters waiting on the table.

Cora was curious. She moved toward the table which held over thirty letters. They were folded into different sized squares and sealed with wax. She selected one and broke the seal.

Rhedyn looked at the bottom of the page and realized Laird Grant had written on behalf of his son.

Her belly knotted. Laird Grant was attending to the details of securing the only sibling of the Mackenzie laird for his son.

So cold.

Cora locked gazes with her. The look in the girl's eyes was one Rhedyn understood.

Helplessness...

And the glitter of rebellion.

Rhedyn took the letter and held the corner of it over the candle flame. The parchment caught easily, a bright flame eating away at the letter until she had to drop it onto the floor.

"Let the Grants receive no letters for a change," Rhedyn said.

"I like ye Rhedyn," Cora remarked softly.

"Cormac might feel the same as ye do," Rhedyn remarked.

Cora offered her a sad smile. "True. Yet, he will no' be leaving his home or promising to obey."

She looked at the little pile of ash on the floor. "Aye, let them wait for a change."

Cora was gone a moment later. Rhedyn might have liked to go after her, but she discovered she had no words to offer the girl. She'd done all she might.

Now, Rhedyn would have to hope fate offered Cora more than a groom who only saw her as a necessary component of a business alliance.

⤜⤜⤜⤚⤚⤚

"WASTE OF THE laird's time, that's what she is."

Cora had learned to hide in the shadows only recently. Rhedyn seemed to be the only one who really looked at her as a woman. But those around her, her kin, they wanted to keep her blind to what reality would eventually deliver to her. The truth was, she allowed them to think she was immature when in fact, she understood far more than they realized. Playing dumb was very effective in being able to hear things which were meant to be kept from her.

She wasn't going to the Grant land like a lamb to the slaughter. And she wasn't going to be naive either. Men liked virgin brides, but she'd come to understand that it wasn't just about being innocent when it came to her maidenhead. Men also wanted to be selfish and keep her from knowing bed sport could be enjoyed by women as well. Yet, everyone told her it was a duty.

Was it so terrible to want happiness in life?

Cora refused to think otherwise. If that made her unbridled, so be it. She pressed her back against the stone wall and listened to the maids.

"I hear he's bedded her repeatedly..." Another maid was adding her opinion to the conversation in the kitchens. "But she still started her monthly courses."

Fenella was gone to the hall, so the maids were using the time to chat. Cora had learned a great deal from them since she'd started doubling back and hiding after already bidding them all good night.

"What do you expect?" another asked. "Her mother only produced two girls, and Laird Lindsey is known for his fidelity."

"Useless creature."

"Barren, no doubt."

"Mackenzie will be made sport of for certain now," Innis was taking the lead in the conversation. "We'll have a bastard for the next laird, if even that much."

There was a round of grumbling. Cora felt her belly heave. It sickened her to hear the animosity. No one spoke up in Rhedyn's defense. There was no mention of the fact that they had been wed less than a month.

No, there was only judgement.

The fate of a noble bride.

Her future...

Oh yes, everyone assured her that she would not be treated in such a way. They petted her when she questioned them, consoling her like a child.

Only, it would be her who would have to face the expectations of the Grants. And what if her husband didn't do his part? The failure to conceive would still be shackled around her ankles.

Cora felt something shift inside her. A firm sense of resolution. She would not be an innocent lamb. If Cormac Grant didn't impress her, well, she wouldn't wed him. They were hardly the first couple betrothed to one another by their parents for the sake of good business.

The difference was that she was not going to suffer a husband who had no interest for her or even detested her. No, Cormac would have to prove himself, or she'd refuse him.

And she would be making certain her brother knew it.

⟫⟫⟫⟪⟪⟪

It was a full moon.

Rhedyn escaped to the north tower the moment Muir had finished his supper. Guilt needled her as she left the hall because the Retainer shot her a look of irritation. Still, he stuffed some cheese into a round of bread and stood. She felt him trailing her through the passageways.

The room in the north tower was clean. The moonlight offered her enough light to see by. She picked up the flint and struck it, causing sparks to fall into a small bowel with tinder in it. The delicate, dry husks caught easily. Picking up a candle, she held it so the wick would catch.

A warm pool of yellow light enveloped her. She placed the candle in a small, ceramic holder. But she didn't light the other candles. Instead, she moved toward the window and opened the shutters. The night air was cold and misty. The scent of rain teased her nose. The moon was large and bright in the sky, casting a glow on the crops beginning to rise up from the ground.

"Why are ye here, Rhedyn?"

She gasped and turned, but Buchanan was already behind her. He clamped his arms around her, his body warming her.

"Umm...." He was nuzzling at her hair, making her loathe the idea of conversation.

"Ye would have me known as a man who cast ye out because I cannot take me ease with ye?" he asked bluntly. He made a scoffing sound under his breath before releasing her.

"Can we not move past ye thinking me a villain?" Frustration edged his tone.

She blinked as she faced him. "That isn't what I meant..."

"But it's what yer actions proclaim," he cut back. "Ye know well our every action will be picked apart by the staff."

"I do know it," she muttered in irritation. "This entire day has been naught but judgment against me."

"So why are ye here?" he demanded. "Ye intend to make it appear that I also find ye lacking and put ye out of me chamber?"

His question stunned her.

"I'm sorry," she exclaimed, feeling tears prickling her eyes. "Everyone has been glaring at me all day...and supper was more of the same...and...and..." She was making a motion with her hand, but her mind went blank on just what else she wanted to say. Instead, she felt like her control was spent. Composure shredding away and dropping her into a heap of emotions on the floor.

Surprise flashed through his eyes before he was suddenly gathering her close again. "Here now, lass. I meant to reassure ye, no' wound ye further."

But she pressed her hands against his chest, wiggling against his hold until he released her. Shame prevented her from accepting his embrace.

"It's my fault," Rhedyn exclaimed. "I made sure I wouldn't conceive."

Shock took over his face.

"I just wasn't sure if things would work out or not..." She was babbling. Caught in the grip of a storm of emotions. Everything she'd locked behind her resolve and composure was just spilling out. "I didn't know what to do when offered the chance to make sure I didn't conceive, so I made sure it wouldn't happen and now everyone is…"

"I do nae care what everyone else is thinking on the matter," he declared sternly.

Rhedyn shut her mouth. His tone was hard, and his eyes had narrowed. She stiffened but kept her gaze on his.

"Ye have the right to be angry with me."

Buchanan was shaking his head. He held up a single finger as she felt like an icy grip was tightening around her heart.

"I committed the crime, Rhedyn," he said. "When I stole ye from yer father. It was the wrong thing, done for the right reasons. I do no' blame ye for being hesitant to bind yerself to me forever with a child."

"Ye don't?" she asked in astonishment.

He shook his head.

She'd never realized how lonely life was until moments when he was pressed against her. It felt as if she'd found the other half of herself.

"But I hope to give ye reason to trust me in the future, Rhedyn."

He scooped her off her feet, carrying her to the bed. The shutters were still open, allowing the night air in. It chilled the chamber, but that just made her want to huddle close to Buchanan more. He pulled the bedding up to her neck and pressed her head down onto his chest while he lay on his back in the middle of the bed.

"I know it will take time, Rhedyn," he muttered in the darkness. "Please give me the chance to be yer husband."

He was a proud man. Laird of the Mackenzie. He didn't have to ask her for anything.

Yet, he did.

There in the bed they seemed to be only a man and a woman. Fresh tears spilled from her eyes as the moment tore at the last layer protecting her heart. No one had ever been inside her private space like he was. She'd never cared so very much about another person's feelings.

"I won't take it anymore," she promised.

He stroked his hand over the side of her head.

"I just needed some time."

"Aye, lass. 'Tis understandable."

She lifted her head and looked at him. He held his expression tight for a long moment before he lost the battle and snorted. He rolled over, pushing her onto her back.

"I swear to Christ I want to throttle ye for drinking poison," he growled. "I know what women take to make certain they do not conceive and it's damned dangerous, Rhedyn! If it's brewed incorrectly, ye can bleed to death. I've half a mind to have Innis sent out from the castle for agreeing to give it to ye."

"How would ye know?" she demanded. "What I took?"

Her question caught him off guard. His expression became guarded. Rhedyn poked him in the chest.

"Did the woman who taught you to be a man tell ye of it?" she asked.

He didn't want to answer her. There was no way she might make him do so, either. His silence made her feel exposed, though, and she set her teeth into her lower lip.

"Aye, it was the woman who taught me how to be a man," Buchanan spoke slowly. His expression darkened slightly, drawing her attention to it in fascination.

Somehow, she'd never thought a man might squirm over such a topic.

"She wasn't me mistress."

Rhedyn felt her eyes widen.

"At least, no' in the sense of the word that is most often used." Buchanan's expression went darker still. "Me father had her brought to me...with instructions to see to me education."

"Ye're blushing." Rhedyn truly hadn't intended to make fun of him, but she was astonished by the darkening of his skin. She reached for his face.

He caught her hand before she made contact, closing his fingers around it.

"My father did nae want me inexperience to be used by a calculating woman. As the heir to the Mackenzies, he said there would be plenty who would use deceit to gain power by getting into me bed."

"Oh." As far as responses went, her's lacked a great deal.

"It was nae a choice, Rhedyn." His hand tightened around hers.

"It had been expected of ye," she muttered. "Just as everyone always minded their tongues around me, keeping me innocent of just what I might find after I was wed. We were both prepared."

"How can ye read me so well, lass?" he asked. "No one sees my personal thoughts the way ye seem to be able to."

She let out a scoff. "I know that difficultly meself."

His expression softened. There was a hint of shyness in his eyes.

"But Innis didn't brew it for me." Rhedyn felt the need to protect the maid.

His eyes narrowed slightly. She didn't get a chance to ask any further questions. He lay down on his back and pulled her close. Her head was on his chest, his heartbeat lulling her to sleep as he stroked her shoulder.

⟫⟫⟫⟪⟪⟪

"I DO NAE wish to wed," Cora spoke clearly.

The head table went quiet. The captains looked to one another and then to Buchanan. Cora looked her brother in the eyes. "And do nae lecture me."

Buchanan laid his knife down. "Ye can be certain I will tell ye I do no' care for yer tone, Cora. Or for having this conversation at the supper table."

Cora appeared unaffected. "I do nae care to see Mistress Lindsey suffering yer men watching her every move."

"It is necessary," Buchanan answered firmly.

"Let us discuss this, Cora," Rhedyn attempted to be the voice of reason.

"Oh, aye," Cora responded heatedly as though Rhedyn hadn't spoken. "It is very necessary for women to be made to bend to the whims of men. Well, I will no' go to the Grants as some lamb to be tormented. I will enjoy me life."

She shoved her chair back and left the table.

Buchanan grunted.

Rhedyn laid her hand on his forearm. "This might be best for women to discuss."

His gaze locked with hers for a moment before he nodded once. Rhedyn pushed her chair back and went toward the kitchens. Cora might be upset, but Rhedyn doubted the girl would go hungry. She'd just gather something up for a meal from the kitchens while the maids were out tending to the Retainers sitting at the tables in the hall.

Rhedyn hadn't made it very far when Cora ran past. Her face was red with fury, and she disappeared quickly into the yard.

"That girl needs a mother."

Rhedyn turned to see Fenella standing near. The Head-of-House wiped her hands on her apron before looking toward Rhedyn.

"A woman who understands the position she was born into," Fenella advised softly.

Rhedyn felt the subtle reprimand. It wasn't unjust, either. Life was hard. Everyone had something they had to do in order to survive. From the lowest scullery maid to the lady of the manner. Each and every one of them had to have a place.

"My mother taught me to recognize the blessings around me," Rhedyn replied. "As well as my responsibilities."

There was a flicker of approval in Fenella's eyes. "As did me own. Cora has been too long in the company of men and thinks fighting is the way to gain what she wants from life."

"I'll see to her," Rhedyn stated.

The Head-of-House nodded. As Rhedyn started after Buchanan's sister, Fenella stretched out her arm in front of Muir. "Best allow the women to talk among themselves for a wee bit."

Rhedyn didn't wait to see what Muir would do. If he trailed her, well, there would be nothing she might do to dissuade him.

She ventured into the yard, heading toward the stables.

"Cora?"

The stables were quiet. Rhedyn looked both ways but ventured further into the darkness. She knew she hadn't imagined seeing the girl go toward them. There was only a sliver of scarlet on the horizon now. It was no time for anyone to be riding out.

"Cora?" Rhedyn called once again. "I know I saw ye."

"Aye," Cora spoke near the far end of the stables. "Ye have good instincts, Rhedyn."

Buchanan's sister pointed at a horse. "And I am repaying yer kindness to me. Ye can go now, and I will not raise the alarm. Everyone will assume ye are with me."

Another chance to leave.

Only this time, Rhedyn was certain she didn't want to go.

"Yer brother is kind to me, Cora."

Cora tossed her head, intent on arguing. But she suddenly stiffened, her face frozen in a stunned look before her body just dropped to the floor.

"Cora?" Rhedyn was reaching for the girl when she saw the man who had been standing behind her. His right hand held a thick length of wood that he raised up. Rhedyn realized his intent to attack too late. She'd put her effort into moving toward Cora, now, as she struggled to reverse course, the man leered at her as he brought the wood down on her head.

There was a dull thud as it connected with her skull. The pain was blinding. But she only felt it for a moment before collapsing like a sack of grain.

⇶⫘⇜

INNIS COULDN'T CONTROL her smile. "Kill her quickly."

"Do nae be foolish, woman," Egan chastised her.

He turned and pulled a horse from its stall. "She is the bait Hamish needs to draw Buchanan outside of this stronghold. Right glad I am to no' have to use Cora."

He bent down and scooped Rhedyn's form off the floor. With a grunt, he tossed her over the back of the horse. Egan used a length of rope to tie her securely in place before he placed a blanket over her.

He turned around and pulled a note from his jerkin. He tucked it into Cora's bodice before nodding with approval. Egan looked at Innis.

"Ye are helpful inside the stronghold," he said. "Best for me to knock ye across the head as well."

Innis's eyes widened. She took a step back.

"Do nae make me chase ye woman," Egan warned her. "I thought ye were loyal to Hamish. Time to prove it."

"Ye will tell Hamish I helped ye?" Innis squeaked.

Egan had grasped the log he'd used to fell Cora once more. "Aye. Ye'll have yer reward when Buchanan is dead and Hamish is laird."

Innis nodded. She turned around and grasped two handfuls of her skirt. The log hit her skull with a dull sound.

⇶⫘⇜

SUPPER WAS THE last meal of the day. It was a time when the Retainers were allowed to rest. In the summer, the days were long and there was more work to do than there were men to do it. Inside the great hall, there would be conversation and drink. The other meals throughout the day were consumed quickly because every man and woman had some pressing task to get to before the sun set.

Even the kitchen staff had time to linger in the hall and enjoy their friends at night. It was a time when smaller children were rubbing their eyes but fighting against falling asleep. Old men would tell stories or sing songs as mugs of ale were passed down the length of the tables. A Retainer didn't make a lot of money, but he was ensured good meals and a place to sleep in the hall once the tables were cleared to the side.

Egan made use of the lack of people in the hall. Up on the walls there would be Retainers still standing at their posts, but their focus was on making certain no one tried to enter the stronghold. He pulled a leather hood up to shield his face and hunched over as he led the horse through the kitchen yard. There was a small gate which lead to the pasture where the cows who gave milk were. In times of trouble, it would be secured, but tonight, there was only a single Retainer posted. He was looking toward the horizon. Egan lifted his hand, as though he knew the young lad.

The Retainer was young. He hadn't experienced much of life and was left on watch because he was the lowest ranked. Egan's wave had the desired effect on the lad. The Retainer mistook the greeting for innocence, never thinking it was a ruse.

He passed through the gate and out of the stronghold. The darkness swallowed him up, allowing him to make his way toward the place where Hamish waited.

A whistle came out of the night. Egan stopped and waited.

Hamish was careful in his approach. Egan didn't hear even a footstep before there was suddenly a knife at his throat. He barely felt the kiss of the sharp metal before Hamish recognized him.

"Ye have her?" Hamish inquired.

"Aye, the Lindsey bitch."

Hamish slowly grinned, and it sent a chill down Egan's back. Hamish looked toward the covered form on the back of the horse.

"Well done, man." Hamish reached out and patted Egan on the shoulder. "Well done, indeed."

From around them, there was a shifting. Men materialized from the darkness. They were a grim bunch, their purpose seeming to taint the very wind with the feeling of treachery.

None of them had sympathy for their bait, and even if they had, taking her would have been something which they considered a necessary evil.

※》》《《※

CORA OPENED HER eyes and blinked.

The darkness she expected but not the pain throbbing in her skull. She lifted her hand, intending to rub her head but stopped when she saw the straw clinging to her fingers. The air was moist, far too much for her bedchamber.

And she was still fully dressed.

She rolled over and stood. Her knees felt weak for a moment as everything seemed to swim in a dizzy circle.

Her memory flooded back in a rush. She looked around as fear clawed at her, but there was no one nearby. But there was a note lying on the floor of the stable. She plucked it off the ground before catching sight of the maid.

Innis was lying closer to the stable doors. Her chest rose and fell though, calming Cora. The note in her hand drew her attention.

"If ye want yer sister back, come alone. Hamish."

Her fingers trembled but only for a moment before her temper flared.

She was not a weakling!

Nor was she some child.

Rhedyn's words rose from her mind, filling her with guilt as she realized Hamish had intended to use her to lure her brother out of the stronghold.

Hamish had targeted her because he thought her a child.

Cora straightened up. Something felt like it snapped inside her. All of a sudden, the tears which had been filling her eyes evaporated as her mind began to whirl with ideas of how to turn the situation in her favor. She looked around. A long dagger was lying on a work table where someone had left it in a hurry to get to supper. She picked it up and hiked her skirt so she might tuck it into her garter.

Another rapid search netted her a jerkin which had been hung on a peg near the door. Likely the thick garment had been discarded during the heat of the day. She shrugged into it and rolled the sleeves up to bare her hands. She grabbed a knitted bonnet and stuffed her hair into it.

She moved toward a stall, reaching out to run a hand over the muzzle of the horse standing there.

Weak? Rhedyn was correct; Cora needed to take charge of her life because a good life required effort to create it.

Hamish was expecting Buchanan. Cora dropped the note next to Innis on her way out of the stable. Her brother would still be along soon, but Cora planned to get to Rhedyn first. Hamish had underestimated Rhedyn before.

Tonight, Cora was going to prove to him that she was twice as much trouble as her sister-in-law.

※»»»⋘⋘※

"ANOTHER SLICE OF pie?" Fenella asked.

Muir was just stuffing the last bite of what he had into his mouth. The meat and vegetable pie was hot and savory. The Head-of-House was smiling as she used a large knife to cut into the pie waiting near the hearth.

"Nae," he forced out. "I really must check on the mistress now."

Fenella carried the new slice over to his plate anyway. The scent of warm meat and flaky crust filled his nose. His belly rumbled as though he'd had nothing in days.

"Women..." Fenella continued as she turned and reached for a pitcher of ale. "Women, tend to take a bit longer when talking."

She poured the ale into his mug. It was more than his measure. A second helping that, by rights, she might deduct from his quarterly earnings. But she only smiled and winked at him.

"Enjoy," Fenella said. "Then ye can be about yer duty."

Muir settled back down onto the bench. It really would be a shame to waste such a treat. There were lads up on the walls, and everyone else was in the great hall. He lifted a bite of the meat pie to his lips with his confidence high. Women did tend to talk longer than men. Muir had never been one to voice his opinion when it wasn't asked for, but young Cora had been allowed to run wild. Like everyone else in the clan, she had a duty to uphold. The mistress would be the perfect person to put an end to Cora's willfulness.

>>><<<

SHE WAS INCORRIGIBLE.

Willful.

Oh, yes, Cora knew well what was said about her. The maids often wondered if she'd turn into a woman who was unbridled. She'd walked away from Shona when she tried to insist Cora learn to keep the account books. Cora had stayed only long enough in the kitchens to learn to turn bread and do the basic cooking. She lacked the patience to stand by and boil a pudding.

But she knew how to track.

And the night didn't frighten her.

She knelt down and stuck her hands into a pile of horse droppings without hesitation. They were still warm, telling her she was close to the horse carrying Rhedyn. With the help of the moon, she found the footprints of the man leading the horse. Clouds were beginning to gather though, promising rain before sunrise.

The tracks would be long gone by first light.

➤➤➤◄◄◄

RHEDYN WOKE TO a headache.

Honestly, it was worse than any headache she'd ever had. She wanted to rub her eyes but discovered her wrists bound behind her. Her back was against a rock as she lay across the ground, the chill of night coming through it to send a shiver across her skin.

In front of her there was a fire. It had burned down, red embers glowing when the wind blew across them. She froze as she watched the men around that fire. They'd chosen a spot among an outcropping of large rocks. In the darkness, the shadows of the large stone created perfect hiding places for them.

She started to shiver, but clamped her mouth shut to prevent her teeth from chattering. The memory of Cora's face flashed through her mind. Fear was attempting to strangle her, but she fought against it, straining to maintain her composure. Keeping her wits would mean the difference between surviving and certain death.

Well, they didn't kill you in the stables...

What she'd meant as a bolstering thought had the opposite effect. There was only one reason she would still be alive—to be used against Buchanan.

Hamish.

She didn't bother to waste time on questioning it. He would have killed her in the stable without a thought for her soul.

The night grew darker as clouds covered the moon. Rhedyn could smell rain in the air. It might serve to cover her tracks, but it would also wake the men sleeping close by. She scanned those nearest to her.

Something touched her leg.

Rhedyn jerked but kept her mouth shut. She looked down, blinking when she thought she spied Cora.

But even after she blinked, Cora's face remained.

The fear Rhedyn had been holding back broke through. Cora was so young, but she reached forward with something. Rhedyn felt her sawing at the rope which bound her ankles. It gave way, sending a shaft of hope through her.

Cora pointed around the rock before she disappeared from sight. Rhedyn rolled over, fighting her impulse to do it quickly. She held her breath as she watched the sleeping men.

It seemed to take forever before she felt the knife working at the rope around her wrists. But when it gave way, she discovered herself panting with disbelief. Cora reached down and took her hand, pulling on it. Rhedyn fought against her skirt as she crawled. Every inch felt like it took too long to cover. Each tiny sound grated on her ears like thunder.

But she made it around the rock, flattening herself against the surface for several long seconds as she looked at the area in front of her. The mist turned to light rain, urging her forward. Cora clasped her hand, keeping pace with her as they scurried around rocks, hunching low to conceal themselves in the darkness. The wind whipped up, slapping branches and leaves against each other.

"Hurry," Cora urged her. "They won't sleep through this storm."

With the wind whipping, they yanked up their skirts and ran. The grass was tall, and it scraped against their shins. Rhedyn grew hot in spite of the chill in the air. Her heart was pounding as everything inside her was focused on moving faster.

Escape...

But the land suddenly fell away. They stood two feet from the edge of a ravine, looking down at the churning water of a river. Rhedyn looked behind her, reaching for Cora's hand when she saw the men closing the gap between them.

"I will not be bait," Cora declared.

Rhedyn looked at her. "Nor will I."

They might have both been choosing death, but Rhedyn squeezed Cora's hand before she ran the final two paces to the edge and jumped.

Whether God would have mercy on her or not, it was a better choice, for she knew without a doubt that Hamish would have none.

⟫⟫⟪⟪

WATER APPEARED HARMLESS.

It was anything but soft. The moment Rhedyn plunged into it, the strength of the current took hold of her. It pulled her under. She fought against it, straining to get back to the surface. The battle was intense, but she broke through the water just long enough to gulp at the air. She was yanked back down again, but the tiny success gave her hope, and hope was the fuel for determination.

She refused to die.

Hamish didn't deserve to succeed in ending her life.

The problem was, the river wasn't planning on losing either.

⟫⟫⟪⟪

THE RIVER'S STRONG current flung Cora onto the bank.

She landed hard, jabbing the side of her face into a broken branch before she reached up and felt her fingernails tearing as she dug her fingers into the earth. She pulled herself away from the water. Chilled to the bone, her teeth chattered. Her body began to shake violently, but she opened her mouth and laughed in the face of her pain.

She was alive.

The price of success was pain. A great deal of it. Cora struggled to her feet, smiling in victory. Behind her, the water was crashing. Like a demon snarling at her as she escaped.

Let it gnash its teeth…

She lifted her skirts because the water made them too long and heavy. The bank was littered with chunks of wood and uneven stones. She threaded her way along as the horizon was brightening with dawn. She made it up the bank of the river, her reward was seeing the crimson glow of the rising sun. Warmth hit her nose and frozen cheeks. All of the pain throbbing in various points in her body was overshadowed by the sight of daylight.

She felt herself being reborn along with the new day. Somehow, the person she'd been yesterday was no more.

Cora looked around, scanning the bank for her sister-in-law. But there was no sign of her.

At the approach of horses, Cora dropped down, hunching low as she strained to see the colors the men were wearing. She easily recognized the Mackenzie tartans.

She stood back up. There would be no outward sign of weakness.

"Cora!" Buchanan was off his horse before it stopped completely. His long legs carried him across the space between them. He reached out, clasping her shoulders.

"Christ in heaven," he exclaimed as he looked her over.

"I freed Rhedyn from Hamish." Cora refused to acknowledge the concern in his tone. "We had to jump into the river to avoid being caught."

One of the Retainers had pulled his doublet off, intending to put it over her shoulders.

"I am well," she informed him.

"Ye are not," Buchanan argued as he nodded to his man. "But the moment ye are, ye had best have a good explanation for why ye went after Rhedyn yerself."

Cora shot her brother a hard look. "I went because I know how to track. Innis was stirring and time was precious. I am no longer a child."

Buchanan went still. Cora walked past him, pressing the doublet back to its owner. She felt everyone's eyes on her as she took the bridle of one of the spare horses and mounted. Buchanan swung up onto the back of his stallion and guided the animal around so he was close to her.

"It seems ye have skills I have failed to notice, Cora," he said softly.

She sent him a proud smile. "Let us find yer wife, for ye can be certain I will not be keeping the books. And if Cormac Grant does nae like me as I am, he can find another bride."

It was an ultimatum. One she was overly bold in voicing, but it simply felt correct. She shot her brother a look, but his attention was on recovering Rhedyn.

Buchanan turned his horse and lifted his hand. With one motion, the entire, double column of Retainers set into motion. Cora kept pace with them, feeling more alive than she had in years. Her skull still throbbed from being smashed in the barn, and the cold was bitter on her toes and fingers. It all paled against the knowledge that she'd freed Rhedyn. The men around her might argue whether or not she'd been foolish or helpful, but in her heart, she'd risen up when circumstances had been dire. No one could take the sense of accomplishment from her.

Because she would never allow them to.

———※———

RHEDYN WAS GRATEFUL.

But she was still lying on the riverbank, searching her mind for every scarlet word she had ever heard. Her father's men had done a good job of shielding her from true profanity, but there were still plenty of outbursts she'd heard.

"Piss on it," she uttered as she flattened her hands on the sand and pushed her upper body up. "Curse and rot it all."

She hurt, but she was free.

Perhaps she was little better looking than a half-drowned kitten, but she drew in a deep breath and looked at the marks left from the rope around her wrists.

She *was* free.

The knowledge gave her strength. She gazed up and down the river, but there was no sign of Cora. Concern for the girl needled her. She climbed up through a tangled mess of dead trees to make it out of the ravine.

"Here now woman!" a man exclaimed.

He dropped his kilt as she appeared, shooting her a disgruntled look. But it melted away as he swept her from head to toe.

"Did ye fall into the river, lass?" He offered his hand to her.

Rhedyn pushed her wet hair out of her face. "I jumped."

He was taken aback. "Were ye drunk?"

"Rhedyn Lindsey."

It wasn't a question. Rhedyn looked further ahead to see Rolfe Munro. He was every bit as imposing as Buchanan. With broad shoulders built up through harsh training, she saw the large claymore hilt of over his left shoulder. His hair was golden with a touch of copper.

He swept her from head to toe with his blue eyes. "I would say I've seen ye looking better, but if ye tell me ye jumped into the river, well then, I think ye appear to have won the day to be on yer feet."

"My thoughts precisely," she answered as though she wasn't dripping wet and likely crowned with a tangle of hair. She felt chilled to the bone, but there were more important matters to focus on.

Cora...

Rolfe had made it to her. He took a couple of steps past her and peered over the edge of the ravine. When he turned back toward her, his expression had turned serious.

"What sent ye fleeing into the water, Rhedyn?" he asked.

"A man intent on murdering me and my husband," she answered. More than two dozen Munro Retainers were watching her.

Rolfe reached into his doublet and withdrew a small flask. He twisted the cap loose and offered it to her.

The liquor burned a path down her throat. Rolfe grinned as she tried to avoid coughing. She tipped the flask up a second time, just to prove she could stomach the strong brew before handing it back. "Hamish Mackenzie was stripped of his colors for trying to murder me. He sent his men back to kidnap me and lure me husband out so he could kill him and take the lairdship."

"I doubt the Mackenzie would have followed him." Rolfe took a drink from the flask before replacing it in his doublet. "But for a man who was stripped of his colors, I suppose a longshot is better than nothing at all."

There was a murmur of agreement from his men.

"I'm grateful to have ye be here," she told him.

Rolfe nodded. "There is a village no' too far from here. Best for us to get ye there before Hamish and his men find us."

"I lost Cora in the water," Rhedyn informed him. She again searched the riverbank with a desperate hope, but there was no sign of the girl.

"Buchanan's sister?" Rolf asked.

"Yes. She followed me and cut me lose, but we had to jump into the river or be captured."

"So, that's the way it went." He'd gone back to the edge of the ravine to look for Cora. Rolfe gestured for two of his men to come forward. "Brawley, take half the men and escort Mistress Lindsay to the inn."

"I can't leave Cora," Rhedyn argued.

"I'll stay and look for her," Rolfe assured her. "Best ye are no' here.

That way, if Hamish finds us, there will be no reason for the man to start spilling blood. He will no' know I have spoken to ye. If the man was planning to become laird of the Mackenzie, it stands to reason he's amassed as many men as he can."

"Oh." Rhedyn understood his logic. "I see."

Rolfe looked toward his captain. "Keep a watch on her and send someone back for more men."

"Aye, Laird," Brawley answered with a tug on the corner of his cap. "Here now, mistress, let's be gone."

Rhedyn found leaving the ravine hard. Her feet dragged as she forced herself to see the logic of Rolfe's orders. The Munro Retainers split, half of them surrounding her as she sat on top of a horse. Their close ranks should have filled her with relief, but there was a tingle on her nape that persisted.

Out in the open, it would be simple for Hamish and his men to cut them down. Hamish had needed to lure her out of the Mackenzie stronghold to have any chance of killing Buchanan. Such was the reason strongholds were built and taxes paid to the laird to maintain them. Stone walls provided shelter and security.

Something she felt the lack of as her escort kicked their horses into a faster gait.

⇒⟫⟪⇐

LUCK FINALLY OFFERED Rhedyn some of its bounty.

The sun shone bright throughout the day. The Sparrow's Nest was run by a widow and her three daughters. They whisked Rhedyn abovestairs after Brawley tossed a handful of silver onto the table. A good bath and scrubbing later, Rhedyn sat down to spend the next two hours combing the knots from her hair. The time was needed for her dress to dry. The mistress of the inn had just brought it back up when Rolfe arrived.

Rhedyn hurried to look down from the top of the stairs, but there was no sight of Cora. Rolfe didn't fail to notice her. He shook his head before lifting his leg and climbing over one of the long benches in the common room to sit down. He reached for a round of bread sitting in the middle of the table and broke it.

Cora might be fine.

Rhedyn tried to bolster her confidence as she returned to the loft to finish dressing. The sturdy wool of her dress had come through the ordeal rather well. Only a few dark stains remained after the innkeeper had washed it and spread it out to dry.

Cora might also be dead.

No, Rolfe would have found her body.

Rhedyn tried to find hope in that thought. She finished braiding her hair and pinning it up before there was a rap on the door. Rolfe gave her only a moment before he opened it.

"We searched a great deal of area," Rolfe began. "There was no sign of Cora."

Rhedyn nodded. "I'm grateful for yer time."

"I sent word to yer brother that we have found ye," Rolfe continued.

Rhedyn blinked a few times. "I've heard of the wedding."

Rolfe shrugged. "Better late than never, I suppose. But considering Vychan is breathing and no one doubts he is yer father's son, a wedding seems a good way to keep the blood from flowing when yer father dies."

"Aye." Rhedyn remarked, still half in thought.

Rolfe pulled a chair around and sat down in front of her. "It will prevent fighting, Rhedyn."

"Oh...aye." Rhedyn returned her full attention to Rolfe. She suddenly realized he'd closed the door behind him, making them very much alone.

It was improper.

"I have a husband now, Rolfe," she enunciated each word. "I am grateful to ye for finding me and keeping me safe, but ye should return below."

Rolfe kept their gazes fused. In his blue eyes, she could see him thinking something through. "Aye, I heard ye wed, but yer father did not give his blessing to the match."

"The Church did."

Rolfe's expression remained stony. "But there are no contracts."

"Couples wed without contracts, Rolfe."

"No' a daughter of a laird. An eldest daughter, as well."

"Well, I have a brother now, the contracts are not so important as they were when ye came to negotiate with me father for my hand," she explained slowly. "I'm glad we didn't come to an agreement, for ye'd be disappointed now."

Rolfe's lips twitched into a small grin. He pointed at her. "That logical mind of yers is one reason I was seeking to make ye my bride. I like the way ye think matters through."

Rhedyn felt a prickle of apprehension on her neck. Rolfe was set-tled on a point. She could see it in his eyes. But he was talking her around, trying to get her used to his way of thinking.

"Marriage with you was always a matter of business, Rhedyn," Rolfe said. "The matter of gaining an alliance with the Lindsey is something me father has charged me with doing. Yer sister is too young, and with me father's health failing, I cannot afford to wait for her to grow up."

Rhedyn struggled to control her emotions. Rolfe was thinking his moves through with the finesse of a chess match. The only way to beat him was to apply logic to her arguments.

"My wedding was consummated," Rhedyn made her words come out evenly in spite of the personal nature of the information. "As the next Laird of the Munro, ye need a pure bride."

"I am nae a virgin," Rolfe informed her. "Hence, it seems rather arrogant of me to insist ye be untouched. Ye are no' a whore, that is all which is important and the fact that ye are nae carrying Buchanan's babe." His expression sharpened. "The mistress of the inn confirms ye are bleeding."

Rhedyn felt the breath freeze in her chest. The hospitality so graciously given to her over the last few hours suddenly took on a more sinister nature.

Rolfe nodded. He appeared to consider the matter finished. He stood. "We'll be heading back to Munro land now."

"I won't wed ye."

Rolfe had turned toward the door. He stopped and looked over his shoulder. "Are ye going to say ye prefer a man who stole ye to one who went to yer father?"

There was distaste in his expression but determination in his eyes. He was frustrated and fighting the impulse to let her see it. She watched him master his temper and smooth out his expression.

"Women are more fragile when it comes to being abducted. The experience muddles yer thinking." He nodded, seeming to come to some sort of decision. "Ye are safe in me company. Me men will see to it. After some rest in a safe, secure place, I expect ye will begin to think clearly. I went to yer father Rhedyn, in front of yer clan. That is how a man should approach a good woman."

There was a warning in his tone. What made her clamp her mouth shut was the irritation she witnessed flickering in his eyes. She couldn't escape inside the chamber. So, she clasped her hands together and held her tongue.

Rolfe Munro nodded once again. "I will always afford ye the respect due me wife, Rhedyn. In me home, ye shall be the mistress."

To Rolfe, marriage was a business matter. She'd been raised to expect precisely that from a union, too. Now there was something burning in her heart which refused to allow her to fall back into the sort of arrangement Rolfe wanted with her. It flared up inside her, panic nipping at her as she rotated around, looking for any possibility of escape.

When she found none, tears flooded her eyes.

She had to get back to Buchanan.

The alternative was so unpalatable, she felt nauseous.

Many would agree with Rolfe that she'd suffered, that she wasn't thinking clearly. That she needed to come to her senses.

What she needed was her husband...

But why?

The question begged to be asked. The woman she'd been just six months ago when Rolfe had come to her home to court her was still inside her, wondering what manner of transformation had taken place. It was her and yet, the person she was at that moment was different somehow.

Vastly different.

For there was no possible way for her to accept a future with Rolfe now. Two months ago, she could have seen it working out.

Nausea gripped her again, harder.

She couldn't bear the thought of anyone's kiss but Buchanan's. The idea of Rolfe touching her filled her with icy dread instead of heat.

She wasn't a wanton...

No, she was in love.

Strange the way such a small word made her feel. It made her want to smile. To twirl around in a hundred circles. She felt like she could fly.

But the reality was, she couldn't. The walls around her began closing in, collapsing on her, smothering her joy. But the warmth in her chest persisted. It didn't seem effected by Rolfe imprisoning her.

Instead, it fostered hope.

She'd survived on hope before. So now would be no exception.

⇜⇝

"RIDERS!" RORY CALLED out.

Buchanan turned his head to see the four men making their way across an expanse of rocky earth.

"Munro," Graham observed.

Buchanan and his men had the high ground. The Munro Retainers were almost upon them before they pulled up. They looked between one another, clearly nervous.

"The Munro are nae fighting with the Mackenzies," Buchanan spoke clearly.

One of the Munro jutted out his chin. "The Mackenzie raid Munro land. We're here on the border to keep our crops safe from the likes of the Mackenzie."

Buchanan felt his jaw clenching. "Me half-brother Iain visited wrongs against more than one clan."

Two of the Munro spit on the ground. "Our laird sent his black soul to hell."

"Are ye saying Rolfe Munro killed Iain?" Graham asked.

The Munro didn't seem to be concerned about their lack of numbers compared to Buchanan's men. One of them nodded.

"Aye. That bastard was bragging long and loudly about his raiding. Word made it to us, so we rode out to protect our own."

There were stern looks among the Mackenzies. Buchanan shot his men a look of warning. "I am Laird of the Makenzie. Iain did not act with my permission. I will personally meet with Rolfe to discuss the matter."

Rory suddenly whistled. He was sitting further up the road and pointed at something. Whatever it was, the four Munro Retainers grew nervous.

"Munro!" Rory yelled.

"Is that yer laird?" Buchanan asked the Retainers.

They clamped their mouths shut. A moment later, they were wheeling their horses around and kicking them.

"Now what was that about?" Graham asked in confusion.

"Let's find out," Buchanan said as he put his heels into the side of his mount. Something was needling him. His gut was telling him to go after the Munro.

So, he did.

The Munro Retainers were riding hard to catch up with the rest of their kin. Buchanan rode just as hard. The four reached their kin, but they'd barely had time to point at Buchanan and his men before the Mackenzie were too close for the Munro to avoid.

As Buchanan pulled his horse up, he saw the reason for the Munro Retainers flight. Rolfe Munro's Retainers turned and faced the Mackenzie but not before Buchanan spied Rhedyn sitting on a mare near the back of the riders.

Buchanan felt something ignite inside of him. Fighting had never been something he craved.

Today appeared to be different.

⟫⟫⟫⟪⟪⟪

FATE HAD ONCE again made its choice known.

Rhedyn thought she imagined the Mackenzie riding toward them. But the Munro she rode with were getting nervous.

Very nervous.

She looked up, spying Buchanan. The hope which had refused to be smothered by Rolfe's determination doubled.

"My husband is here for me," she told Rolfe. "Let us not have bloodshed."

Rolfe's eyes narrowed. He was thinking again. She could see him contemplating the situation. "He stole ye, Rhedyn. How can I hand ye back to him and call meself an honorable man? How do I face yer father?"

"I wed him freely."

"Ye weren't in yer right mind, lass." Rolfe shook his head. "Stealing a woman…it is no' the act of an honorable man."

"He did the wrong thing…for the right reasons, Rolfe," she explained. "Sometimes a laird must choose an action for the sake of the bloodshed it will prevent."

Rhedyn watched her words impact him. Rolfe closed his mouth before he was moving his horse around to face the oncoming Mackenzie. One of the Retainers leaned over and snatched the reins of her mare from her distracted grasp. He pulled her mare back as the Munro closed ranks around their laird.

She was so close and yet, fear was trying to gain a hold on her as she watched the way Rolfe appeared determined to hold her.

Fate couldn't be so cruel…

The problem was, she knew that it could very well be, and there would be nothing she could do to prevent it.

CHAPTER EIGHT

"ROLFE MUNRO," BUCHANAN greeted his fellow laird.
Rolfe nodded. "Laird Mackenzie."

Rhedyn held onto the mane of her mare, setting her teeth into her lower lip to keep her mouth shut.

All she wanted to do was cry out.

She knew how to conduct herself, yet it seemed to be falling away like leaves in late autumn. There was only the man she loved and her need to be reunited with him.

"It seems I owe ye a debt of gratitude for finding me wife." Buchanan wasted no more time in making it plain what he wanted.

"A wedding with no contracts," Rolfe didn't hesitate to make his opinion known. "I was in negotiations with her father last season."

Buchanan leaned forward. "She is me wife now."

"So," Rolfe began. "I am to suffer yer half-brother raiding me land and now, ye stole the woman I planned to make me bride."

The men around them were silent. The tension was tightening as the two faced off. No one was ignorant of the stakes.

"Iain," Buchanan answered, "acted without me knowledge. I will pay whatever ye deem fit for the losses suffered. Let us agree to not continue the fighting."

The Munro Retainers looked between themselves, many of them nodding agreement. But the sound of approaching horses distracted them all. The road dipped off to their right, which meant the approaching riders didn't get a look at what was ahead of them.

Hamish and his men had to pull up to avoid colliding with the Mackenzie and the Munro. Horses screamed and men cursed as the dust was stirred up and the birds in the trees went scattering.

"Hamish!" Buchanan roared. "Ye'll no' be escaping me!"

Hamish was fighting to control his mount. The horse danced in a wide circle before Hamish got the animal under control. "Escape? Ye are the one who hid behind the walls of yer castle while putting me out!"

"Ye tried to murder a woman in the stable." Buchanan pointed at him. "I should have hanged ye!"

Hamish smirked. He looked at Rhedyn, his features twisted with evil.

She was certain she'd see that expression until her dying day.

"But ye didn't," Hamish flung back at Buchanan. "Because ye are weak! That Lindsey witch has ye by the balls! The Mackenzie need a laird who is strong enough to lead them!" Hamish's anger was making his steed nervous. The stallion fought against the tight hold he had on the reins, rearing up and snorting.

"Ye should have run Colum Lindsey through for causing Iain's death!" Hamish declared. His men roared with approval.

"I'm the one who killed Iain Mackenzie," Rolfe Munro raised his voice. "And I call it an end to pestilence. He was raiding me land."

Hamish grunted. "A bit of raiding is harmless enough."

Rolfe shook his head. "If he'd kept it to cattle, it would have been. But he took to raping."

"That is a filthy lie!" Hamish declared.

Rolfe shook his head. "I saw it with me own eyes. And ye only further prove it with yer actions against women. Men should fight between men. No' send a lass jumping into a river to avoid ye."

The Munros and Mackenzies growled with approval.

Hamish scoffed. "She's the daughter of a coward traitor. Her father told ye where to find Iain."

"Donnach Munro heard Iain Mackenzie with his own ears," Rolfe declared, "and followed him back to me own land to see if he'd sober up and turn for home. He set fire to a home and wouldn't allow the family to escape unless the wife came out and whored for his men. I ran him through and will no' apologize for it."

Hamish was shocked silent for a long moment. He slowly shook his head, refusing to believe what he'd heard.

"No, no, ye..." Hamish pointed at Rolfe. "Ye want to wed this Lindsey bitch to secure a dowry, so ye will say anything to keep her father's reputation sound."

"I do nae deny I want to wed her," Rolfe responded. "But it has naught to do with defending me land from raiders. Or that Iain was heard by one of me captains. There were plenty of witnesses, man. Laird Mackenzie is wise no' to judge the case quickly."

Rolfe dismounted and pulled his sword free. "If ye want a fight, I am yer man."

Hamish wanted blood. The lust for it burned in his eyes. But he wasn't planning on fighting fairly. He drew his sword and kicked his stead at the same time. The stallion screamed as it reared. When its hooves crashed down, Hamish released the tight hold he had on the reins and the animal bolted forward. Hamish swung his sword, intending to strike Rolfe from above.

Buchanan knocked him from the saddle. Leaping across the space between them as Hamish ventured by him. The two men hit the ground hard, rolling over one another in a tangle of limbs. The afternoon sun flashed off a long dagger as Hamish brought it up high, intent on driving the blade into Buchanan's chest.

Rhedyn felt her heart stop.

Everything around her slowed down. Both men were straining, struggling against one another in deadly combat. It was harsh and vicious. Buchanan twisted away from the blade as he drove his fist into

Hamish. Hamish heaved, tossing Buchanan off him and diving after him to lock his hands around Buchanan's throat.

Rhedyn slipped from the saddle, unable to watch.

Rolfe caught her, hooking his arm around her midsection and lifting her off her feet. "Don't distract him," he whispered in her ear.

Rhedyn bit down on her lower lip again. Rolfe deposited her behind him, blocking her with his body.

Buchanan kicked the dagger away. "Still taking the coward's way, Hamish?"

"Strength is what matters!" Hamish declared.

He lunged toward Buchanan. But this time, Buchanan turned his body and hooked him around the throat. There was a crunch as Buchanan twisted the other man's head. Hamish stiffened and dropped like a stone.

So quickly.

Just a moment and it was over.

Buchanan looked toward the men who had ridden with Hamish. They wheeled their horses around and kicked them into a run.

"Let them go," Buchanan ordered. "But remember their faces."

The Mackenzie nodded in approval. Buchanan turned, still breathing hard. There was a slice through the fabric of his shirt on his upper arm. Fresh blood was seeping into the cream-colored material.

For some reason, the blood struck her as a sign of life.

Of his victory.

She tried to duck around Rolfe, but the Munro laird stuck out his arm. Rhedyn ran into it and a moment later, Brawley was pulling her back. She tried to dig in, to resist, but the Munro Retainer simply lifted her off her feet.

"Let go of me!" she snarled.

The Munro Retainers didn't listen to her. No, their obedience was for their laird. They formed a circle around her, making a wall with their bodies. It was all she might do to master the urge to fly into their backs like a startled bird who could only think of fleeing.

Panic wouldn't help her.

And distracting Buchanan might just be the cause of his death.

She forced herself to stand in place, gripping her skirt as helplessness nearly choked her.

⇉⇉⟨⟨⟨⟨

ROLFE MOVED FORWARD.

Buchanan faced off with him. "As I said, I'll pay the Munro what ye deem fitting."

Rolfe looked into the distance where the men who had ridden with Hamish had disappeared. "There will be more trouble from that lot."

"They are clanless," Buchanan declared. "Ye will have to face the same sort of thing when yer father passes. Someone will covet what ye inherit."

"Fools," Rolfe muttered.

Buchanan stepped closer to Rolfe. "Return me wife."

"Her father agreed to my wedding her."

There was a gasp from Rhedyn. "He would not."

Rolfe kept his gaze fused with Buchannan. "He did. The contracts were drawn up. Column wanted to have me court her this season, to make the matter easier for her. But between us men, the deal was struck."

"Do ye expect me to call ye friend after ye take me wife and point to contracts with her father?" Buchanan asked in a low tone.

Rolfe had squared off with him. He leaned in, his expression hard. "Aye," he uttered in barely a whisper. "And for this."

Rolfe landed a hard blow on the side of Buchanan's jaw. It sent him back a step before he was growling and lifting his arm in retaliation.

"Ye shall not fight over me!" Rhedyn declared. There was a flurry of movement as she stomped on Brawley's foot and broke free.

Buchanan turned and swept her behind his body to protect her from Rolfe's next blow.

"I am his wife!" Rhedyn yelled.

Rolfe drew himself up. "He stole ye. Are ye going to tell me that ye choose him over me? A man who went to see yer father and ask for yer hand?"

Rhedyn was trying her best to get around Buchanan. But Rory had gripped her by two handfuls of her skirt and was pulling her back.

"That is precisely what I am saying, Rolfe Munro!" Rhedyn raised her voice to make certain she was heard. "Ye'd better listen to me, for I swear I will never love ye as I do him."

"Love is for fools," Rolfe answered her. "Buchanan does nae return yer affection."

"I do, Rolfe Munro!" Buchanan charged at Rolfe.

They both went rolling across the ground. But Buchanan suddenly realized that Rolfe wasn't fighting back. Flat on his back, the other laird was choking on his amusement as he put up a halfhearted defense. Buchanan leveled himself upward. Rolfe winked at him.

"Ye'd best thank me, Buchanan Mackenzie," Rolfe muttered as he rubbed his jaw. "I'd no' let just any man hit me."

There was a gasp from Rhedyn. Buchanan got to his feet and offered his hand to Rolfe.

"Go and kiss yer woman, Buchanan," Rolfe muttered as he wiped the blood from his nose. "And remember ye owe me a favor. A *large* one."

"I do." Buchanan offered him his hand.

They clasped wrists in a solid hold before Buchanan turned and started toward her. Rhedyn was suddenly free, Rory releasing her and hightailing it away from her.

Buchanan closed the distance between them, the look on his face stirring her temper.

"How could ye get into a fight…"

The rest of her demand got caught between their lips. He pulled her against his body, binding her to him as his mouth took hers in a kiss that stole her breath.

It was hard.

Fierce.

And absolutely perfect.

She reached for him. Without a care for how many pairs of eyes were on them. He was her husband, the other part of her soul. When he lifted his head, her heart was hammering, but she wasn't alone. With her hands on his chest, she felt his heart keeping perfect time with hers.

"Ye are the most frustrating man I have ever known," she informed him.

His lips lifted into a grin. "And I am all yers, Rhedyn."

"You'd better be," she warned him. "I choose ye Buchanan, so don't think I will be tolerating any mistresses."

He stroked the back of her head, his eyes turning serious. "I have never once played the villain with ye, lass. And I never will."

It was a promise she felt all the way to her heart. It warmed her from the inside out, banishing every last doubt. Was there logic to her feelings? Yes and no. But she wasn't choosing a life based on negotiated terms.

No, she was taking flight with love.

And there was no looking back.

⇛⇚

THE LAIRD HAD brought his bride back.

Innis tossed and turned throughout the night as her mind refused to grant her any peace with the matter. At first light, the boys who laid the fires in the hearths came into the kitchens. She heard their steps as they hauled wood in and stacked it. The first scent of smoke teased her nose as she rose. The two youngest maids looked at her, but they didn't dare question her.

It was their task to begin the process of making bread. The rest of the kitchen staff might linger in slumber until true dawn, which was a privilege earned by years of toil.

Innis made use of the water the younger girls heated and scrubbed her face, neck, and hands. The soap was strong and stung her skin, but it was a strict rule in the kitchen. Everyone washed three times a day.

The castle was quiet. There was precious little light in the passageway as Innis made her way toward the stillroom. Years spent working in the kitchens meant she knew precisely how many steps it was from the kitchen to the stillroom door. She was forbidden to go inside without permission because of the expensive and rare spices kept there.

She looked both ways before venturing inside.

"I'd hoped ye would not come, child. Truly, I did not wish to see ye here."

Fenella stood inside the stillroom. The rod she used to punish those who broke the rules was in her right hand.

"Ye have been warned, Innis," Fenella began. "I take some of the blame for putting the idea into yer head of being the laird's mistress, but I cannot look the other way while ye seek to harm the mistress."

"But…"

"No more." Fenella sliced through the air with the rod. "Colum Lindsey is innocent. Iain was raiding…." The Head-of-House paused for a moment as she drew in a heavy breath. "And so, the men who rode with him must also accept the risk they ventured into. The marriage will stand, and the laird has pledged himself to his wife."

Innis looked at the floor for a moment before she raised her face. "Am I to be put out?"

Fenella sighed. "Ye've already ignored me warning, Innis. How am

I to trust ye? I know ye believe ye understand the way of making concoctions to keep a waistline slim, but I warn ye, lass, it is nae simple. One little mistake can have dire consequences. What would ye have me do?"

"Wed her to me."

Fenella looked up as Innis whirled around. Tyree stood in the doorway. His scarred face had an oddly uncertain look on it as he ducked beneath the doorway and entered the stillroom. He looked at Innis.

"I am not much to look at...but I can afford a wife," Tyree declared as he made an attempt to soften his features with a grin. On the face of the hardened Butler, the welcoming expression made both women stare at him.

"Ye have never approached me," Innis said shyly. Her heart was suddenly misbehaving, thumping and jumping inside her chest.

Tyree offered her a half shrug. "A Butler is best no' seen until it's too late," he said. "I'm good at me duties. No one knows just when I will appear. That way, they don't get it into their minds to thieve."

He looked past Innis at Fenella. "Innis is no' a bad sort. Just young with no one to look out for her. As me wife, I will make certain she causes no trouble."

Innis felt tears welling up in her eyes. It had been so long since anyone had offered to give anything to her. Guilt tore at her insides. "Wait," she said.

Tyree turned a startled expression toward her. "Ye won't have me?"

Innis was stunned to see a wounded look in his eyes. Never would she have believed the huge Butler might have tender emotions which could be hurt if she hadn't seen it with her own eyes.

Her guilt doubled.

"I have to tell ye that I did something very wrong..." Innis stammered. "It wouldn't be right to wed ye if I don't confess." She gulped in a breath but realized Tyree deserved the truth from her. "Egan gave me a letter in the stable one night. I didn't report it. I just did nothing. It was wrong of me. The laird could have taken more precautions to protect the mistress and Cora if I had spoken. I don't deserve anyone standing up for me. I am selfish."

Tears trickled down her cheeks. Why had she not seen what was important? How could she have been so dim-witted as to long for a position of mistress when Tyree was there the whole time.

"I am too foolish to be worthy of ye, Tyree."

"I think ye might just have taken the first step toward being worthy, Innis," Buchanan emerged from the shadows in the passageway.

Innis sniffled but kept her chin level. Buchanan looked at her for a long moment. "My wife…" he stressed the word, "gave me the benefit of forgiveness."

The laird looked at Tyree. "Ye have served this house faithfully for years. I asked a hard thing of ye in keeping me wife locked up. I owe ye an apology."

Tyree reached up and scratched his head. "I had faith in ye, laird. That ye'd no' hurt the lass."

Buchanan looked at Innis and back at Tyree. "Do ye want Innis, or are ye stepping up to shield her?"

Tyree suddenly smiled. The expression transformed his face as his eyes glittered with happiness. "I'm right glad ye never took a liking to her, Laird. I was waiting for her to grow past her infatuation. All the maids fancy themselves in love with the laird at some point. It passes."

Buchanan looked at Innis. "Will ye have him?"

Innis suddenly nodded. "I will."

Buchanan looked at Fenella. His Head-of-House nodded. "Innis is a good lass. Being alone in this world is hard to suffer. She got a bit off the path is all."

"Aye, I know such can happen," Buchanan agreed. "I will provide the dowry."

Innis gasped. Tyree appeared stunned as well.

"She is the daughter of one of me father's Retainers who died protecting this land," Buchanan explained. "The Mackenzie take care of their own."

Innis clasped her hands over her mouth as a sob escaped her lips. Her eyes were filled with tears, but now they were ones of joy. Tyree smiled at her once more, and she lost track of who was in the room. All of them melted away as she locked gazes with the man who looked back at her with eyes filled with adoration.

There was absolutely no one else she would rather look at.

≫≫≪≪

"I WONDERED WHAT made ye rise from bed so early."

Buchanan came out of the still room to find his bride in the passageway. Her hair was still flowing down her back as she hugged her arisaid tightly around her upper body to ward off the early morning chill.

He moved toward her, reaching out to stroke the side of her face. "I could not sleep when there was any possible threat to ye."

Tyree was coming out of the room. He had Innis's hand clasped tightly in his own. He stopped when he spied Rhedyn, reaching up to tug on his cap. "Don't worry, mistress. No one will harm ye on Mackenzie land."

"Blessings to ye both," Rhedyn offered.

The Butler flashed her a smile before he was hurrying away with Innis in tow. They disappeared into the shadows, sending a touch of heat onto Rhedyn's cheeks as her mind offered up precisely why the couple wanted some privacy.

"Do ye have any need of the stillroom, lass?" Buchanan asked softly.

Rhedyn looked at her husband. There was no warning in his tone, no reproach in his gaze. Just a steady question that he stood waiting for her to answer.

She slowly shook her head.

His lips began to curl up. She'd seen him grin before, but this was something different. The expression on his face was radiant and so full of love, she felt a shiver go down her back. Buchanan wrapped his hand around hers and winked at her before he turned and pulled her toward the stairs.

FENELLA SMILED, BUT tears welled up in her eyes, too.

The rod in her hand felt terrible, magnifying the chill she seemed to notice more and more. She shook her head and made her way back to the kitchens. She was lonely.

And old.

There would be no wedding for her or any more children.

She sniffed and drew herself up straight. Never had she failed to face what life challenged her with. The days ahead would be filled with duties, if not with family. She had a place.

"Mistress Fenella," Una said.

"Yes?"

"There is someone to see ye." Una turned her head and gave it a little jerk to get the girl hovering beyond the doorway which led out into the yard moving.

She was a half-starved thing. But she drew in a breath and squared her shoulders. She moved through the doorway and stopped to lower herself in a reverence.

"Rise child, and tell me what ye seek. The dawn is fully broken and there is much to do."

The girl lifted her hand. Neatly folded on it was a length of linen. Its edges were carefully rolled and sewn. On its ends were embroidered flowers which Fenella knew every stich of. It was a binding tie which had been draped over her wrist on the day she wed her husband, and the priest gave the blessing of marriage to her.

"Conrad was my man," she whispered. "He promised to bring me to ye when he received his earnings on quarter day."

Fenella reached out to take the binding strip. There was a new set of stiches on it now. A small bird was embroidered above one of the flowers which she had sewn herself.

"But he did nae return," the girl finished. "I have only a sister. Her husband has put me out." She laid her hand over her belly. "He can nae afford to feed us both."

Fenella stared at the little bird and then looked at the girl. She felt like something brushed her back, in just the same place her son had always patted her before he went off. The girl was looking at her with wide brown eyes. Fear was swimming in them as she wrung her hands and waited.

"My son." Fenella lost the battle to keep the tears in her eyes from falling. They trickled down her cheeks as she clasped the binding stripe to her chest. "Conrad would never have given this to anyone except his wife."

The girl drew in a ragged breath. "I can work hard. I swear it." She held up her hands. "Me skin is tough."

"Ye will sit right down and eat," Fenella declared. She pointed at Una. "Get a plate for her…she is eating for two."

One of the other maids brought a stool over to the edge of the long work table. All of the maids began to bring things to it. A glass of fresh milk from one of the buckets newly arrived. A bowl of steaming porridge from the large cauldron simmering over the fire. A thick piece of cheese appeared on a plate along with a handful of fresh berries.

"Sit down now." Fenella cupped the girl's shoulders, ushering her toward the stool.

"But...I can earn me keep." The girl was on the stool before she finished.

Fenella shook out a cloth with a snap and laid it over the girl's shoulder. "Time enough for that after ye have filled yer belly. My grandchild must be healthy and strong, and ye must have the strength to suckle the babe. What do I call ye, lass?"

The girl had the cheese in her mouth already, her belly rumbling loudly. Fenella clasped her hands together and smiled. Laughter bounced around the kitchen as the maids shared in the moment of joy.

And Fenella felt that pat on her shoulder one again.

>>>—<<<

The Sow's Troth...

COLUM LINDSEY WAS waiting. Sandra was in her customary location in the loft abovestairs.

"I do nae care for this," Vychan informed his sire. "We are exposed."

"Buchanan will come," Colum voiced his opinion.

"I do nae doubt he will," Vychan answered. "I question if he's coming to talk or take advantage of the fact that ye have made yerself available."

"He has wed yer sister," Colum offered. "The Mackenzies are an ally worth a small risk to acquire. And I do nae think Buchanan will be any more willing to venture into our stronghold than ye would want to ride into his. So, we'll wait here."

Whatever Vychan might have said was cut off as horses approached. Buchanan rode in with only a dozen Retainers. He dismounted and stomped on the steps to dislodge mud from his boots before he entered the inn. He spotted them immediately. Every man in the common room was watching to see what he'd do.

Buchanan Mackenzie, laird of the Mackenzies, reached up and

tugged on the corner of his cap while inclining his head toward Colum Lindsey. The respect being offered wasn't lost on anyone. It cut through the tension in the room.

Colum slowly chuckled. "Come…" He gestured with his hand. "Come and sit, lad."

The rest of the common room was filled with Lindsey and Munro Retainers. As Buchanan settled in front of Colum, the men grinned and looked toward the kitchen for ale to be served. Rolfe Munro stood up from where he'd been sitting in a far corner. He offered Buchanan a grin as he settled at the table with Column.

Mackenzie men made their way inside after caring for their horses. They sat among the other clansmen, uncaring about the mixing of colors. Above them, Sandra smiled and waved her girls forward to serve their guests.

It was time to celebrate the new peace.

❯❯❯◀◀◀

The next year…

"YE'RE WORRIED HE won't come."

Rhedyn cast an annoyed look at her husband. "We've been over this, Buchanan. Ye should ask me what I'm thinking. No' simply act as though ye can read me thoughts."

Buchanan cocked his head to one side.

"Oh…why do I bother?" Rhedyn asked with her hands propped on her hips. The posture made her swollen belly stick out even more. "It is not that me father won't want to come, I just worry that Vychan won't allow him to venture into our stronghold."

"Cora brought up that same thought," Buchanan muttered.

Rhedyn's shoulders slumped. "It won't be yer fault if he doesn't visit." She rubbed her distended belly. "I will just have to wait until next season when I can travel."

Two months away from the birth of their first child, her emotions were turbulent. Rhedyn drew in a deep breath, attempting to fend off a flood of tears. It would be foolish to venture onto the road so heavy with child.

And reckless.

Besides, there was no way her husband would allow her to. Or any of his Retainers. The Mackenzie had taken to following her everywhere. When she glared at them, they grinned and refused to disperse. One little frown on her face was cause for Fenella to come in a hurry to make sure nothing was wrong.

Buchanan was suddenly beside her, wrapping his arms around her and pulling her close.

"He will come," he spoke softly.

"Ye cannot be so certain."

Buchanan gently raised her chin. "Since I allowed Cora to go and be yer brother's guest while Colum is in my stronghold, yer father had better appear."

Rhedyn gasped. "Ye allowed Cora to go to Lindsey land?"

Buchanan wiped the tears from her cheeks. "Well now, it was Cora's suggestion. And it's the truth I thought I should agree before she took it into her head to go without me permission."

Rhedyn sent her husband a knowing look. "Yer sister is unbridled."

"Aye," Buchanan agreed. "But I have no desire to break her." He tapped her on the tip of her nose. "Nor do ye, wife. I have a deep affection for yer willfulness in choosing me as yer husband, so I cannot tell me sister to be any different than ye are."

One of the Retainers up on the walls started to ring a bell. The sound announced the approach of riders. Rhedyn hurried out onto the top step of the great hall doorway. The sound of horses made her clasp her hands together in glee.

Buchanan watched it all from a few paces behind his wife. Everything he'd ever been taught pointed at their union being doomed to fail. Doing wrong shouldn't have produced such joy.

And yet, it had.

He soaked up the sight of Colum Lindsey riding through the gates of the Mackenzie castle.

Aye, somehow, joy had risen from misdeeds.

He was properly grateful.

⇥⟫⟪⟻

"YE ARE BUCHANAN'S sister?"

Cora turned and contemplated Vychan Lindsey. He was huge. She was considered tall for a female, but Vychan still topped her by a full head.

"I am," she answered.

Vychan's hard gaze swept her from head to toe. "And yer brother sent ye here as a hostage?"

Cora refused to be intimidated. "I suggested it." She moved to a chair and sat down. "I did not want my sister-in-law to be disappointed. Rhedyn misses her father."

Vychan chuckled. "Ye are everything the rumors claim ye are, mistress." He stopped at a small table. Several bottles of different liquors sat on it. He placed his hand on the French wine.

Cora shook her head.

It earned her a half-grin from her host.

His hand moved onto the whiskey.

She rewarded him with a smile.

"Precisely as the rumors say," Vychan said as he poured her a double measure of the strong liquor.

"Ye are well informed," Cora remarked as she took the glass from him and inhaled the aroma of the brew.

Vychan didn't sit in the chair facing hers. He leaned against the wall. Cora sipped at the whiskey and didn't squirm. She wasn't going to allow him to rattle her. The man was curious. So, let him look his fill. The gossips did like to talk about her. She didn't fit into their idea of what a well-behaved girl should.

But then again, it seemed there were plenty of good girls striving to perform to the standards of those same gossips and yet, the tongues wagged away.

What was the point of attempting to embody the ideas of someone else? Cora was herself. To apologize for it seemed a greater sin.

Vychan's eyes narrowed before he moved forward and sat down. He raised a toast to her before they drank in silence. A sense of ease filled the room. Neither of them felt the need to impress one another which had resulted in both of them succeeding in doing precisely that. Without posturing or grand words.

Cora placed her empty glass on the side table. "So, what will ye do with me Vychan Lindsey?"

He sat his empty glass down as well. "Truth to tell, I'd planned to send ye off to sit with Bree."

She sat forward. "And now?"

"I'm half afeared ye'll teach her tricks to use against me if I force ye to sit out the next few days learning stitchery and bread turning."

"And the gossips said ye were no' a very sharp-witted man."

Vychan grunted. "Ye're unbridled and good at it. God help the man who falls for ye, lass."

Cora fluttered her eyelashes. "They can fall all they like, but I am not the wife sort of woman."

And part of her didn't care for the truth of the matter.

Still, no one had everything. Some girls were fair and others were clever. She? Well Cora was restless. She felt like her spirit was forever attempting to catch the wind. Like a ship as it unfurled its sails. As the wind caught in the canvas, the first jerk forward was marked by creaks in the wood of the masts. In that moment, there was always the possibility that the mast would snap and the ship would be left floating with no way to join the wind, just a wounded creature waiting for its death.

But while the mast held, the wind would carry the vessel far and wide, to places of enchantment and mystery. It was a gamble. A bet against the hand of fate. And she seemed to have been born for it. So, she would live it. And be true to herself.

About the Author

Mary Wine has written over twenty novels that take her readers from the pages of history to the far reaches of space. Recent winner of a 2008 EPPIE Award for erotic western romance, her book LET ME LOVE YOU was quoted "Not to be missed..." by Lora Leigh, New York Times best-selling author.

When she's not abusing a laptop, she spends time with her sewing machines...all of them! Making historical garments is her second passion. From corsets and knickers to court dresses of Elizabeth I, the most expensive clothes she owns are hundreds of years out of date. She's also an active student of martial arts, having earned the rank of second degree black belt.

Manufactured by Amazon.ca
Bolton, ON

11976934R00157